# A HARD TIME
# TO BE A FATHER

## BY THE SAME AUTHOR

### Fiction

THE FAT WOMAN'S JOKE
DOWN AMONG THE WOMEN
FEMALE FRIENDS
REMEMBER ME
LITTLE SISTERS
PRAXIS
PUFFBALL
THE PRESIDENT'S CHILD
THE LIFE AND LOVES OF A SHE-DEVIL
THE SHRAPNEL ACADEMY
THE HEART OF THE COUNTRY
THE HEARTS AND LIVES OF MEN
THE RULES OF LIFE
LEADER OF THE BAND
THE CLONING OF JOANNA MAY
DARCY'S UTOPIA
GROWING RICH
LIFE FORCE
AFFLICTION
SPLITTING
WORST FEARS

### Children's Books

WOLF THE MECHANICAL DOG
PARTY PUDDLE

### Short Story Collections

WATCHING ME, WATCHING YOU
POLARIS
MOON OVER MINNEAPOLIS
WICKED WOMEN

### Non-fiction

LETTERS TO ALICE
REBECCA WEST
SACRED COWS

# A HARD TIME
# TO BE A FATHER

## Fay Weldon

BLOOMSBURY

Published by Bloomsbury Publishing, New York and London.
Distributed to the trade by St Martin's Press

A CIP catalogue record for this book
is available from the Library of Congress

ISBN 1-58234-011-0
First US Edition 1999
10 9 8 7 6 5 4 3 2 1

Typeset by Hewer Text Ltd, Edinburgh, Scotland
Printed in the United States of America by
RR Donnelley & Sons Company, Harrisonburg, VA

# CONTENTS

## OUT OF THE PAST

What the Papers Say                          3
The Ghost of Potlatch Past                  21
Once in Love in Oslo                        29
GUP – or Falling in Love in Helsinki        42


## SCHEMING WOMEN

Come on, Everyone!                          59
Percentage Trust                            67
Inside the Whale – or
   I Don't Know But I've Been Told          77


## MOVING ON

Move Out: Move On                           87
New Year's Day                              97
Inspector Remorse                          105


## MOTHERS AND SISTERS

My Mother Said                             115

A Libation of Blood                          124
Pyroclastic Flow                             140

## OTHER PLACES, OTHER GENDERS

Spirits Fly South                            149
Stasi                                        173
A Great Antipodean Scandal                   182

## HOSPITAL

New Advances                                 203
Noisy into the Night                         204
A Hard Time to be a Father                   218

## Skipping Rhyme

My mother said
I never should
Play with the gypsies
In the wood
If I did she would say
You're a naughty little girl
To disobey
Your hair won't curl
Your boots won't shine
You're a naughty little girl
And you shan't be mine!

So we all went out to the wood, to play with gypsies.

# OUT OF THE PAST

WHAT THE PAPERS SAY

THE GHOST OF POTLATCH PAST

ONCE IN LOVE IN OSLO

GUP – OR FALLING IN LOVE IN HELSINKI

# WHAT THE PAPERS SAY

New York was hot and soggy and you couldn't smoke, so they checked out of their hotel where the air-conditioning groaned and shuddered, and took the train to Boston. Damask thought the journey would be pretty but it wasn't. Just indeterminate August trees, and the only spot of romance was the whoo-whoo of Amtrak, as they'd heard it in a hundred black-and-white movies, floating back from the engine. How painfully slow and bumpy anything seemed these days if it was not air travel, and after you'd been in Concorde, apparently even ordinary air travel irritated. Ariel had flown in Concorde, though because he'd had to go stand-by, only in the rear section where the noise and vibration already begin to get to you. Stand-by on Concorde! Damask marvelled. She was always marvelling. That was what he said he loved about her, so she did it a lot.

Ariel was fifty-two and called after the archangel, not the blithe spirit of Shakespeare's *The Tempest*, nor the soap powder, as Damask, who loved him newly and passionately, would tell everyone who didn't already know (and quite often even if they did) from the press cuttings. Ariel King, Irish film star, Oscar-winner. Married. Not to Damask. Ariel was meant to be in Hollywood for promotional purposes but had managed to take a week out in order to show Damask Vale-Eden America. His wife Elspeth was on holiday with the children in the Seychelles. Elspeth liked a flat, watery place with a known circumference. Elspeth marvelled at nothing, grieved at everything. Elspeth was Ariel's conscience, and Damask his delight.

Damask was a model of the plumper kind, though thin enough by ordinary standards: she was the one they liked to use when accused too savagely of heroin chic. Damask was twenty-two, and smoked like a chimney.

Boston was even hotter and soggier than New York: the clam chowder was good, if oddly grainy, and Damask tried to light up in what she assumed was a bar area of the hotel restaurant. An angry woman in a blue sequined dress snatched the cigarette from her mouth and accused her of murder, and said she was a slut and a whore. The woman was crazy, everyone agreed, but it was a nasty incident, so Damask and Ariel flew down to Chicago where the Catholics cluster and the sense of sin is not so great – it being traditionally purged by confession and so having no way of accumulating over long periods – and the rich and successful are allowed to be fatter and happier than any-where else in the States. You could smoke, mostly, but after you'd been to the Art Institute and the John G. Shedd aquarium and walked in the parks and taken a boat out on the lakes, there didn't seem much to do. How could anywhere be so hot and windy at the same time? They couldn't go to grand hotels, in case Ariel was seen by someone he knew: so they went to the run-of-the-mill kind, where there wasn't a concierge to tell you what was what, and they had to depend for their entertainment on tourist traps, as if they were just anyone. The hotels were OK, but there was no swanning about, no half-mangoes with giant

4

strawberry for room-service breakfast; and sex felt oddly perfunctory: not overwhelming, now for once there was time for it. Ariel was guilty about Elspeth, so his performance led them to joke about Viagra, and Damask was, frankly, not all that keen on anything that tended to take her by surprise, making her screw up her face: she didn't want to get wrinkles. But that was OK. 'This thing,' as they assured each other, 'is about more than sex.'

After Chicago they went to Washington DC and on a guided tour of the White House, and even caught a glimpse of Bill Clinton himself, in the midst of a posse of security men, whose necks seemed wider than their heads. 'Isn't he handsome?' marvelled Damask, and a fellow tourist remarked, 'Well, yes, a girl like you would think so.' Damask did have Lewinski-like qualities, it is fair to say: a kind of buoyant overflowingness, a spontaneity, and a rich, loose, red mouth. She had been named Damask by her mother, with just that same kind of spontaneity, only somehow messier. Damask was one of five sisters, by four different fathers, none of them ever resident. They'd all lived in Cornwall in a pretty bohemian house on a cliff top, but rising seas had eroded the coastline and they'd had to leave when Damask was sixteen: such eccentricity no longer suited the times, and even the ocean knew it.

Damask and Ariel left Washington DC and went to Nashville on SouthWest Airlines, an August-only deal, only $42 a head, and by coach to Memphis and Gracelands, because Ariel had a thing about Elvis Presley, and where it would be a very good idea indeed if he wasn't seen. Ariel had won his Oscar for playing Beethoven in *Prometheus*. And in his new movie *Pure of Heart* he played a Christian Scientist prepared to lay down his life for his faith. The studio had high hopes for it: the sequel, *Heartlands*, was about to go into production. Ariel was indeed seen at Gracelands, as it happened, by a passing fashion photographer, who recognised them both and double took, in every sense of the word, but when it came to it neither Damask nor Ariel noticed. Lovers always tend to believe they are invisible.

Back to Nashville for a night out at The Old Opry, which Damask couldn't stand. New men in black hats and girls singing twangy therapist songs. She was an acid-house girl herself: she couldn't bear lyrics.

'Did you know,' said Ariel, 'that if they want to prevent fish from getting sucked into grills they play acid house into the water. The boom, boom, boom, drives them to the far end of the pool.'

Yes, this relationship was cooling off. Neither wanted to admit it, but both knew it. He from experience and she because she knew perfectly well he was too old for her and in taking up with him in the first place had only been trying to annoy her mother. It is not nice to find yourself with no home, albeit it is the ocean's fault, at sixteen, and to have to go to live with an aunt, along with your twin sister Velvet, with whom you do not get along though everyone thinks because you are twins you must. And your mother, though remaining fond, seems to have simply given up on her role, and no longer sees it as her responsibility to provide board and lodging. She has to be punished, just a little, as the years go by.

Velvet had recently become pregnant by a Rastafarian, which was a far more drastic kind of thing to do than merely going off secretly with a man thirty years older than herself, as Damask had done. But Velvet had always taken things to extremes: she was alleged to be Damask's identical twin but during their growing years was always fatter or thinner or taller or shorter than Damask: Velvet too had tried to start a career modelling, but was too inconsistent in shape and behaviour, too scatty in attitude, and the rich red lips seemed to look bad-tempered rather than to pout; how two people so nearly alike could be so different in photographs was a marvel to their mother Caledonia. Velvet and Damask Vale-Eden. School had been a torment. 'Take no notice,' said their mother. 'They're just envious, all the Annes and the Joans and the Marys. The Browns and the Smiths and the Joneses. Don't try to be like other people, girls, because you're not.'

Perhaps Ariel and Damask got together not just because sudden fame went to his head, and the brave must surely deserve the fair, and not just because she rated a man who won Best Actor about as high as Lewinski rated the President, which was just about as high as you can get, but because of this question of the names. Ariel's father was an Israeli out of Germany, a socialist of the pre-war kibbutz movement: his mother a nice girl called Anne from Dublin, but they'd had no more mercy than had Caledonia. How mixed up everyone becomes!

The soft green grass and the fireflies and the low, full moon of Nashville made outdoor love-making tempting: they walked back to their hotel from The Old Opry and into what was either a park or someone's front garden, what did they care? They fell upon the ground and embraced, and he sang 'Moon River' and she wished he didn't. The photographer had followed them all the way from Gracelands, patiently, pitter-pat. Lawn sprinklers suddenly started, security lights flared, dogs barked, the errant couple started up in surprise, Damask's fine cotton dress, drenched, clung to her body, all her fine bosom revealed, his cotton chinos to his manly form; the couple fled into the dark, re-arranging clothes as best they could.

# A HARD TIME TO BE A FATHER

That was Nashville.

They flew to San Francisco but there was no air-conditioning. Really, August is not the best time for cities. Then Hollywood lost patience with its errant star and tugged the cord and Ariel obeyed, and it was time for Damask to fly back to Heathrow. She would arrive back first thing on Sunday morning, ready for a shoot her agent arranged for the Monday. She looked forward to it. Swimsuits for the *Living Family* magazine and its Mail Order Catalogue: but a classy catalogue for once, and the more unclothed Damask was, the better she always looked. The creamy curves of her shoulders and arms, the smooth stretch of long full legs – she would never be totally chic, everyone agreed, but chicness in itself was beginning to feel unfashionable. Once skinny, attitudey chic reached the high streets, things had to go the other way.

At the British Airways Terminal of LA airport Ariel and Damask kissed and hugged each other goodbye.

'I'm no Humbert Humbert,' Ariel said. They'd seen the remake of *Lolita* in Chicago. 'I can't do this to you. This week has been the happiest of all my life, and it breaks my heart. But I renounce you, I set you free, find the man you love, my darling, be happy always. And call me when you can. Use the mobile number.'

Mobiles are best for clandestine phone calls. You can switch them off in your spouse's presence, switch them on when privacy is available.

Damask resisted the temptation to winge and sulk. To be happy, she knew, is always the best revenge. It is only natural for a girl to want the man she's just spent a week with to yearn passionately to spend the rest of his life with her, but she could see it was unrealistic. Had she already been a well-established world figure she might have had a chance; to

8

share headlines keeps a relationship afloat – look at Mick and Jerry. But if they tilt either way too sharply and suddenly, there's bound to be trouble sooner or later. No, let him go back to Elspeth, who'd never had a headline in her life but only made body text, and was two stone overweight, three by most people's standards, and pale and plain and reclusive and terribly, terribly serious. Damask had her future to think of, and besides she was a good, kind girl and knew how to behave.

'I shall never forget you,' Damask said softly to Ariel, 'never. Whoever I'm with for the rest of my life I'll remember you: the best and tenderest first lover in the whole world. My mother always says I'm lucky and so I am!'

A nice girl indeed, Damask, though of course Ariel wasn't her first lover, but it was pleasant for him to think he was and that he had made such a fine and lasting impression on her. Damask became a little fidgety and wanted to go off to the smoking area, so she did not hold him back when he kissed her for the last time, and left, leaving her with an hour to catch her flight.

On the flight back – Club-class: Ariel had paid – she thought of him with affection, but no longer with love. She felt more mature and more experienced now: that was the thing about older men; you osmosed worldly wisdom from their bodies. She hated using condoms. Such a waste. Everyone knew – alas, there was no word for it that didn't put you off – that coital bodily fluids were the best thing for the complexion, whatever orifice was engaged. So she used an old-fashioned cap. The pill made you put on weight, and she couldn't afford to, her size being so finely tuned to the needs of the market – enough for wow! But not enough for yuk! – as her agent put it. Damask was not afraid of AIDS; she believed in a benign fate; all she wanted was not to be pregnant and not to have to take time off for a termination which would interfere with her bookings.

Velvet, her twin, had had two abortions, each more traumatic than the last: the previous Christmas when the whole family had for once gathered together, in a borrowed house, there was Velvet, the youngest by twenty minutes, making everyone miserable by weeping and groaning and lamenting. What a sight the family made! Six pairs of red lips around the table, straight firm noses, clear skins, wide blue eyes, firm chins – Caledonia has had a face-lift – so like one another some swore the mother must have given birth by parthenogenesis – there really should have been nothing in life to complain about. Only Velvet was given to fits of misery: the others felt she lacked style. All the girls save Velvet were doing well: Chenille was a practising lawyer; Satin, who these days called herself Joan, was an analytical chemist; Georgette was doing a PhD on the influence of the Napoleonic Wars on figurative painting; and Damask's modelling career seemed to be taking off.

But now it was the end of August. And Velvet was pregnant again, though this time happily, if drastically, and engaged to be married. Having got rid of the genes of a racing driver and a professor, as Georgette had crossly observed, she had settled for those of a yardie. A Rastafarian rock star.

'All men are equal, none of my girls are racists, I am so proud of my Velvet,' Caledonia had crooned when they'd all got together at Easter, and she'd taken another whisky, and inhaled marijuana for her nerves, but her eyes looked slightly cross-eyed with the effort of not worrying about the polyglot nature of the future. It was an embarrassment. When young white women run off with beautiful black men it is seen as if lust is uppermost in their minds; and lust is not ladylike. Such a difficult line to tread when bringing up children: you want them to absorb your own intellectual, sexual and artistic messages in the proportion in which you yourself enjoy them, and which works well enough for you, but the children never quite seem to get the proportions right. Velvet interpreted a joyous sexuality as the alrightness of being sex mad. Encourage Satin to read a book and she ended up a misogynist scientist. One rash overnight visit for the mother, taking Georgette along to a painter's studio, and the girl spends the rest of her life amongst paintings, knowing everything, but so far as Caledonia is concerned, appreciating very little. Preach forgiveness and Chenille spends her life protecting the criminal classes from their just deserts. Only Damask seemed to get everything just about right: the balance poised in the daughter as it was in the mother. So what if Damask went off on holiday with a married actor, at least you knew she'd be back in time for work. Of the twins, it was always Velvet had the unluck and Damask the luck. A single slip-up from Velvet and she'd be pregnant and you'd know in advance there'd be a power cut and a botch-up should she be whisked into hospital for some emergency operation. Whereas Damask – Damask rode the crest of any wave going: Damask would be swept along on the tide of popular taste: the *Living Family* catalogue today, but tomorrow's Ms Versace, as bosoms and smiles became the rage, and there was no more profit in poky ribs and puncture marks. Yes, Damask, second to last, was the most successful, the most balanced, of Caledonia's daughters.

Caledonia, herself the younger daughter of a former Foreign Secretary, now deceased, and executor of his estate, was involved in a long-running lawsuit with the publishers of his biography, a book full of disgraceful and humiliating tittle-tattle, most detrimental to his memory. The estate claimed damages for various posthumous insults to the elder statesman's reputation. It would make a legal precedent if it succeeded: the past claiming damages from the future, as it were, rather than the other way round. It was at a sensitive stage. The family hoped for £$\frac{1}{2}$ million at least: Caledonia would at last be able to buy a proper new home. For five years she had been house-sitting for absent lovers, or staying with friends, or one way or another putting off her domestic duties.

And Damask? Damask just wanted the family to be happy and all together. She was a good, sweet girl. And now she had sensibly parted from Ariel, and allowed him to go back to his serious wife, as a good, sweet girl should.

And that was that, or so Damask thought. She loved the flight back with its endless unnecessary servings of dainty snackettes, and its little movie screens, and Ariel was on one of them, playing the faithful husband of a faithless spouse. He always played the good guy, the old-fashioned hero: Harrison Ford the younger. Me, me, she thought, that man on that screen loves, loved, well, something, once, me. It was thrilling. She slept. But the past is never over, no matter how much we might wish it were.

When she came out into the light at the end of the Heathrow tunnel it was into a mob of paparazzi, news crews and press men: grabbing and snatching, pressing forward like the surge of the waves which once carried her home away: crashing into her happiness. What can be happening, she wondered, what's going on, it can't be me. But it was. Photos of Damask coming out of Arrivals, stunned and staring, jaw dropped, looking far from her best, not even any eye shadow, made the front pages the next day. And alongside Damask, re-runs of Saturday's pics of Elspeth back from holiday, two stone the lighter and for once looking fabulous, if of course grieved. And the captions ran the gamut from 'Fury Wife Chops Out AK' to 'Daffy Damask Steals the King' to 'Face of a Marriage Breaker'. Elspeth was suing for divorce through a PR firm, and claiming untold millions. And there were the two sweet blonde King kiddies too, weeping all over the pages, front, middle and back. And everywhere, everywhere, was the pic that had got Elspeth going. Damask drenched to the skin, bosom half-bared, rising like Venus out of long grass, fireflies glittering her hair, from her horizontal embrace in the Nashville night with the clothed Ariel King. Picture of the year. It made the photographer half a million. It ended the King marriage. *Cheesecake sur l'herbe*, as it was known, after Manet, and became the trigger for great media debates on everything from the selfishness of parents, to adultery as sin, to the merits and otherwise of love-making out of doors and the life-cycle of fireflies. But that was later, and only after what Damask had said at the airport, and when Georgette had made her rash comparison to *Déjeuner sur l'herbe*. None of the sisters were to be left alone. Pitter-pat, pitter-pat, went the sweet tough newsgirls after the lot of them: do you have any comment, don't you want to put your side of the story? We'll be nice to you, the others won't. You, the five beautiful sisters with four different fathers (and if the last two hadn't been twins no doubt it would have been five), do we blame you, pity you? Can you just tell us where your mother is? Caledonia? What kind of name is that? Caledonia's father was once in the running for Tory Prime Minister: haven't we some old pics of some old scandal: hasn't the daughter got some ongoing lawsuit? And there were the biographer's calumnies all over the literary pages again and the book selling like hot cakes but the profits to the biographer. Out came the therapists, the geneticists and counsellors: the infidelities of the father visited unto the second generation: compulsive marriage-breaking in the genes. The media couldn't believe its luck.

Because of course at the airport Damask, instead of reacting with appropriate shock, horror, confusion and apology to her uncovering as a bad girl, had coolly observed, 'Why blame me? Why not blame him?' And had fled to take refuge with Velvet, press pursuing. Otherwise it might all have died away sooner.

On the Sunday, Damask and Velvet prowled up and down in their besieged apartment in Parson's Green in South London. Damask had made her escape through the kindness of a couple of journos from the *Mail* who had whisked her into their car, evaded the following pack, and delivered her to Velvet's place for what they had hoped would be a quiet interview. Only Damask had managed to slam the doors in their faces before they could follow her in. They shouted at her through the letter-box: all they wanted to know, they said, was what Ariel was like as a lover? How did he rate? Did she wish to comment on Elspeth's statement that she'd have been happier with a dildo? Didn't Damask want to comment on that? Eventually they went away. Damask and Velvet pulled the curtains, locked the doors, took the phone off the hook, and smoked a couple of joints.

In the middle of Sunday night Velvet started to miscarry, and had to go to hospital in an ambulance. The press were still there outside. Velvet – when finally she wrote the story of her abortions for a miserable £5,000: 'I Murdered My Unborn Babies' – attributed the disaster to the shock of it all, though actually she had been bleeding on and off for days, and no one in the family knew, frankly, whether to be glad or sorry, and anyway concern for Velvet's emotional state was not currently at the top of the family's agenda. 'Velvet Loses

Rasta Baby' had almost become a so-what. Though it gave rise to yet more column inches – dire warnings from health experts saying that for every two abortions, expect one miscarriage.

It was as if the nation had gone to sleep one night careless and randy, as usual, and woken up the next in such a fit of respectability you couldn't believe it. Cruel Damask, the media reported, couldn't even be bothered to go to hospital with her own sister: perhaps she was too busy making phone calls to married men? Oh yes, they knew her sort!

Caledonia had gone into hiding but broke radio silence by getting through to Georgette, also under seige, and saying of Damask, her one-time favourite, 'Darling, it's so vulgar for a woman to have her name in the paper. I can never forgive Damask for this.' And then, relenting. 'But don't tell her so, Georgie. She has enough to put up with.'

On Monday morning early, Damask called a taxi and fought her way through the ravening cluster on the steps and got to the studio with only a small crowd following. She was met there by her agent and the client. She was no longer needed on the shoot. She was notorious, and notoriety was not needed on *Living Family*: they had a young, wholesome image.

'But the magazine won't come out for a month,' pleaded Damask. 'It'll all be forgotten by then.'

The client shook his head. He knew better. Her agent raised sceptical eyebrows. Her dewy implorings counted for nothing. She wasn't looking her best. Jet lag, shock and terror at her new image as perceived by the world, had rubbed the bloom off her. A nice damask plum. Her agent raised sceptical eyebrows. Versace had been on the phone first thing. They didn't want the association. Sure, ribs and drugs were on the way out, and health and sex on the way in, but why use a model the whole world hated? Her bosom was way too big anyway, they'd assumed it was silicone and could be easily diminished: but real flesh? It might go wrong and she'd sue. So thank you, Miss Vale-Eden, but no thanks. And only twenty-two, poor girl, and trusting. She who'd once believed in her own good luck.

Stories are spun out of nothing and sink back to nothing, leaving a few ruined lives behind, living sacrifice in the cause of headlines, being there first, getting the exclusive. Or else see it as a horse race, a starting point and a finishing point, when the Editor finally says enough of that: and a mad gallop in between. Who's to blame, the man or the woman? And they're off, like horses from the starting-post, ripping up the turf as they go! Others see it as feeding frenzy: piranha fish at work. Nothing once it's over but the bare bones of the victim, glimpsed on the riverbed, whitened and bleached and thin.

On the other side of the Atlantic, meanwhile, from coast to coast, Ariel was the brute, the monster, the seducer, Damask the young victim. Wrongly described in one paper as being sixteen years old, facts picked up like Chinese whispers, she ended up little more than a child. King the paedophile, though nobody quite used the p-word in case he sued. *The New Yorker* ran pieces on the media as the new morality and the innate helplessness of New Woman in the face of her own sexuality. *The New York Times* linked the scandal with Clinton. Great Lives, Silly Loves, Poor Wives: CNN did a special out of Atlanta. There was a report that Elspeth King had sold her story for $500,000, and had met up with her (married) PR agent while holidaying in the Seychelles: but it suited nobody to know that. That story quickly died. The studio stopped production of the new Ariel King movie *Heartlands* out of sensitivity to public feeling, throwing away $30 million and a dozen new hopeful film careers on the way.

On the Heathrow side of the Atlantic Damask became the hate figure, the girl all other women fear (or are said to), the stealer of husbands, the marriage breaker, the careless, selfish, dangerous bitch. The media dug up family photos, decided her upbringing was not to blame. Caledonia was exonerated. Blame the daughter, not the mother! Caledonia, lone mother, doing her best in the face of personal disaster. A series of wicked abandoning men. She'd brought up a family, hadn't aborted a single one (or none that anyone discovered) and had never been a charge on the state. Caledonia, pursued, gave herself up to the *Mail*, offered them her story if they'd only keep the others off her back. She gave the £100,000 to the Prince's Trust charity. Bred a lady, always a lady, the papers agreed. So long as it's the aristocracy, bad behaviour is allowed to turn into a delightful eccentricity. So much remains of *noblesse oblige*. Caledonia was off the hook. Except the law then swung against her. She was a public figure, wasn't she? How could she claim loss of privacy? She got damages of one penny and the biographer laughed all the way to the bank.

All this because of one love-making observed and interrupted amongst the fireflies and the green grass of Nashville, Tennessee, after a night out at The Old Opry. A longing look from Damask, English Rose, a bosom unconfined, a lusty clasp from Ariel, film star out of Hollywood, and pow!

Someone looked up Ariel's birth certificate back in Dublin. Barry turned out to be his given name. 'If I'd known it,' Elspeth was reported as saying, 'I wouldn't have married him. It was Ariel, archangel, which so enchanted me.' A hundred new features were spawned. The power of the name! The Israeli father turned out to be a fantasy. The true father was an absentee builder. Elspeth's sued him for $8m he hasn't got.

An Oscar he might have, but until *Prometheus* he hadn't been a huge earner and now *Heartlands* was being withdrawn. His agent advised, 'Lie low for a year or two, restart a career as a villain, what are your options now? When will you guys ever learn?' The agent shook his head but he was just going through the motions. He was on Viagra, he had his own problems: in love with a twenty year old who wasn't responding, Viagra or not. He couldn't be bothered with a client who'd fucked up, and would in all likelihood never earn any money again. Ariel tried to change agents but only the real shysters would take him on. He thought back to the day he'd first met Damask. It had been at some fashion show in London: it was the mother who'd interested him until the daughter showed up: 'a titled family', someone had told him, though being fierce egalitarians, they never used the title. Dubious motives, Ariel suddenly saw, brought with them their just deserts and more. It was wrong of him to have taken advantage of the sexual pulling power of an Oscar. He was ashamed of himself. He was a more serious person than he had imagined. Perhaps the Studio knew what it was doing, type-casting him the way it had. He began to feel not so much oppressed by the Devil as saved by God, taught a necessary lesson. When Damask got through on the mobile, weeping, he was kind and fatherly. All things pass.

For two and a half weeks the story ran before the editors said enough, within which time lives and fortunes changed. Then someone showed up in LA from the Seychelles – a beach guard. He came with snapshots, which could not be denied. Elspeth in *déshabillé*, on holiday, embracing her PR man on the beach. He was slipping a slice of pineapple from his lips to hers, and they were not pretty lips. Behind them one of the little girls had her hand to her mouth in horror. One final outburst, the manic squeal of a balloon deflating, shooting round the room. And the life just went out of the story. The goods and the bads became blurred, and that was a disappointment. And another story broke: an aircrash and a royal divorce, and no one cared about the Vale-Edens any more. The thick, wodged envelopes from the Cutting Agencies became thinner, thinner, slowed to a trickle through the family letter-boxes, stopped.

Caledonia re-appeared. While in hiding, she had found a new rich lover, twenty years younger than herself. A Scottish land-owner, a laird of lairds, bored by fog and cold, wanting warmth and central heating, too grand and rich to be afraid of publicity. He came south with her; they married and set up house together.

Velvet and Damask went home to their mother; Velvet developed ME and had to be waited on by Caledonia hand and foot. At the end of the year she got better and after the horror of 'I Murdered My Unborn Babies' became first a serious feature writer, then an almost intellectual columnist, and actually married a banker. All the sisters came to the wedding. Satin had become spokesperson on ethics for an international drug company and earned a fortune, Georgette had given up detecting art forgeries and ran a gallery, and Chenille had given up law to write legal thrillers. The lot of them, in fact, were in the media. If you can't beat them, join them.

One day Damask got a phone call from Ariel. He was in Scotland, playing the lead in a major Hollywood special-effects movie. He was an alien on the run; a kindly being who could control the weather. It meant big money. His agent had been wrong. He had a week off. They went to Edinburgh together and saw the Castle and ate Arbroath smokies, and to Glasgow to see the Mackintosh chairs, and to the Isle of Skye to taste the home-made whisky, and to Dundee where they stood on the Tay Bridge and recited McGonagall, and as far down as York to visit the Roman Museum there. They shared a bed for warmth and companionship but nothing else. She had stopped smoking, and was training as a photographer. Ariel kept dropping in at Catholic chapels for a quick Ave Maria, but Damask didn't mind that. Once he'd put up with her smoking: now she put up with his religion. They had a wonderful week and when they got off their respective flights, he at Aberdeen and she at Heathrow, no one took the slightest notice.

# THE GHOST
# OF POTLATCH PAST

Miss Jacobs, retired psychoanalyst, heard a scrabbling at her door at five o'clock one Christmas Eve and found a young woman folded on her doorstep, weeping. All around, fallen from her hands, were carrier bags from department stores, out of which tumbled glittery gift-wrapped packages of all shapes and sizes, many of them awkward. Miss Jacobs, although she had never seen the girl before, asked her in, and moved her many possessions inside the door, out of the rain. The girl was in her early twenties, clean, well-dressed in the contemporary fashion, and pretty enough. She had a ring through each nostril and twelve in one ear. Miss Jacobs, fascinated, counted them while the girl, who said her name was Clarissa, drank the tea Miss Jacobs offered. She drank it black, without sugar. Milk, Clarissa said, was known to contain organophosphates and possibly wrongly-folded prions, the source of BSE, and sugar was empty calories. Clarissa stretched her white damp disfigured fingers – string from the heavy carrier bags had bitten into them – and advised Miss Jacobs never to eat dairy products if she valued her health and sanity. She sat across the table from Miss Jacobs and sipped the unkind liquid and spoke.

'I was going to knock on your door like a proper person,' said Clarissa, 'but when I came to it I couldn't. I didn't have the strength to knock and didn't have the strength to leave, so I stayed where I was and cried, and rescue came. I was surprised. Rescue so seldom comes.'

'But why my doorstep?' asked Miss Jacobs.

'My mother was once a patient of yours,' replied Clarissa. 'She would point out your door while we passed, usually by taxi, and would tell me how much you had helped her.'

'I am happy to hear that,' said Miss Jacobs. 'What is your mother's name?'

'Juliet Penrose,' said Clarissa.

'I have seen many patients in the course of my working life,' said Miss Jacobs. 'I'm sorry. I don't instantly recall the name.'

'I expect it happens much as it does in a family,' said Clarissa. 'A child has only one mother, and is conscious of her all the time, but a mother can have many children, and is conscious of each only a little of the time.'

'Quite so,' said Miss Jacobs, relieved. 'But tell me, why are you quite so exhausted? Is it the season or is the problem more than this?' Though indeed Miss Jacobs was fairly tired herself. Not even being Jewish can save you from Christmas, and Hanukkah only just dealt with.

'So long as you don't charge me for my telling you,' said Clarissa, fine eyes flashing.

'Of course I won't,' said Miss Jacobs. 'I am retired now and my pension is quite adequate.'

'Potlatch,' said Clarissa, 'Potlatch has exhausted me. Four o'clock on Christmas Eve and the shops slam shut their doors, and turn off their lights, and the frenzy of shopping must stop, like the frenzy of killing when the blue UN helmets appear –'

'If only it were so,' murmured Miss Jacobs, but Clarissa did not hear, so bent upon her theme was she.

'– and a forlorn peace descends upon the land, and the streets empty, and the taxis vanish. I walked all the way here.'

'Poor you,' said Miss Jacobs.

'But if you watch the darkened shop windows you can see dim figures the other side of the glass, bending, stretching, reaching, putting up the New Year sale notices, bargain screamers, prices slashed. The battle is over but the dogs of war sleep for only minutes, already they are stirring, whimpering for a fresh attack. Warfare by way of gifts. Slaughter by generosity. Potlatch.'

'I don't quite understand what you mean by potlatch,' said Miss Jacobs.

'Perhaps just half a teaspoonful of sugar in my tea after all,' said Clarissa, 'and just a drop of milk. I do feel a little faint. With any luck there won't be a faulty prion in the particular drop you give me. Do you understand about prions? Minute particles of protein; they normally fold in a rather pretty, attractive corkscrew whirl, but this way of folding leaves them vulnerable: heat can destroy them, or radiation or mould, or the simple entropy which affects us all. But now another prion has arisen, a rogue prion, which cares nothing for charm, but puts self-interest and survival first: it has flattened out its whirls to present a straight, sharp, flat, almost fascist surface to the world, which nothing so far known can destroy. And every gentle, old-fashioned prion this immortal, indestructible being encounters, gets the message at once, and flattens its own shape. It is not infected: it simply imitates, copies, in the interests of its own survival.

23

The growth of the flat prion is exponential. The news spreads like wildfire in the prion world: merely flatten and survive! If a flat prion, and there are more and more and more in existence, encounters a brain cell in man or beast, it locks, apt surface to apt surface, and stays and lies in wait for new-comers, and then holes begin to appear in the brain – spongiform encephalitis – and all reason evaporates –'

'We were talking about potlatch, not prions,' said Miss Jacobs, 'though I can see it is very frightening.'

'They are linked,' cried Clarissa, passionately. 'Don't you see? Potlatch is the extravagant ceremonial distribution of property by North Pacific Indians, in particular the Kwa-kiutl. Potlatches are given by chiefs by way of wreaking vengeance on an enemy. The one who gives least is humi-liated and shamed. *"Take this war canoe, my friend; finely painted and beautifully carved: see how subtly-shaped the paddles!" "We much admire the gift, friend, but here we have a many-coloured tepee for you: six squaws lost their sight embroidering its fringes, and take as well this humble war canoe, with simple filigreed prow and paddles silver-tipped!" "Thank you, thank you! Now take these six virgins, reared specially for you, friend. See how plump and sleek they are!" "How thoughtful of you, and surprise, surprise, we have twelve virgins for you and all your tribe, and all our virgins can read and write, and see here, the heart of a slaughtered slave."* And so on, until the one outdone by the other, the poorest in generosity, creeps away disgraced. My mother practises potlatch. And I, like the prion who has discovered how to survive, now practise it too. I cannot help myself, but hate myself.

'I was born on Christmas Day 1972, and the earth moved. Ten thousand people died in an earthquake in Nicaragua. I was the youngest child of six, an afterthought, born when my

24

mother Juliet was forty-two. She only became pregnant with me, my mother once told her friends, and I overheard, to give herself an excuse to stop seeing you.'

'Really,' remarked Miss Jacobs, puzzled, 'can that be so?'

'It's what she told me,' said Clarissa, 'which makes you responsible for my life. I have always felt so, and never passed your door without a certain *frisson*. Anyway, my mother's guilt was such, great sums of money were spent converting a box-room into a nursery on my account, the better to welcome me into the world. It would have been better sent to the victims of the earthquake. I could have shared with Severo, aged two at the time of my birth.'

'Perhaps your mother just wanted to welcome you into the world,' observed Miss Jacobs, 'it may not necessarily have been guilt that motivated her.'

'On my first birthday,' said Clarissa, ignoring this, 'the nation was in the middle of a three-day week; the power stations closed; TV programmes stopped at ten-thirty, and my mother bought me a teddy bear so big it could hardly get through the door. It sits at the end of my bed to this day. My father left home on Christmas Eve; he'd found a lover in my mother's bed. The couple were both asleep and I had crawled in beside them. I don't remember the scene; I have buried the memory, no doubt. But the teddy bear from my mother was guilt on her part, of course it was. Only spend, my mother thought, and all will be well. She should have given the money to the striking miners.'

'Should, should,' murmured Miss Jacobs.

'Potlatch only happens when there is plenty,' said Clarissa. 'The North Pacific Indians lived in a pleasant, fertile land. Deer were plentiful, edible roots were at hand, and salmon ran up the rivers. My father made millions as a designer of contemporary furniture. And of course he felt guilty too, for his five abandoned daughters and one abandoned son. Tax never took enough away.'

'That is quite a rare response to tax,' said Miss Jacobs. 'In fact in all my working life I have never heard anyone say such a thing.'

'By Christmas 1974,' said Clarissa, 'inflation in Britain had reached 25 per cent. Teachers that year got a 32 per cent pay rise. And what was my mother's response? Spend, spend, spend! The Sex Discrimination Act and the Equal Pay Act came into force three days after my birthday in 1975, and did my mother get a job? No, she just asked for more alimony. By my third birthday my leisure years were considered over, and while a Rhodesian terror gang killed twenty-seven of their own – how puny massacres were in those days – I was finger-painting Christmas cards for my four sisters, my one brother, my absent father, my new stepfather and his three sons. And after that, it was downhill all the way. My mother's generosity and kindness increased my annual present list exponentially. Thanks to you she never quarrelled with husbands or lovers, she simply left or was left, and kept on good terms with everyone, even my father. Like wrongly-folded prions, those in need of gifts and friendship latch on, and I, like her, spend the Christmas season, when so many world disasters happen, wrapping presents and attaching baubles. Warfare by generosity. Potlatch: who gives, wins.

'On my seventh birthday the Vietnam boat people took to the seas and my mother adopted a little Vietnamese boy. She always preferred sons. On my eighth, the Iranians rose against the Shah and welcomed the Ayatollah Khomeini (out of the kettle into the fire, some say) and I was given the most expensive bicycle Harrods could offer. For my ninth my mother was away in the States for John Lennon's funeral; on my tenth my mother should have been at Greenham, but she wasn't. My mother was not the kind to damage her nails linking hands with muddy women, not even to save the world.'

'Perhaps this obsession with birthdays,' remarked Miss Jacobs, 'is because you feel deprived by fate. Children whose birthday is near or on Christmas Day often have to make do with one set of presents.'

'You must have told my mother that,' said Clarissa, 'and she believed it. I always got at least five times as much as my many and varied siblings, and they know it, and dislike me for it, and the more they dislike me, the more I feel obliged to give them.

'In December 1980 at least two thousand people were killed by Union Carbide at Bhopal, but nothing daunted my mother's gift-wrapping fervour. Could we have bread and cheese for Christmas dinner, and do without on their account? No. In October 1987 a tree fell through a conservatory roof in the great gale so that Christmas we ate in the kitchen and the maid stayed home, but that was our own misfortune, not the world's. In December 1988 an earthquake in Armenia wiped cities off the face of the earth and a hundred thousand died, but my family's annual Christmas fund remained undented. On my birthday in 1991 Gorbachov resigned and the Soviet Empire came to an end, and our turkey was too big to go into the oven. In December 1993 the South African parliament voted itself out of existence and over the Christmas Day sherry, I heard my mother ask someone, "What is apartheid anyway? Is it a city?"

'Do you know what I have in all those wet shopping bags? I have gifts for my sisters Saffron, Jubilant, Cleopatra and Severo, and my brother Aurelius, and my little adopted brother Min, and presents for my father Harry, and his later wives, Mandy and Debbie and Peacock, a transsexual, and my ex-stepfather Richard, and his boys Charles, David and Bill, and my new stepfather Gavron and his sister Cassandra, who'll be upset if she's left out – she is suicidal. And there are so many grandparents on all sides, not to mention aunts, uncles, cousins, I don't know what to do, but those you forget don't forgive. And Saffron and Jubilant are both pregnant and what worries me is that now the next generation is coming along and, as with the flat-folded non-destructible prion, growth of family members will be exponential and potlatch frenzy never be at an end, and how will I ever find time or strength to save the world? I blame my mother. And the shops are shut and I have no gift for Saffron's partner or Jubilant's husband and I can't even remember their names. I'm so tired.' And Clarissa's tears were renewed.

'What we regret for the dead, the poor and distressed,' said Miss Jacobs, 'is that they are not alive, spending and happy. We might as well have a good time while we can, in their honour, if indignation will allow. There's such a thing as going too far, I do agree, but all will yet be well.'

When Clarissa was calm again she and Miss Jacobs both put on raincoats, and went down the street to where there was a skip and emptied out the contents of the carrier bags – a myriad packages and parcels, gold and red and green, all glittery with Christmas goodwill – so they tumbled down into wet rubble and in between paint-peeled planks of worm-eaten wood. And if the minute Miss Jacobs and Clarissa were gone a host of shadowy figures stretched skinny arms out of the damp dark to retrieve them, so much the better.

# ONCE IN LOVE IN OSLO

The woman drove. The man was the passenger. She was English. He was German. She was in her fifties, tough and bright and not yet finished with sex. She wore a vivid green shirt and jacket. His hand rested on her knee. He was thirtyish, blond, gentle-eyed; sharp, childish features clouded by a soft fuzzy beard. He thought she was invincible, wonderful, and often told her so.

Stella had things to do in Oslo, she said: a couple of people to see: a few loose ends to tie up. She'd appreciate company. Lothar was a children's book illustrator; a couple of commissions had fallen through: he had time to spare. They'd met in a bar in his home-town, Berlin, and gone home together. She was in business, she said; he was not sure what it was. She lived in Ipswich, England.

She knew her way through the backstreets of Oslo; the ship had docked at 6 a.m.: early: they'd picked up the hire car at the port, a BMW, executive style, glossy black, bullet-proof windows. Lothar didn't drive – he did not, he often said, wish to be an accomplice in the pollution of the planet; besides, he enjoyed his passenger status. He thought her hands gripped rather tightly on the wheel as they approached Grunnerloek-ka.

'I hate this place,' she said.

Early sun shone on snow-sprinkled trees. Lothar looked round for any possible source of her hate, but could find none. It was a district much like the one he himself lived in, only in Oslo, not Berlin. A run-down, attractive village-within-the-city, where artists and academics clustered, and now the immigrants moved in because rents were cheap. Already people were about. A bouncy blonde mother wheeled out twins in a high, well-sprung pram: a group of shrouded Islamic women hurried by; a pale young man with ringlets played folk-songs on a flute. A Turkish foodstore stood next to a shop selling Japanese paper lampshades and beeswax candles: there was an espresso bar next to a clinic offering Chinese medicine and acupuncture. A gang of chil-dren raced along the shop fronts, banging hands against shutters and doors as they went – clang, clang, reverberating – but otherwise they kept silent, as if like a flock of birds they could read each other's minds. Vietnamese, he thought: lithe, graceful and dangerous; those, you could be sure, whom earlier generations had wronged, now thriving on the guilt of the descendants.

'It seems much like anywhere else,' said Lothar cautiously.

'It's going down in the world,' she said. 'Black faces everywhere.'

He felt shocked. He'd been on the verge of falling in love with her. He moved his hand away from her knee. She felt it go and smiled.

'I am concerned for property prices, that's all,' she said. 'Rentals and so forth.'

\*     \*     \*

They came to a park. An untidy slope of snow, thawing, green and brown tussock showing through the white, ran down to a partly frozen stream, tree-lined. Ducks swam in patches where the ice had melted, milling around, uncomfortably close to one another. Stella parked the BMW on the gravel verge. On the other side of the road, overlooking the park, stood turn-of-the-century apartment blocks, balconied, shabby but attractive in their deep Hanseatic colours. They had been built in an age where there was more space, fewer people; the buildings stood at a leisurely distance from one another, their proportions pleasant.

'How attractive,' said Lothar, who would always rather praise than blame. Good humour, he felt, made the world go round.

'I lived here for eleven years,' said Stella. 'Up there on the fourth floor. The balcony with all the house plants. I was married to a musician.'

'What happened?'

'He betrayed me,' she said, and seemed disinclined to say more.

'Did you love him?' he pressed.

'Oh, yes,' she said bleakly.

She made no move to get out of the car. They sat there in silence. A duck made an aborted landing on the ice down below, and took off again directly. That made her laugh.

'I moved out so she could move in,' said Stella. 'It was the sensible thing to do. So sensible, the Norwegians. She was Miss Oslo, a long time back. She had a degree in anthropology, and could play the bassoon besides.'

'Miss Oslo?' He was confused.

'I'm talking the old world, not the new,' she said. 'I'm talking Beauty Queens. Hers was the female face and form

31

Norway chose to present to the world. My husband served the same function, but as a musician. He would take his orchestra abroad: how everyone applauded: cut out clippings back home. They were made for each other. Though I think now there are financial problems. They are getting older: the young tread hard upon their heels. Incomes fall. You know how it is.'

A man came out of the wooden doors of the apartment block. He was in his early sixties, perhaps: thin, a little bent, gentle, elegant, a man of some dignity and authority. He carried a violin case. He did not notice the BMW or its occupants, though they should have been noticeable enough.

'There he goes,' said Stella. 'There goes George. His mind on other things, as usual. Music, most likely. Miss Oslo had to all but lie on her back and wave her legs in front of him, before he so much as noticed. But such long legs, in the end he couldn't help it. I don't blame him, I blame her.'

'Don't you want to speak to him? Shouldn't you go after him?'

'More fun to speak to Miss Oslo, 1970,' said Stella.

A blond boy of about twelve came out of the apartment door, and ran after George. He too had a violin case; it banged against his legs when he ran. He took George's hand.

'That will be Tora,' said Stella. 'They had a boy, later, a half-brother for Karianne.'

'Karianne?'

'My daughter,' said Stella. 'She chose to stay with her father. This is Norway: children have rights too, you know. She's seventeen now. It seemed best to keep out of her life one way and another.'

*     *     *

A dark-eyed boy came out of the apartment block and stared at the car. He was Turkish, or perhaps Kurdish, with smooth plump, dusky cheeks; beautiful, rather girlish. Lothar thought he would be perfect as a model for the child in his next book. When the boy had enough of staring, he went in again.

'He'll have gone to fetch his friends,' said Stella.

'Don't leave me alone here,' said Lothar, suddenly nervous and a long way from things familiar. The sun had gone in: such snow which still rested on branches stopped glittering, and the white had a kind of deadness.

'Don't be so nervous,' she said.

She reached across him and opened the glove box. She felt beneath papers and brought out a hand weapon, squat, dull and black, showed it briefly to Lothar, smiled, and tucked the gun back under the papers again.

'A gun?' he asked, incredulous. 'A real one?'

'Yes, and it's loaded,' she said. 'So don't be stupid with it. But guns make anyone feel safe. Just knowing they're there.'

He remembered she'd made some kind of deal with a couple of young men in a bar the night before they left Copenhagen. A box had changed hands. She'd insisted on going to that particular bar, though there were better, smarter ones near-by, and the night was chilly. Click, click, her heels had gone down the cobbled harbour alleys.

'Copenhagen's cheap for weapons,' she said. 'I got it for a couple of hundred dollars. I'd have had to pay nearer eight back home.'

'But why?' he asked. 'What can you possibly want a gun for?'

'I'll sell it to help pay for the trip,' she said. 'Since there's a personal element in us coming here, I don't like to charge it to my business. I hate being out of pocket.'

'How do you get a weapon through customs?'

She looked at him sideways: eyes still bright and long-lashed; delinquent.

'I have a friend in every port,' she said. 'It's how I make my living.'

He supposed it to be a good living: her bracelet was solid gold; the buckle on her belt likewise. Her cases were soft leather. She'd paid cash for the car hire: she kept a wad of notes in her bag, rolled and in a rubber band. Too many for a wallet.

He could see he was of no practical use to her: she must sincerely want his company, or at least his body. He was flattered. This powerful, dangerous, effective person, with so much history, her body melting into his at night.

Now a young woman came out of the apartment block: pretty, and healthy, long-legged, black tights, short yellow skirt, leather jacket. A willowy black youth came out after her: shaven headed, well featured. They walked off hand in hand, black and white.

'There goes the future,' said Stella, without bitterness.

'My daughter and what they've made of her. I'm going up.'

And without further ado, she left the car and vanished through the doors of the apartment block. She left the gun where it was: he was relieved. He had thought perhaps she was on some mission of vengeance. A group of boys, some nine or ten of them, had come out to stare at the BMW. They kept to their side of the road, reverential, passive and well behaved enough. They'd moved aside without protest, to let Stella by.

Lothar found his mouth was dry. He felt trapped. He realised he had no krone, only marks. He wished he could drive. Perhaps when he got back to Berlin he would give up the more extreme of his ecological principles, and take lessons. But would he be going back to Berlin? Past and future seemed to retreat. Supposing this alarming woman asked him to join her in England? What then? He might even accept. In theory, it was easy to work and earn in any European country.

He adjusted the driving mirror the better to see his face. He looked tired: the last couple of nights' exhaustion showed. He took a compact out of his travelling bag, and opened it: dark blue eye-shadow. He applied a little to his eyelids with his fingers and smoothed it in. The action calmed him: he found people seldom noticed. Now a little mascara on the lashes. Soft, young, dark eyes looked back at him, but they weren't his, they were out of the side mirror. The boy and his friends had crept up to the car. Now they pointed and laughed, white teeth sharp in wide mouths. He knew enough about vehicles to switch on the BMW's ignition and close a crack of window, which he saw was open on the driver's side. With a casual elbow, he triggered the central locking system.

He felt safer. He switched on the radio and stared fixedly ahead. The radio gave him rock music. Making as little movement as he could, he changed the station. Jerome Kern. When he allowed himself to look again the children had retreated to their own side of the street. Hostility now seemed to be mixed with curiosity. Avoid eye contact, he thought.

Where were their mothers? Their fathers? Was there no one about to disperse them, send them about their business? Did the police never come down here?

On the fourth floor of the apartment block Miss Oslo opened her front door, thinking it was the dry-cleaning delivery, and saw George's wife standing there. Most people by the time they arrived up here were panting a little. But Stella's breath came easily.

'I didn't know you were in Oslo,' said the former beauty queen. She had the sculpted face of so many Scandinavian women past their first youth: the hair scraped firmly back; handsome, all character, no nonsense.

'I was just passing through,' said Stella, and laughed. All kinds of things seemed to amuse her.

'No one goes to Oslo on the way to anywhere,' observed Miss Oslo. 'You've just missed the others. What a pity! Little Tora went off with his father: they play such good music together. And Karianne's off with her boyfriend for a couple of days. You should have given us some warning.'

'It's you I've come to see.'

'I'm delighted,' said Miss Oslo, backing into the layers of foliage which broke up the cold clean lines of the apartment. 'You are always welcome here.'

Nothing was disorderly, nothing was out of place. Even the papers on Miss Oslo's desk, at which she had evidently been disturbed, were neatly arranged: her reference books evenly placed. Old books. *A Small Hut in Bali. The Penang Peninsula in the 1920s: Art and Habitat. Asian Myth, Eurasian Artefact.* Distant places, distant years, collected, confined and organised, here in this Northern city.

'I am not in the least welcome,' said Stella. 'I don't want to be welcome.'

36

'Ah, Stella,' said Miss Oslo, kindly, 'still the naughty little girl!'

And she made the Englishwoman sharp black coffee and they talked about George's health and Karianne's new black lover, and anything other than why Stella was there. Stella enquired about the possibility of marriage between her daughter and the black man, and Miss Oslo laughed and said Stella was old-fashioned: these days in Oslo, marriage was a rare occurrence. 'But George would like her to,' said Stella. 'Or so he wrote and told me.'

'I didn't know you and George corresponded,' said Miss Oslo, taken aback.

'He writes to me,' said Stella, 'when you have an affair, or he's upset in some way.'

'How strange,' said Miss Oslo, 'that he should turn to you, when he and I can discuss everything freely.'

'He doesn't want to discuss,' said Stella, 'he wants to complain.'

She went out on to the balcony, and stood there, to look over the frozen park and the hapless ducks, and the city she once knew so well. Miss Oslo came out after her.

'It's quite chilly out here,' she said. 'Wouldn't you rather be inside?'

'I felt I couldn't breathe in there,' said Stella. 'But that's just Oslo, isn't it? Airless.'

'I don't understand what you mean,' said the younger woman. 'Oslo is exceptionally unpolluted for a major city.'

'Even out here it's airless enough,' said Stella. 'I remember standing here one day while you explained to me how my marriage was over, and George nodded and agreed. I thought

I was suffocating. So much sense, so little passion, it was hard to breathe.'

'It was all for the best,' said Miss Oslo.

Looking down, Stella could see the shiny roof of the BMW and the children who circled it.

'Is it school holidays?' she asked.

'No,' said Miss Oslo. 'All the children are in school. Do come in and finish your coffee. It's strong, but it's decaffeinated.'

'One is always so safe in Norway,' said Stella, but she didn't go inside. 'More and more things to be safe from. Caffeine, nicotine, alcohol.'

'These things are bad for one, or put others at risk,' said Miss Oslo primly hovering.

'These things are beautiful,' said Stella. 'It is one's right to self-destruct before time.'

Miss Oslo's face stayed blank.

Stella lit a cigarette and puffed. Politeness and distaste warred in Miss Oslo's face; politeness won: she said nothing. Ash from Stella's cigarette span in the wind and landed on the soil of a potted plant.

'You can remove it later,' said Stella, 'flake by sinful, uncivilised flake! I see you have a string of nuts hung out for the birds. How kind you are, Miss Oslo; even the birds of the air experience your goodness! But Miss Oslo does not work out what happens next. She is naive. Those you do good to hate you. The birds of the air and the beasts of the earth will eat your crumbs, and return to take everything you have.'

'I have a deadline,' said Miss Oslo. 'An article to deliver by this afternoon. I really have to get back to my desk. But it was wonderful to see you.'

Stella came back inside, but made no move to leave.

*       *       *

Downstairs in the front of the BMW, Lothar stared fixedly at his knees. The children circled. There must be nearly twenty of them now. There were a handful of girls amongst them now, he noticed, not so good-looking as the boys; they had more crowded, cramped, sullen faces. Surely someone would come along soon. The boy he assumed was the leader – the one he had hoped to draw – drew out a coin and scratched it along the side of the car, slowly and deliberately. The children laughed. Lothar froze. He did not know what to do, or what would happen next.

'Tell me why you're here,' said Miss Oslo.

'I thought perhaps you'd like to know,' said Stella, 'that George has been sleeping with your baby-sitter, Camilla. Sometimes he writes to boast as well as to complain. It happens when you're away, on your case studies.'

'I don't believe you,' said Miss Oslo eventually. 'George and I are totally open with one another in sexual matters. If there was anything to tell me, he would have discussed it with me.'

'Disloyalty takes all forms,' said Stella. 'What you citizens of Oslo have to fear is not the enemy without, but the enemy within. It's not the Russians creeping down from the tundra, or the Germans seeping up from the lowlands; it's the serpent in your bosom, the snake you saved from the cold. George writes to me to say he wishes to marry Camilla; but he does not know how to break it to you.'

'You're lying,' said Miss Oslo, white as a sheet: she had run her hand through her hair, and wisps had escaped from their confining band.

'I wrote to him; why! I said, just to be honest about it, civilised. Do it in Camilla's presence. Explain to her that her relationship with you is finished, dead. Your turn, Miss Oslo, to stand on the balcony, and try to breathe. Tora is so close to his father, from what you say, no doubt he'll choose to live with his father and his new mother, not you and your no one.'

Some six or seven of the children had coins in their hands: they ran them in patterns over the car: the paint on bonnet and doors split, blistered and flaked as in their poison hands the sharp metal edges of the coins crissed and crossed. The children laughed to see the damage. Lothar reached for the gun in the glove compartment. He pointed it at the circling enemy, first this side then that. The children laughed louder and jeered and pointed. Either they thought the gun was a toy or they didn't care what happened next. That last was the most frightening thing.

'What goes around, comes around,' said Stella, upstairs.
  'As life goes by, it becomes apparent there is some justice in it.' Miss Oslo wept.

The leader of the boys leaned over and pressed his face, gargoyle-like, against the windscreen of the BMW. Lothar screamed aloud in fear and fired the gun; the bullet hit against toughened glass, failed to pierce it: instead ricocheted around the inside of the car, bouncing off walls and seat backs and dashboard, finally hitting and lodging in Lothar's right shoulder. He screamed again, and the children scattered, scared off by noise, and running feet, and the wail of approaching police cars. By the time the ambulance had arrived, there was no sign of the children. Lothar freed the locks with his one usable hand, and even that was bloody. Someone opened the car door, and helped him out.

*       *       *

Stella came out of the apartment block in time to see the commotion: Lothar saw her and called out, but Stella could see it was not in her interests to be involved. She didn't cross the road to him, but turned away and walked swiftly round the corner and out of sight.

# GUP – OR FALLING IN LOVE
# IN HELSINKI

You'll never guess what happened to me in Helsinki. How my life changed, when I was there last October. Let me tell you! The trees in that much-islanded, much-forested Northern country – you've never seen so many islands, so much forest, so low and misty and large an autumn sun – were just on the turn; the rather boring universal green giving up and suddenly glowing into reds and yellows and browns. 'Ruska' is what the Finns call this annual triumph of variety over uniformity; something so dramatic they even have this special name for it. It is, I suppose, the last flaring surge of summer: like a woman of fifty who throws out the black shoes she's worn all her life and shods herself in greens and pinks, feeling she'd better make the best of things while she can. Not that I'm fifty, in case you're wondering, I'm twenty-nine; but twenty-nine can feel pretty old. Older, I imagine, than fifty, because around thirty the tick-tock of the biological clock can sound pretty loud in a woman's ear.

My mother wants me to stay home, get married, have children.

'Settle down, Jude,' she'd plead. 'It's what I want for you.'

'I can't think why,' I'd say. 'You never did.'

'That's different,' she'd say, and pour another whisky and light up her cigar. My mother is a professional golf coach, and has been ever since my father walked out twenty-five years ago. She had to do something to earn a living. She's a healthy and athletic woman, though she must be over sixty, and men are still for ever knocking at her door, though she doesn't often let them in. The whisky and cigar syndrome is no problem (or only to my sister Chris). I see it as just my mother's rather old-fashioned way of saying to a man, 'I'm as good as you. What do I want you for?'

'Christ,' I say to my sister, 'Mother's whisky is always well watered. The cigar goes out after ten seconds. What are you worrying about?' But Chris is a nurse. She was seven when my father left. I was four.

My mother's determination that I should settle down seems to me a fine example of GUP. What do I mean by GUP? It's the Great Universal Paradox which rules our lives. See it at work in any obstetric ward, at the very beginning of things. There you'll find a woman who only ever wanted a baby but hers was stillborn, and another who's just had a living baby she doesn't want, and someone in for a sterilisation and another for a termination, and another with a threatened miscarriage, and another resting up before sextuplets, having taken too much fertility drug – and all will be weeping. All want different things so passionately; and nature takes no notice at all of what they want. Nature just rumbles on insanely, refining the race.

What you want you can't have: what you do have, you don't want. That's GUP.

When I arrived in Helsinki I was in love with Andreas

Anders, who didn't love me. And I was loved by Tony Schuster, whom I didn't love. My loving of Andreas Anders loomed large in my life, and had done so for six years. Tony Schuster loving me, which he had for all of seven days, meant to me next to nothing; that's the way GUP goes. Andreas Anders not loving me made me feel fat and stupid: so if Tony Schuster was capable of loving someone as fat and stupid as me, what did that make Tony Schuster? Some sort of wimp? In other words, as famously spoken by Marx (not Karl, but the third brother) tearing up the long-sought invitation to join – 'Who wants to belong to a club of which I'm a member?' GUP.

Finland is just across a strip of sea from the Soviet Union, though the government is of a rather different kind and in Finland women seem to run everything, whereas in Russia it's the men. Finland is noble but Russia is exciting. Little Finnish children always look so healthy, bright-eyed, well-mittened and properly fed to keep out the cold. Yes, yes, I know. I'm broody. Bright, bright clothes they wear, in Helsinki. Terrifically fashionable. Lots of suede, so soft it looks and acts like linen.

We were in Helsinki to make a six-part thriller called *Lenin in Love* for BBC TV. Helsinki's Great Square is the same period, same proportions, same size as Moscow's Red Square, so it gets used by film companies a great deal. Filming in Red Square itself is always a hassle: there's a lot of worried security men about and they like to read the script and object if it says anything detrimental about the Soviet Union – and the script usually does: that being the whole *point* of cold-war thrillers. Their wrongness, our rightness. The queue for Lenin's tomb is always getting into shot, and you can hardly ask the punters to move on, when they've railed all the way in from Tashkent or Samarkand to be there. So off everyone goes to Helsinki to film the Moscow bits. *Doctor Zhivago* was made in Finland.

Andreas Anders is the Director of *Lenin in Love*. Tony Schuster is the cameraman. I'm the PA. I have a degree in Politics and Economics and moved over from Research to Production five years ago; seeing I had a better chance of being close to Andreas Anders. You'd think a bright girl like me would think about something other than love, but at twenty-nine it gets you, it gets you! Twenty-nine years old and no children or live-in-lover, let alone a husband. Not that I actually wanted any of those things. In the film and TV world there's not all that much permanent in-living. You just have to pack up and go, when the call comes, even when you're in the middle of scrambling his breakfast eggs. Or he, yours. Men tend to do the cooking, these days, in the circles in which I live. Let's not say 'live'. Let's say 'move'.

I'd been the researcher on Andreas Anders' first film. I was twenty-three then and straight out of college. It was a teledrama called *Mary's Son*, about a woman's fertility problems. It was during the first week of filming – Andreas took me along with him: he said he needed a researcher on set though actually he wanted me in his bed – that I both developed my theory on GUP and fell in love with him. At the end of the second week Andreas fell in love with his star, Caroline Christopherson, the girl who was playing Mary. And I was courteously and instantly dismissed from his bed. Nightmare time. I'd got all through college repelling all boarders: now this.

*       *       *

45

But Andreas Anders! His face is pale and haunted: he has wide, kind, set-apart grey eyes, and he's tall, and broad-shouldered. He has long, fine hands, and what could I do? I loved him. That he should look at me, little me, in the first place! Pick me out from all the others? Even for a minute, let alone a week, let alone a fortnight, what a marvel! At least when he fell for Caroline Christopherson it was serious. They got married. And now she's world-famous and plays the lead in big budget movies, and is a box-office draw, which irritates Andreas, since he's so obviously the one with the talent, the creativity, and the brains: Caroline just has star quality. When it gets bad for Andreas, why there I am in bed with him again and he's telling me all about it. They have a child, Phoebe, who gets left behind with nannies. Andreas doesn't like that either. I don't say, 'But you're the one doing the leaving too,' because I seldom say to him what I really think. That's what this one-sided love does to you. Turns you into an idiot. I hate myself but I'm tongue-tied.

How can I compete with C.C., as he calls her? That kind of film-starry quality is real enough: a kind of glowing magnet-ism: a way of moving – just a gesture of a hand, the flick of an eye – which draws other eyes to itself. I don't look too bad, I tell myself. Though I suppose where C.C. looks slim I just look plain thin. Both our hair frizzes out all over the place, but hers shines at the same time as frizzing. I do not know how that effect is achieved. If I did, friend, I would let you know. I look more intelligent than she does, but that's not the point. On the contrary. Andreas Anders once complained I always looked judgemental. That was when we were doing a studio play up at the BBC's Pebble Mill studios, *Light from the Bedroom*. My first PA job. C.C. was giving birth to little Phoebe in Paris while we were taping in Birmingham. Andreas couldn't leave the show: well, how could he? He and I stayed at the Holiday Inn. He is the most amazing lover.

I don't let on how much I care. I pretend it means nothing to me. If he thought it hurt, he'd stay clear of me. He doesn't mean to be unkind. I just act kind of light and worldly. I don't want to put him off. Would you? GUP again! If you love them, don't let them know it. 'I love you' is the great turn-off to the uncommitted man.

And now here's Tony Schuster saying 'I love you' to me, publicly, leaning down from his dolly as he glides about in the misty air of Helsinki's Great Square. The mist's driving the lighting man crazy. The scenes are intended to be dream-like, but all prefer the man-made kind of mist to the one God has on offer. Man's is easier to control.

'Let's leave this life,' Tony says. 'Let's run off together to a Desert Island.'

'You mean like *Castaway*?' I ask. I know film people. Everything relates back to celluloid.

'How did you guess?' He looks surprised. He's not all that bright. Or perhaps I'm just too bright for everyone's comfort. For all his gliding to and fro on his great new black macho electronic camera with its built-in Citroën-type suspension – 'This camera cost £250,000,' he snaps, if anyone so much as touches the great shiny thing – I can't take Tony seriously. He has quite an ordinary, pleasant, everyday face. He's thirty-nine, and has a lot of wiry black hair. Andreas's hair is fair and fine. 'I love you!' Tony Schuster yells, for all the world to hear. 'Run off with me, do!'

I think his loving me so publicly annoys Andreas, but he doesn't show it. Tony's one of the top cameramen around:

they can be temperamental. It's as well for a Director to hold his fire, unless it's something that really matters – a smooth fifty-second track in for example – not like love, or desire, which everyone knows is just some kind of by-product of all the creative energy floating around a set.

'I love you' is a great turn-off for the female committed elsewhere. GUP.

Sometimes I do agree to have a drink with Tony, when it's a wrap for the day, and we all stagger back to the bar of the Hesperia. Except for Andreas, who's staying at the Helsinki Inter-Continental. When I heard C.C. was coming to join her husband and hold his hand through the whole month of Helsinki shooting, I put them in a different hotel (I do location accommodation, *inter alia*) from the rest of us. I thought I couldn't bear their happiness too near me. We'd be going off to Rome presently, anyway, and C.C. wouldn't be following us there. She'd be going, not back to little Phoebe, but to Hollywood for some rubbishy block-busting new series, which Andreas despised. He had the Art, she made the money.

'It's so clichéd I can't bear it,' Tony would moan. 'The PA in love with the Director! You're worth more than that.'

More than being in love with Andreas? How could such a thing be possible?

Tony's wife had just left him, taking the children. He'd been away from home just once too often. When she wanted him where was he? Up the Himalayas filming *Snowy Waste* or under the Atlantic with *Sonar Soundings* or in the Philippines with *Lolly a Go-Go*. When he didn't turn down *Lenin in Love* because he couldn't miss an opportunity of working with Andreas Anders, the Great Director, Sara waited for him to say 'yes' to the call from his agent, and he did, of course, having said he'd say no, and at that point she packed. The wives do.

'You love films more than me,' she said. And so Tony did. Now he thought he was in love with me. I knew what was going on. His wife had left, he was sad and worried; love on the set's a great diversion. On the whole, you last as long as the project does; not a moment longer. Sometimes it sticks – look at Andreas and C.C.; me and Andreas – but mostly it's all, as I say, just surplus energy taking sexual/romantic form. I know so much, and so little too. GUP!

'You have no pattern for a happy married life,' laments my mother. 'All my fault.'

'I don't want to be married,' I say. If I was married how could I follow Andreas round the world? But I don't tell her that. His favourite PA! I'm good at my job: by God, I'm good at it. He won't find fault with me.

'Without you!' he once said (that was *Love in a Hot Climate*: we were in a really ritzy room at the Meriden in Lisbon: C.C. was off in Sydney and Andreas thought she was having an affair with the male lead), 'Without you, Jude, I wouldn't be half the director I am!' A real working partnership we have, Andreas and me, oh, yes! His fingers running through my hair when there's nothing else to do, and hotel rooms in strange cities can be lonely; you need your friends around.

Before I left for Helsinki my mother said something strange. 'Your father ran off with a girl from Finland,' she said. 'Our au pair. Just make sure you come back.' Now my mother never said anything at all about my father if she could help it. And my sister Chris and I seldom asked. Questions about our dad upset her. And it doesn't do to upset a woman who is a golf coach by profession. She gets put off her stroke, and if she loses her job, how will any of you live? Our house went with the job. On the edge of the golf course. Thwack, thwee, muted shouts – to me the sound of childhood.

I expect if your husband ran off with the Finnish au pair you wouldn't want to dwell on it much. This was the first I'd heard of it. Chris and I had tried to trace our father, when she was twenty-one and I was eighteen, but we never got very far. I can't say we tried hard. Who wants to be in touch with a father who doesn't want to be in touch with you? Apart from the fun of the thing, I suppose. Sister Chris had been oddly worried about my going to Helsinki.

'You and your lifestyle!' she said, when I rang the Nurses' Home to say I was off to work on *Lenin in Love*. She'd just been made Night Sister of Men's Orthopaedic. Quite a cheerful ward, she said. At least they mostly got better. 'Can't you ever stay in one place, Jude. You'll get AIDS if you don't watch out. You film-people!' Chris had my lifestyle all wrong. I was astonishingly sedate. There'd only ever been Andreas Anders, apart from a few forgettables. It was pathetic, really. But somehow men seem to know if your emotions are occupied elsewhere. You send out 'I belong to someone bigger than you' signals, just as much if you're wretchedly involved as if you're happily married.

My mother and sister were right to worry, as it happened. Because a strange thing did happen to me in Helsinki. I was walking with Tony in the Rural Life Museum one Sunday and explaining why I wouldn't go to bed with him, and what was wrong with his psyche. He was looking quite wretched and pale, as men will in such circumstances. The Museum is in fact an open-air park devoted to the artefacts of Finland's past. We were admiring an elegant wooden church boat which could hold a hundred people – entire villages would

row themselves to church in these boats if they so chose –
when my attention was caught by one of those familiar
groups of people, complete with cameras and sound equipment. This lot were clustered round and filming one of the
enormous orange toadstools with yellow spots they have in
these parts. Proper traditional pixie toadstools. Hallucino-
genic, they say.

And the sound man put down his gear – he was taking
white sound, I presumed: a toadstool hardly makes much
noise, even in its growing, which can be pretty rapid – and
walked over to me. He wasn't young. Sixty or so, I suppose.
Quite heavy round his middle: pleasant looking: intelligent:
glasses.

'Hello,' he said, in English.

'Hello,' I said, and I thought where have I seen that face
before? And then I realised, why! whenever I look in the
mirror, or when I look at Chris: that's where I've seen it.
More the latter, because both Chris and he were overweight.
It looked worse on her. He was really quite attractive.

'You're with the English film crew, aren't you?' he said.

'I saw you in the Square yesterday. It had to be you. Jude
Iscarry.'

'Or Judas Iscariot or Jude the Obscure,' I said, playing for
time, because my heart was pounding. 'Take your pick!'

'Your mother said you'd gone into films,' he said. 'Chip off
the old block.'

'You're my father,' I said.

'"Fraid so,' he said.

'I didn't know she was in touch with you,' I said. It was all I
could say. Tony just stood and looked on. Moments in a
person's life!

'I passed by five years back,' my father said, 'but she
advised me strongly to keep away, so I did. Though I'd have

liked to have stayed. Quite a powerful stroke, your mother.'

'She's had to develop it,' I said.

'Um,' he said. 'But she always was independent, wanted to be father and mother too.'

'That's no excuse,' I said.

Tony left us and he, my father, whose name was Saul Iscarry, took me out to lunch. We had pancakes, caviar and sour cream, washed down by tots of vodka. The best food in the world. The Finns have the highest heart disease rate in the world. So Chris had assured me, before I set off for Helsinki.

My father had eventually married his Vieno, my mother's au pair, and actually gone to the Moscow Film School, and now he was one of the best sound men in the world (he said) and had Finnish nationality, but lived in Leningrad. Vieno was a doctor, they had three children, and what with visa problems and general business and so forth there hadn't been much point in keeping in touch, let alone the time. (Roubles are just one of those currencies that make it difficult for a father to support his abandoned children.) But he'd thought of Chris and me a lot.

Big deal, I thought, but said nothing. What was the point?

Now we were in touch, he said, we must keep in touch. He was glad I was in films. The best life in the world, he said, if you had the temperament. But why was I only a PA? Why wasn't I a producer, at the very least? Ah. Well. He said he'd like to see Chris. How was she? Just fine, I said. She'd have to come over and see him some time, since visas for him were so complicated. If you ask me visas are as complicated as you care to make them, but I didn't say that either.

I said Chris would be over to see him next Easter. That gave her six months to lose three stone. She should be able to do that. A girl likes to be at her best when she meets up with her old dad.

'You've grown up a fine handsome girl, Jude,' he said. 'I'm proud of you,' and you know, that meant a great deal to me. More than it should have. If anyone was to take the credit for the way I was it should have been my mother. Oh, Great Universal Paradox which runs our lives – that what should please us doesn't, and what does please us, shouldn't!

He had to go back to work, my father said. The pixie toadstool called. The crew could not be kept waiting. When could it ever, in any country, in any language in the world? We exchanged addresses. He went.

And I took myself off to the little Greek Orthodox church that's tucked away behind the Great Square, and there I sat down. I had to be quiet: absorb what had just happened. I didn't kneel. I'm not very religious. I just sat, and thought, and rested. The unexpected is tiring.

It's a small, ancient building: a chapel rather than a church. But it blazes with intricate icons and gold leaf and crimson velvet; everything shimmers: there's no way it can't: there must be a thousand candles at least stuck all around, lit by the faithful at their own expense. It's a sensuous, somehow Mediterranean place, stuck here as if by accident in this cold northern land. The air was heavy with incense: that and candle smoke smarted the eyes: or was I crying? And in the ears was the gentle murmur of the faithful, the click click of the telling of beads. Yes, I was crying. But I don't think from wretchedness. Relief, happiness almost, at something completed. My father: no longer fantasy, just a man.

And there in front of me, a couple of rows nearer the great glittery altar, was sitting Andreas Anders. He looked round and saw me. I wish he hadn't. I wanted to just go on sitting there, alone, thinking. But he got up and came to sit next to me. How good-looking he was. His bright eyes glittered in the candlelight.

'Well,' he said, 'she's not coming to Helsinki after all. Had you heard?'

By 'she' he always meant Caroline Christopherson. 'I think,' he said, 'I'd better give her up altogether, don't you? Divorce, or something drastic. I can't stand the strain.'

'Let's go outside,' I said. 'This isn't the place for such conversations.' Nor was it. As I say, I'm not one for religion, but some sort of God was here in this place, albeit in heavy disguise, and didn't want to hear all this soggy, emotional mish-mash.

So we went out, Andreas and me. And he tucked his arm into mine and said, 'Shall we go back to the Inter-Continental, just you and me?' and I pulled my arm away and said, 'No, I won't. What a monster you are!' and heard myself saying it, and knew I meant it, and there I was, out of love with him. Just like that. 'A monster?' he asked, hurt and confused. But I didn't even want to discuss it. It wasn't worth it. I'd see the *Lenin in Love* through, of course, because I was a professional, but that was all. The man was an egocentric maniac.

I left him staring after me, his worm turned, and I went back to the Hesperia and found Tony in my bedroom and told him to stop messing about and for heaven's sake somehow get his wife and children back. If he wanted to get out of the business, let him do it with the proper person.

'Is this what finding a long lost father can do?' he asked, as he left. 'And I had such high hopes . . .'

And all I could do was suppose it was: that, and simply Finland itself.

In the past Finland has always been conquered or annexed or governed by someone else – this vast flat stretch, on top of the world, of islands and forests – but now it has its own identity, its own pride: it looks not to its previous masters, Sweden and Russia, but to itself. How odd, to identify so with a nation! Perhaps it's hereditary, in the genes: like ending up in the film business. My dad ran off with a Finn: one mustn't forget that. Perhaps he somehow felt the same connection, and can be forgiven.

And that's the strange thing that happened to me in Helsinki, last October, and how my life has changed. And I called this story 'Falling in Love in Helsinki', not 'Out of Love', because although it's true I fell out of love with Andreas, out of love with love (which is a real blight), somehow I fell into love with life. Or with God, call it what you will, there in that chapel. Whatever, I found myself sufficiently enamoured of just the sheer dignity of creation to realise I shouldn't offend it the way I had been doing. I think everything's going to be all right now. I'll make out. I might even leave the film business altogether. Not go into a convent, or anything so extreme. But I might try politics. It's what I'm trained for.

As for GUP, the Great Universal Paradox, that's real enough. What I marvel at now is how happy so many of us manage to be, so much of the time, in spite of it.

# SCHEMING WOMEN

## COME ON, EVERYONE!

## PERCENTAGE TRUST

## INSIDE THE WHALE –
### OR I DON'T KNOW BUT I'VE BEEN TOLD

# COME ON, EVERYONE!

All kinds of things puzzled Maureen Timson when she was eighteen, and nothing puzzled her more than her friend Audrey Thomas. If Audrey was a friend: Maureen couldn't even be quite sure of that. Maureen and Audrey were both at college, doing languages. They shared a room, being next to one another in the alphabet; a kind of fated closeness. Maureen had all the advantages, Audrey (in Maureen's eyes) very few. Yet Audrey led and Maureen followed, and Maureen could not understand it, and chafed, and was riled. Maureen liked to get to the bottom of things: to work away at them like a knotted shoelace, yet here there was something bottomless, un-unknottable. The tangle stayed. It was not fair.

She, Maureen, was pretty: she only had to look in the shared bedroom mirror to know. (Maureen's mother had discouraged mirrors, being the kind who said it was your character that counted, not your looks, but mirrors are everywhere. Puddles or shop windows will do, or the interested eyes of others, when they reflect back a flattering image.)

Audrey was not at all pretty. She had a face like – as Maureen's Great-Aunt Edith would say – the back of a bus. (Maureen's mother had eight aunts and Edith was the one she most disliked – but then Maureen's mother disliked almost everyone, scorning the weak, the frivolous, the idle, the soft, which meant almost all the human race, excepting only sometimes Family.)

Maureen was an only child, Maureen's mother having scorned her father right out of the house, shortly after Maureen's birth. (Maureen had a vision of him, stumbling with thick boots and beery breath, up the damp path between the sad rhododendron leaves and away for ever, her own infant crying echoing from the right-hand upstairs window.)

Maureen had a tidy little waist, and Audrey had rolls of flesh above and below hers: that is the kind of thing you get to know if you share a room. Maureen had never shared a room before. It puzzled her that for all her bodily imperfections Audrey could wander around it naked and easy. Not only did it puzzle her, she didn't like it.

Maureen was clever: from the age of thirteen she'd never let a past participle not agree with a verb, not once. Audrey could hardly tell a *grave* from an *aigu*. Heaven knew how Audrey had wangled her way into college. Maureen read Machiavelli and Audrey read women's magazines. But still there was something Audrey had, that Maureen didn't. Audrey led, Maureen followed, half grateful, half resentful. Maureen was solitary, Audrey was not. Maureen hated to be solitary.

'You make friends so easily,' said Maureen to Audrey, making it sound like a reproach, some in-built lack of discrimination. 'How do you do it?'

And that seemed to puzzle Audrey, who was so seldom puzzled.

'You just talk to people,' she said.

## COME ON, EVERYONE!

'Anybody?' asked Maureen, with distaste.

'Well, yes,' said Audrey. 'Anyone who comes along. Why not?' Sometimes it was more than talk, it was into bed with just anyone, and then into someone else's, so the first anyone would go off in a huff, and Audrey would weep. But as Maureen would say to her, what did Audrey *think* would happen? Maureen kept her virginity to the last possible moment, and then surrendered it to the Secretary of the Debating Society, a steady and reliable boy with a car. Maureen was sensible, Audrey was not.

Audrey was popular with boys but Maureen could take her pick of them, so that wasn't a problem. But Maureen felt when she looked in the mirror of their eyes she saw something different from what Audrey saw. Now why should Maureen think that? She tried to talk about it to Audrey. 'Well, what do you see?' asked Audrey.

'Lust and self-interest,' said Maureen, before she had time to think. They were sitting together in a Chinese restaurant after a film. Audrey was eating crispy banana in batter, which Maureen of course had declined.

'Oh,' said Audrey. 'I see them liking me.'

Maureen felt such a spasm of rage she swallowed too great a mouthful of too-hot calorie-free China tea and burned her throat, and it was dry for days. But she didn't say anything. What was there to say? She forgot it.

What she didn't forget was Audrey standing on top of a sandhill one day in spring, in a one-piece swimsuit, hair flying in the wind, turning back to the group that followed her, that would follow her anywhere, calling out, 'Come on, everyone!' and everyone followed. Friends. Company. Party

61

times, good times, crowded times, peopled times; the whole human race whizzing round the benign fulcrum that was Audrey. 'Come on, everyone!' and everyone came, and so did Maureen, against her will yet by her will. She thought of the quiet, damp regularity of her childhood home, the single cat shut out at night, breakfast for two, mother and daughter, laid before they went to bed: some blight had entered her soul too deeply. Up the sandhill she ran with the others, and Audrey was in the sea first. 'Come on in, everyone! The water's lovely!' But of course it wasn't, Audrey was joking; it was icy, everyone screamed and Audrey splashed. How dare she! Maureen was furious. But everyone had a good time, and so did she. Orchestrating Audrey, that's what she was: weaving everyone into patterns of pleasure! How was it done?

Eventually their paths parted. Audrey with her two-two went off to muddle through some Social Science course; Maureen, with her two-one, went off to Brussels to work for the EEC, always her ambition. There had seemed something so clear and wholesome and ordered, not to mention well-paid, about the notion of a job in such a city, with a little car of her own, a little flat to be private in. And so it had turned out. Maureen had to chuck the Secretary of the Debating Society, because he went to work for Marks & Spencer in Newcastle, but these things often happen to student relationships. All the same Maureen was quite put out when she found Jim had married within the year, a colleague ten years older than himself. That summer she went home to her mother in Paignton for her annual holiday, but it was miserable and boring; she resolved never to do it again. Twelve years in Brussels, and creeping up in the Agricultural Division, and lonely, and getting herself involved with a married man (but they were *all* married: what was she to do?) which kept her lonelier because of all the waiting about for the telephone to ring and the secrecy and the unkept promises and the no social life. It took her for ever to break it off (what had *happened* to her?) but finally she did.

The very next day she got a letter from Audrey. Could they meet? Just like Audrey, Maureen thought, why should anyone want to keep in touch with anyone just because they'd been to the same college, been close together in the alphabet. But she wrote back. Audrey invited Maureen to stay for Christmas. Yes, Audrey was married (well, she would be, wouldn't she: with three children). They lived in the country, with lots of animals. Just like Audrey, thought Maureen, come-on-everyoneing into something no doubt damp, muddy, messy, noisy, with cat crap in corners. But Maureen went; she had come to dislike Christmas after seven seasons with a married man.

Audrey's house was a mess. Of course it was. Maureen put on rubber gloves and helped clear up; helped get the over-decorated Christmas tree steady on its pins, the stockings done, endeared herself to the children by handing out Mars bars in a sugar-free household, and keeping Audrey's husband Alan entertained while Audrey muddled through the children's bedtimes and prepared four kinds of stuffing for two small turkeys because that was more fun than one stuffing and an apple in a single large turkey.

'But it's more work, Audrey.'

'I know it is, Maureen, but we've all got used to two turkeys. Family life is all ritual.'

Maureen doubted that ritual was enough. Alan was a political journalist with left leanings; he had to reinspect his own political stance at least three times a year. It didn't seem to Maureen that Audrey was taking much notice of what was going on in her husband's head: she favoured a kind of ongoing warm emotional demonstration by way of keeping him happy.

'Darling, what's the matter, what's the matter?' she would cry, flinging her arms round him and embracing him as he stared at the electricity bill (two turkeys cost a third more to cook than one, as Maureen pointed out) until he unwillingly smiled. Maureen understood the unwillingness very well. In fact she thought she understood Alan very well. She looked round the ingredients of the household: the children, the warmth, the animals, the mud tramped in and out, the friends coming and going – they came for miles – and thought, with a little reorganisation this would do me very well. She thought she would have it for herself.

She had to wait four years. In that time she became a frequent visitor to the household. Long weekends, Christmas, holidays, part of the family. Then Audrey had, as Maureen knew she would, her ritual affair with a married man. Maureen knew the anatomy of that very well. 'I feel so bad about it,' mourned Audrey, chopping Christmas nuts for the stuffing of one of the turkeys. 'I love Alan, but I just can't stop myself.'

'I expect you just want attention and flattery and to feel loved,' said Maureen, carefully. She'd read enough women's magazines in her time, oh yes, many a one since her college days. 'The things Alan isn't good at. Such a pity he isn't more demonstrative. Then you wouldn't have to look for love outside your marriage.'

Audrey's tears fell into the couscous and lemon peel, and made the stuffing a fraction soggier than it should have been.

'If only I could tell Alan, if only I could talk to him about it, I'd feel so much better in my mind.'

'Perhaps you should,' said Maureen, not believing her luck. 'You have such a strong marriage. If Alan knew the lengths you'd been driven to he'd be horrified. He'd really work at saving the marriage, to make sure this kind of thing never happened again.'

'You mean, confess?' asked Audrey, her swift hands pausing, some glimmer of common sense illuminating the dark recesses of her lovesick mind, but only for a moment, not long enough. Her lover was as married as she was, glooming over his Christmas Eve whisky in some other household, missing her as she was him, lost to her for the season.

'It's hardly confessing,' said Maureen. 'It's just being honest. How can a marriage as close as yours and Alan's work if you're not honest with one another? I think you owe it to your marriage, and to Alan, to tell him all.' Then Maureen went out for a walk with the children, in the woods, where the leaves were wet with mist, and tried out 'Come on, everyone!' as she produced Mars bars from her bag. How they rushed. It worked.

Audrey told Alan about the affair, as the two of them filled Christmas stockings. She told him all about her secret love, about trystings in the backs of cars and offices, and behind hedges – it had been going on since the summer – and how she really loved Alan. If only he was a bit kinder and nicer to her it need never have happened, but he'd let things get stale and how much she valued her marriage.

'Don't talk like the back of a women's magazine,' was all Alan said, before hitting his wife from one side of the room to another, and by Boxing Day Audrey had packed her bags and gone. She'd had to go, screaming and hysterical, leaving the children, the matrimonial home and all, but it didn't help her a bit in the divorce. Technically, she'd deserted. And her lover decided to stay loyal to his wife, as married lovers will. They want excitement, not legality. Just as well there was Maureen there to help the family through the rituals of that dreadful Christmas Day – Maureen knew the domestic ropes so well, as Alan's mother had observed. And by the next Christmas Maureen was not just installed in the house but pregnant as well, with her first child, and calling out 'Come on, everyone!' at meal times, along with the best, though she didn't often cook herself, having help in the house, and a very good job (considering the local wage structure) running the local branch of the Farmer's Union.

'Don't say that!' Alan would beg. 'Don't say "Come on, everyone!" '

'Why not?'

'It irritates me. I don't know why.'

'Then you're just being irrational,' said Maureen firmly, and went on doing it. For a time her 'Come on, everyone!' was rather less peopled than Audrey's had been – but the family friends soon drifted back and everything was just fine, and the damp and droopy rhododendron leaves which rustled in her past, in her dreams, stood up fine and straight and glossy in some glorious imagined sun.

# PERCENTAGE TRUST

He came to her out of the desert, like Valentino, wearing not robes but a well-cut coat in camel cashmere. He had a solid gold pin in his lapel, in the shape of a Lear Jet. His cravat was pure silk, deep red and bright blue, and his black shoes were pointy and highly polished.

She met him at Heathrow; she was waiting and waiting for an uncle from Johannesburg to come out of immigration. He was waiting, similarly, for a business colleague from Lagos.

His face was narrow and his nose aquiline; as if carved by hot winds driving over an arid land. He was perhaps fortyish, but when people are from foreign parts you can never quite tell. He was a member of a Saudi Royal Family, he said; a cousin of the King, but he chose to live in Rome. Though he had offices in London. He loved the way she laughed, he said. The world did not contain enough laughter. His teeth were perfect.

He asked for her telephone number. A girl needs only about 60 per cent trust to part with that. Trust that the man isn't a nutter, and will simply go away if you decide not to continue the acquaintance. She wanted to hear more of the voice. It was soft, and delicately, sweetly accented. She wrote her number down for him, before he was whisked away in a limo with the colleague from Lagos, who was tall, impressive, shiny black, beautifully tailored, wearing rather a lot of gold. She did not really believe he'd call. What would a man who could have, and probably did have, girls with legs up to their navels, big blue eyes and masses of blonde hair, want with her, Elspeth Gray, children's book illustrator, late thirties, living alone and happily in a flat in Camden, if having a problem with the rent?

'Love,' he said, when he called the next day. 'Love. I fell in love with you at first sight. I loved your laughter, I loved your grace, I loved the elegance of your ballerina neck.' A ballerina neck! What her mother had always called 'your neck the giraffe'. Of course she melted.

'Now how can I help you?' Aziz asked Elspeth. Elspeth's uncle was not to be allowed into the country. His visa was not in order. Aziz said he would take the matter up with the authorities, and did. But her uncle decided to go home anyway. Elspeth felt apologetic to have put Aziz to so much trouble, for nothing.

'My dear,' said Aziz, 'anything in the world I can do for you, I will.' They were having supper at a little Italian restaurant round the corner from where she lived.

A girl needs only 65 per cent trust to have supper with a man; trust that his table manners will be good, his conversation lively, he'll pay his share of the bill and not put her under any kind of future obligation. Elspeth insisted in advance that they both pay their own way, and chose Chez Luigi, where it was cosy and quiet and the food was OK.

'I love this place,' he said. 'I love it because I'm with you. Who wants grandeur, chandeliers and caviar when they can have the simplicity of happiness?'

He ate with care and delicacy; spaghetti wound perfectly round his fork, helped by his spoon. If you lived in Rome, as he explained, you got good at spaghetti. His marriage to an English girl, a sports-shoe heiress, had failed three years back. He had two teenage sons who lived in Canada: he saw them whenever he could, but he was so busy about his cousin the King's business, it was not often enough. Import–export.

'Of what?' she asked, and he laughed, a little, complicit, sexy laugh.

'Not drugs,' he said. 'Don't worry. Gold, diamonds, precious stones.'

He was in disgrace with his family, of course he was, living away from home the way he did, marrying outside his religion, his children lost to them. But he preferred the Western way, though it could break your heart. He had thought after the end of his marriage he would never love again, but now he had met Elspeth. Her laughter had rippled through the Heathrow halls like streams through the stately pleasure domes of Kubla Khan, and worked its magic. Her head had turned, so gracefully.

He made love with the practised care, delicacy and enthusiasm with which he ate. You can always tell from the meal how it will be.

A good girl like Elspeth needs 80 per cent trust to go to bed with a man on the first date, that's if she doesn't love him. Trust that he won't turn out to be a serial killer or try to rape her; that he's not doing it for a dare, or to be revenged on a wife, or to prove to himself that he isn't impotent: in other words that she's unique, that she's somehow involved in this transaction, that she's not just a woman, all women. Trust that he'll be in touch afterwards. Of course if she loves him trust can fall even below 60 per cent and still she'll do it.

Elspeth loved Aziz a little bit before and a lot more after: but for some reason the trust never soared to 95–100 per cent, as you'd expect. As it has to be if you mean to marry. Trust he won't leave you, won't live off you, isn't after your money, your name, your nationality; trust he is what he says.

Not that marriage was mentioned. Good Lord, they'd only known one another a week, and who got married these days anyway? He took her to dinner at the Ritz to celebrate. He paid, with a platinum card. She let him. They ate oysters. He waved to an affluent-looking man two tables away who waved back and smiled.

She introduced him to a friend or so, back home.

'You look so well,' they said, 'and happy, which is the main thing. But he is rather foreign.'

'He's very helpful and so polite,' said Elspeth's daughter Angela, who was nineteen and in college, living in York. 'If you married him what fancy relatives I would have! I suppose he is on the level.'

'Why shouldn't he be? Is there any evidence that he isn't?'

'But is there any evidence that he is? Have you met his family, his friends?'

Well, no, she hadn't. Nor seen where he lived. Nor been to his offices. He travelled so much. To Paris, to LA, to Hong Kong. He'd call her from these places. Hurry to meet her on his return, to slip between her cool, ironed sheets. Elspeth ironed her sheets. She was a good girl. Her work went swimmingly. She paid off her credit cards. Sexual satisfaction cast a glow over all she did.

But he'd make a date and then just break it without warning. She hated that. She'd leave messages for Aziz on his office answerphone. He'd call back from wherever, full of apologies.

'He has a wife tucked away somewhere,' said her friends, 'that's what it is.'

Trust wavered, and fell to somewhere between 55 per cent

70

and 60 per cent. She almost broke it off. She tried; he wept. He'd been so busy, about his cousin the King's business. And in his country the rules were no different. A woman waited for her man, if she loved him.

'He must love you,' said Angela, 'or why would he bother? It's not as if you had money to steal, or a title to offer, or were a raging beauty. You're just a middle-aged, poverty-stricken illustrator of children's books.' Oh thank you, daughter!

But trust rose again to 70 per cent. He was back in her bed. He'd brought her legal documents, bonds, to prove he was who he said he was. There was his name; there were the columns of figures, descriptions of jewels, pharmaceuticals, so many noughts everywhere, littering the stiff formal pages. She wanted to trust, so she did. She laughed at her own suspicions and he rejoiced in her trust. He borrowed her mobile phone. He'd left his in Rome. The office was so busy: simpler to borrow hers than organise another.

He took her to stay the weekend at Claridge's. They drove down Bond Street in a limousine, and he bought her elaborate designer clothes, evening gowns, low-cut, and a little jewelled bag for £1,200. He said it was a cheap throwaway thing.

'But where will I wear these things?' she said.

'I like to show you off,' he said.

That night at dinner at Claridge's she wore a deep red heavy silk gown with a strappy top and no sleeves. People looked at her in admiration.

'You're really meant to wear sleeves when you dine,' she murmured (she'd been so well brought up), but all he said was, 'You have perfect skin; the more you show the better.' And it was true, she realised: she had a skin so white it seemed to glow. She'd covered it up all her life: in dull greens and browns, cotton and denim, anything that was virtuous, not flash. Dull, in fact.

An American crossed over from another table to say hello. Hogan McBride from LA, dealer in fine jewellery.

'Meet my fiancée,' said Aziz, and Hogan kissed Elspeth's hand. 'Perfect for diamonds,' he said. 'White background glow, like white sound on a tape. Such truly pale fingers.' Elspeth could see that her hands were perfect, now that a Bond Street salon had attended to them: creamed the skin and polished the nails. 'Your hands the claws,' her mother had said. 'I'll certainly think about that,' said Aziz. 'But perhaps better a necklace, to show off the perfect neck.' Hogan nodded and smiled and went on out.

'Fiancée indeed! I haven't said I'll marry you,' said Elspeth. Trust was running at 90 per cent, but a man shouldn't necessarily know it. 'And now I have to get back to real life and finish a commission. I'm late as it is with my deadline, and I have a tax bill to pay.'

Aziz went to see the concierge: something about a limo. Elspeth went upstairs again to collect her coat. He'd left the mobile phone on the bed. It bleeped. Elspeth pressed OK. It was her phone after all. She told herself for all she knew it might be a call for her. But really it was the 10 per cent between 90 per cent and 100 per cent which bothered her. Perhaps it was the wife or girlfriend calling: the one he was with when he wasn't with her. But it was a man's voice: a rich man's voice: she could tell by now. The voices of the rich have an easy confident flow.

'Aziz,' the voice said, 'pick me up at ten tomorrow for Paris. Take the Mercedes, we'll go by Chunnel. I'll need you for the day.' And that was all.

Trust bottomed out at perhaps 35 per cent. She put the phone into her pocket, and when Aziz returned kissed him goodbye as if nothing had happened. Everyone has a different way of dealing with emergencies. Elspeth's was to smile and hold her fire while she worked the parameters of danger out. Screaming and shouting was simply put on hold. Aziz arranged to meet her for lunch the next day, at Chez Luigi. She had a 25 per cent-ish kind of miserable idea it would be one of the occasions when he didn't turn up and made his excuses later.

She went home and finished her commission. A sweet story about a little girl and a computer with a heart. Then by judicious punching she got the mobile phone to read out the caller numbers over the previous month. They ran at the rate of five or six a day. She checked out their area locations. She marked the map of London; a drawing-pin for every number. They were not random; the gold points circled within the wealthier areas of the city. Well, naturally. She tried a few numbers. Secretaries, receptionists, housekeepers, answered. 'Can I speak to Aziz?' met with a polite non-response. She switched off the phone. If she responded to the bleeps he'd know it was in her possession.

She went at lunchtime the next day to Chez Luigi. Aziz did not turn up. She ate her spaghetti alone. She realised how often she did this. She went home, got on with her work and waited for him to call.

The next morning he rang her from a phone box to apologise. He'd had to go to Paris unexpectedly: a diamond deal. He'd call round that evening. He loved her. Trust almost soared again: desire can have that effect. But she made her excuses. If he couldn't come round to her place, he said, much disappointed, would she come to the Dorchester that weekend? Of course! He said, by the by, he'd lost her mobile phone: he was dreadfully sorry. It must have fallen out of his pocket.

She traced the number he'd been calling from. Press OK and 1471. A call box in South Hampstead. For its own mysterious reasons, the phone company would not tell her where it stood. She called the box again and again until a passer-by succumbed, picked up the phone and told her its location. She went and stood outside the phone box and surveyed the street. Across the road was a car-hire firm, called Classy Cars. A fancy place. Limos were parked in the yard. Chauffeurs came and went. Elspeth hung about the phone box for a couple of hours. About the only place in a city where loitering women attract no attention. Presently a car drove up and Aziz got out of it. She almost didn't recognise him at first, in his chauffeur's cap. She went home.

He had a honeymoon suite booked at the Dorchester. He had her new clothes in the wardrobe. She realised he never took her to the same place twice. Since the credit cards were stolen that of course would be unwise. But if you knew the punter's travel plans you could assess the risks. And whoever curtailed a conversation because the chauffeur might be listening?

They were to meet Mr Hogan in the downstairs bar at six-thirty. So she got to the Dorchester late, at six not five, the better to stay out of Aziz's bed. With trust at 10 per cent desire altogether fails. And that 10 per cent is there only as a kind of generalised burnt offering to faith.

She wore the white silk dress, simplicity itself, that had cost £2,200.

'You might spill something on it,' he said anxiously.

'I won't,' she said.

This dress too was strappy and low-cut. Her neck was so long and elegant and pale, she could see that now. Beautiful, not freakish, just right for diamonds! She understood now why he'd chosen her; of all the women in the world he could so easily have charmed and cheated. She was a good girl, above suspicion, and she had a perfect neck. She felt just a flicker of warmth for him.

They sat and waited for Hogan McBride in a quiet corner of the bar. Hogan strode in; he had just time for a quick drink. His limo was waiting outside, he said; Classy Cars no doubt, thought Elspeth. He put his briefcase on the table, and with his back to the world drew out, layer upon layer, a gold and diamond necklace of great magnificence. He fastened it around Elspeth's neck. Both men breathed deep in admiration.

'Your wedding present,' said Aziz to Elspeth, and to Hogan McBride, 'It hangs about an inch too low. I thought so.'

'It goes back to the workshop at once,' said McBride, 'Leave it to me. Perfection demands perfection!' And he leant forward to unclasp the necklace and as he did so she knocked her red wine all over her beautiful dress, and had to rise and run, benecklaced as she was, burbling about cold water quick, to the ladies' room – and ran straight out the other door, into the lobby extension, and had the doorman hail a taxi and went home.

She changed into her homey dress and was an altogether different person at once. Herself. Unrecognisable as fiancée to a King's cousin. She switched on the mobile phone. Within the hour it bleeped.

'Bitch, bitch!' he said. 'Where are they?'

'Not in my pocket, not in yours,' said she. 'In a safe deposit in the bank. I'll go fifty-fifty, but only because I need your help to sell them on, before I learn the trade.'

'What do I do about Hogan McBride?' he whined, all the stuffing knocked out of him, taken by surprise. Defeated by a girl!

'Just get out of there quick,' she said, 'and don't go back to Classy Cars. We'll make new contacts. Do the disappearing trick.'

As a partner in crime she grew to trust him 90 per cent and the other 10 per cent was just a burnt offering to the Fates, who don't like too much confidence. But she never went to bed with him again. The percentages were too fickle. Crime is one thing, love is another, and much more sensitive.

# INSIDE THE WHALE –
# OR
# I DON'T KNOW BUT I'VE
# BEEN TOLD

This isn't an inside-the-whale story. You know, one of those stories that run round a city like wildfire, something that happened to a friend, or a friend of a friend, so everyone shivers with dread and is glad it didn't happen to them. My friend who fell out of a fishing boat and was swallowed by a whale and was regurgitated (that was one of the earliest – his name was Jonah) or the grandmother on the roof: she died on holiday in the Basque country in very hot weather, so the family strapped the body to the roof-rack and drove a day and a night to the city and parked the car outside the police station where the car was promptly stolen. Or the axe-murderer hitchhiker dressed as a nurse but with hairy arms – you know the kind of tale?

This one is true. Honestly. It was told to me by my best friend Ursula. She has an older sister Wendy, to whom all this happened. Ursula has babies and makes bread and lives in the country. Wendy's very different, they say. I only met her once. She's a control freak, she's something big in the city: a power-dresser who wears shoulder-pads in or out of fashion, with a perfect figure and a sharp nose; one of those non-flat faces that falls away from a prominent middle, so if asked to measure it you wouldn't just run the tape from ear to ear, you'd run it from ear to nose and double it. As a face, it doesn't photograph well, but men like it. When Wendy was twenty-nine, and already vice-President of a bank, the President himself, Sir Larry Hamstock, asked her to marry him. 'No,' said Wendy.

For while Ursula was sweet and kind and pretty, and fell in love with no-good-niks who would exploit her and make her suffer, and the more she suffered the more she smiled, not so Wendy. She was the kind who grew up with suitors, had powerful men with roses on their knees before her and the worse she treated them the more they hung around. Men seem to like a woman without doubt who has nothing to frown about but seldom smiles. That was Wendy. She didn't believe in marriage and didn't believe in children; she liked her career, her wealth, her celebrity, her freedom. So Sir Larry asked her to marry him, so what? No. Not if he expected her to stay home, keep home and have babies, which he had the nerve to do.

Friends urged her to re-think. Let Sir Larry go and whoever better was likely to come along? Thirty-nine, whizz-kid, phenomenal looks, hereditary title, lands, country house, wheeler-dealer banker friend of princes, and what was more a nice guy, almost a New Man, heterosexual and no peculiar hang-ups? Recently divorced after five childless years from Susannah, one of the fox-hunting kind, who'd run off with Peterkin, an Argentinian racing-driver with red hair. Susannah, all agreed, was a bitch. And if now Sir Larry was in love with Wendy, who, come to think of it, on a dark night in a warm bed could have passed for Susannah – same physical type; same ear-to-nose looks – let her capitalise on it. Some opportunities come along once in a lifetime.

'Marry him,' friends begged Wendy, 'before someone else bags him.' Women do talk like this, even in the age of emancipation, even at the turn of the millennium; it's the training of centuries. Women know well enough that a successful woman who reaches forty will seldom have a husband and kids at home: while most successful forty-year-old men will have a wife to bring to the office party and be obliged to take time off at Christmas to go to the school nativity play. Men are romantic: women are realists. 'Grab him,' they said. For once in her life Wendy wavered.

Already the lunching ladies were gathering: the Harvey Nichols crowd: elegant women in pale silks with sensitive souls and infinite charm, widowed or divorced, cast-offs of famous men maybe, but worth a lot, well-diamonded, with names to die for. Suitable second wives for Sir Harry. 'Nab him, Wendy, or someone else will.' Wendy saw the sense of it: she always responded to competition.

'Tell you what,' said Wendy to Sir Larry, 'you pay me the salary I'd get at the bank, taking expected career moves into account, increments, bonuses and all, for the duration of our married life, and I'll marry you, and have your baby.'

'Anything, darling,' said Sir Larry, 'anything.'

Sir Larry loved a tough lady. Some men do. A demanding woman is an erotic challenge: a real man like Sir Larry looks forward to eventual mastery in bed. There is something here worth having, worth reducing to squeals and helplessness. Not a domestic day drifting inevitably towards the mattress, with no great difference between up and down, rather the shock of an elegant, snarky day coming suddenly up against the sensual needs of the night. The contrast, that's the thing, and ceremony. His grey suit neatly folded over the chair: her diamond necklace on the dressing-table: a sharper pleasure than any mixed pile of old jeans and T-shirts on the bedroom floor.

Sir Larry signed the contract. The magazine *Hello* came to the wedding. This mildly disconcerted Sir Larry's family but the new world is what it is and Wendy thought the presence of photographers a small price to pay for the quarter of a million pounds *Hello* offered. The couple moved into Hamstock House in Sussex; so did the builders, the plumbers, the landscape gardeners, the interior designers. Wendy was ruthless: within a year it was a place fit for American friends to stay, not just to say, 'How quaint, how English,' at gurgling water-pipes, cluttered perspectives and draughts, but simply, 'Wow, what a sound system!' Not a floor sloped, not a softened angle anywhere. Everything sharp and new, or if old, like the Jacobean panelling in the library, properly restored, treated and sealed. If the sealant was on the shiny side, so much the easier to clean. Casement windows were replaced by fine sheet glass, to the same end. Sir Larry continued to adore, and it must be said, Wendy grew very fond of him. The parties they gave once the house was finished became quite a number on the social scene: the mustier of the old guard fell away, to be replaced by pop-stars, politicians, fashion people: you know the kind. Both useful and fun.

So much was public knowledge. The rest Ursula told me.

The problem was, you see, that Wendy then had trouble conceiving. She couldn't believe it. She was accustomed to controlling her destiny. All hammer blows from fate, she had believed, of the kind others suffered, could surely be avoided by a little skilful manoeuvring. Not so. Not now. Eggs fell, sperm was delivered, nothing happened. The body she had so carefully nurtured, dieted, exercised, oiled and adorned, now betrayed her. She didn't tell Sir Larry. No, she just told him she was taking contraceptive measures; that they needed a little time, just the two of them, before inviting along the third. 'My darling, my darling, anything you want!'

Three years passed. Wendy had herself secretly prodded, poked, tested, blown; still no baby.

'No, Lady Hamstock, nothing physically wrong. Perhaps your husband should come in for tests?'

'Oh no,' said Wendy, 'I don't think he'd like that.'

'For heaven's sake,' said Ursula, 'tell him what's going on. He loves you.'

But Wendy wouldn't. She could see she was failing in her side of the bargain. Her salary was at risk. In the light of the marriage contract, infertility was not a joint misfortune to be endured by a bonded couple; it was a cause for dismissal, and fair dismissal at that.

Susannah and her husband, the fiery Peterkin, were back in London with their three little children: three in four years. Peterkin had won a couple of Prix Internationales, or whatever it was such people won. He was hero of the hour. Wendy persuaded Sir Larry that the time for forgiveness had come. That all exes in the New Age must be friends. That from such efforts all good things would flow. That Susannah and her Peterkin must be invited to the next party, and *Hello* must come too.

'Anything, my darling, anything! Don't you think the time has come for us to have a baby?'

'Of course, my dearest,' said Wendy. She recognised a bargaining ploy when one was offered. 'A baby it will be!'

Susannah and Peterkin were invited to stay over for a party which just so happened around the time of Wendy's ovulation. Wendy tipped her birth pills (which in fact were aspirin) down the waste disposal and Sir Larry threw the switch.

Susannah marvelled at the changes in the house, and complimented Wendy – whom privately she thought a cow – on her audacity. In return Wendy seduced Peterkin. She knew that, if Sir Larry fancied both Susannah and herself, it would be the same for Peterkin. That's the way attraction works: why second wives are right to fear first wives, and the same goes for husbands too. Never in all her life had Wendy thrown herself at a man and been refused. Nor was she now. Sudden secret intimacy took place beneath the fairy lights, behind the trees, beyond the tables of champagne. Peterkin the Brave deserved the Fair: what better for a hero but to cuckold the same man with two of his wives? Peterkin's shock of red hair glittered above Wendy: his almondy green eyes gleamed: briefly she wondered whether to take him altogether from Susannah, but this man, for all his passion and energy, knew nothing of increments, bonuses, pensions, international markets. It would not do. They were all photographed together. 'All friends again after their painful divorce', ran *Hello's* headline.

Wendy was pregnant. Sir Larry and she rejoiced. The baby was born, was held up for the cameras. A son. A male heir. His eyes were deep blue, his hair was black. Saved! Some risks have to be taken. Don't think Wendy hadn't thought of it. In an ideal world Peterkin would have had ordinary brownish hair. But at six weeks the baby's black hair fell out, as this first crop often will. For a lucky three months the child was bald. At five months the hair began to grow in. Little shafts of red, unmistakably. Wendy shaved the head, in secret. Nurse thought her strange. The baby's eyes lost their deep-blue depths; turned green and almondy. And the more she shaved, the stronger the red growth came through. Anyone who has ever shaved arms or legs as a child, in the face of their mother's warnings, knows this to happen.

Wendy fell and broke her wrist; her shaving hand was useless. One misfortune leads to another. Wendy tried with her left hand but nicked the baby's scalp and desisted. She was tough but not that tough. She knew when she was beaten. Like Canute, she was fighting back a tide. One day Sir Larry stared into his baby's crib and saw a child with Peterkin's red hair and green eyes, and cried aloud in shock and grief, and called his lawyer. Wendy had to go, without so much as a penny redundancy money and with all pension rights rescinded.

Ursula swears this story is true, but I'm not sure. It shows too many of the characteristics of an inside-the-whale tale. It offers the same kind of lesson – 'Never try to palm off a baby on a husband if the lover has red hair' – as do the others I mentioned. 'Never fall out of a boat if there are whales about' or 'Never take your grandmother on holiday' or 'Never pick up hitch-hikers, even if they look like nurses'. It contains the same whiff of moral superiority, requires the answer, 'Personally, I'd never be so stupid.' And Wendy's story contains the same inconsequential but somehow convincing detail (the Basque country, the over-shiny panelling). The same sudden end: the see-what-did-I-tell-you defiant stare of the narrator. Yes, I've changed my mind. The baby-with-red-hair is just another inside-the-whale story. You don't have to believe a word of it, unless there's a lesson in it somewhere for you.

# MOVING ON

MOVE OUT: MOVE ON

NEW YEAR'S DAY

INSPECTOR REMORSE

# MOVE OUT: MOVE ON

It happens to everyone, either from choice or necessity. You do it, or it's done to you. Your parents split; they sell the roof over your head. If it's their time to move on, it's yours as well. Once you're an adult it's either the bank's foreclosing, or you need more room, or you've just got to get out of there fast, the vibes are all wrong. So you move house: move out: move on. It's terrible, but inevitable. Who dies in the same house in which they were born? There must be a nomad hiding in us all: he's not our best friend.

Yet when the ice slabs of the igloo begin to stink and melt, what can an Inuit do but go in search of improvement? Or you're in Sarajevo and there's ethnic cleansing down the road. Or the tanks are rolling in Chechenya. Time to go. Burn the longboat when the Viking dies, for Thor's sake, if only because it's in such a mess. Push the bloody thing out to sea, build a new one. Saw fresh, clean planks. Move on, start over. Except someone always has to sift the past. The dead Viking's girlfriend sorts through his old fur slippers, throws away the rusty shield, wonders whether the lump of stone in the pocket is a talisman or just a lump of stone. She has to make decisions. She weeps. Lucky old Viking not to be there.

# A HARD TIME TO BE A FATHER

Move out, move on.

My bottom drawer: what's in it now? A broken plastic rose, loose batteries, dud or otherwise, foreign coins, shedding dried flowers, blurred receipts, broken pens, cotton off its reel, a dead wasp, an unopened letter from the bank, coffee-stained, guitar plectrums – who was it played the guitar? The tune has long since faded. The bits – oh the bits. The fluff. Is that a mouse dropping? I love you, I need you, I want you, desire you. No, I don't. Actually I don't. Not any more. I accept defeat. Here is the evidence; love never made anything perfect. Forget love, when the spirit goes dross is left behind. Assume the batteries are dud.

My fingernails are broken and grimy. Are you proud of me, Miss Jacobs, my erstwhile therapist? Are you dead or alive? Who can tell me? Do you watch me from heaven? Would you approve of these few neatly-packed and labelled boxes, all I will allow from the past? Nothing to travel with me, to go on into my future, that isn't needed. Is this maturity, coming to terms, or mere acting out? A defiant response where none is needed? How's a girl to know, now that you're gone? You knew so much about me, and I knew nothing about you. What sort of an affair was that?

If I don't do this now my children will have to do it for me after my death. I see I have preserved only what can be sold by them after I'm gone, or turned to useful purpose in their own homes. I have left them neat plastic-wrapped evidence of their descendency, their roots, in the form of certificates – birth, death, marriage, divorce – of the generations before them: the occasional passionate letter, a few proud press cuttings, their great-grand-

father's war medals. It has been a kind of suicide, except I
will go on living.

Moving on, moving out. Terrible, horrible, an internalised
earthquake. Everything gone, except what can be ordered,
clean and neutralised. People tell you this is the second worst
life event. First death – well, yes, naturally, unrecoverable
from – then moving house, then divorce, then redundancy.
How I once scoffed. Not for me, not for me, I claimed. For
me moving house would be simple; a practical matter. I am
not neurotic or over emotional. Am I?

It was I who initiated this divorce, I assure people. Don't
worry about me. I always knew if I went to law it meant I
would 'have to sell the house and split the proceeds'. I
have lived for five years without my husband. I am
accustomed to his absence. It was I who asked him to
leave; and he went without argument, which did rather
upset me, it's true. Five years have gone by and I find I
want things 'tidy'. I want to be legally 'free', not a married
woman with an absentee husband. What a world of
passions confined by the quote marks of shared experience,
have I not entered in here? 'Tidy.' 'Free.' 'Sell the house
and split the proceeds.'

Tony was happy enough with things as they were. And
now, as I sit here sorting through my bottom drawer, I see
the deed for what it is; folly: an act of self-abnegation,
martyrdom, masochism. Acting out, indeed. 'Now see
what you've made me do.' I am damaging myself for
the pleasure of thinking well of myself, doing what the
world admires – brushing aside a marriage, putting it in its
proper place. Hurling it, more like, out the window:

joining the horde to include myself between comforting quote marks.

Yesterday I sat on the floor sorting photographs. I came across one of my husband with the woman I was later to discover was his mistress. It had all the appearances of a family group: he, she, the two children aged about seven and nine, and the dog, then a puppy, out for a country walk. It was just the woman was the wrong one: she, not me. She had the grace to gnaw her knuckles and look guilty: Tony my husband looked handsome and polished and happy; my two sons were diving into his legs, as children are wont to do at that age, in flurries of embarrassed affection. They loved their father: we all did. I must have been away from home; I had to be, sometimes, for work. I couldn't date the year accurately; or be sure about the children's ages; my mind wouldn't focus. I took the scissors and cut the wrong woman out of the picture, and tore her pieces up and added her to the detritus of discarded life which rose about me, and kept the rest.

At floor level you find a different kind of debris than exists in drawers: here on the wardrobe floor are foam shoe trees, puppy-gnawed; boxes of old Christmas cards; scraps of torn fabric, horrible scarves, frayed ties, odd shoes, bent wire hangers, envelopes containing negatives of unremembered trees and nameless babies, and this photograph which I suppose no one wanted me to find but did not want to throw away. Well, nor did I. With my enemy snipped out it is now just a happy family memento, from the time when a marriage was living and vigorous. Photograph of Husband and Children out on a Walk, just rather oddly composed, truncated down one side: Tony's elbow gone, since it coin-

cided with her breast. Was that good or bad, Miss Jacobs?
Did that decisive action show health or neurosis? Cutting the
ties that bind.

When the Inuit looks at the pool of dirty water that was once
his home what does he think? What sort of reflection does it
offer him in return? Move house and you meet yourself. If the
home is swept away by flood or crumbled by earthquake, or
razed or bombed, you are allowed to stand and weep: then
others better off than you collect you, look after you, put you
in tented cities, feed you and clothe you, as if you were a new
born baby. By the time you have acquired a document or so,
a cooking pot and a blanket you have adult status again: you
must fend for yourself. Every bird must have its nest, every
person their address.

I remember packing up my parents' house. My mother had
gone off five years earlier to start a new life. She was fifty-six.
She'd left everything, debris and all, for me to sort, running
off into the arms of a wealthy golfer from South Carolina.
She took only a suitcase, and split. What an abandonment
that was. I was twenty; I took it badly. So did my father: all
he'd done was take my mother off on a cruise, by way of an
apology for an affair with a secretary. What a traditionalist
my father always was: anniversary gifts, silver wedding
ceremonies, affairs with secretaries. In the old days it was
customary for the secretary to act as second wife, making
coffee, coaxing, cosseting, flattering, with sex always just
around the corner knocking on the door, and the wife in the
business circles of the Western world as resigned to the girl's
existence in her life as the Chinese wife to the concubine, the
Muslim wife to the arrival in the household of the second,
third and fourth wives. That is to say, a lot or a little,

depending. Mohammed, they say, came back one day from talking with Allah in the desert with word that it was OK to have as many wives as you wanted. But the prophet's advisors, those grave and powerful men, though without a direct line to God, decided he had heard wrong. Surely Mohammed was mistaken; surely Allah said no more than four? Otherwise, wouldn't family life collapse? The prophet's remembrance under pressure, collapsed. OK, OK, only four; that's what Allah said, have it your own way. And so it goes, to this day. Only four.

These days, though too late for my mother, the secretary calls herself a PA, is more likely to be loved by her boss than to love him, finds it beneath her to make coffee, or service her boss's emotional needs. Things change, but don't necessarily get any better. My mother, not satisfied with the superior status offered as compensation to first wives everywhere in the world, ran off to play golf and have exclusive sex in South Carolina. It was five years before father gave up hoping for her return and sold the house; he broke his ankle on the day he contacted the estate agents; the house sold quickly he so under-priced it, and I had to do the sorting, the packing, the moving out and moving on for my father. And he not even dead.

There's the same length of time, I observe, between Tony's leaving and my own decision to divorce, and move house. Is there a connection here? Is it my father's drama I re-live, not my mother's after all? Who cares? Miss Jacobs, where are you? I want a debriefing. I need my Day of Judgement.

The detritus of my parents' house was of a different generation of trash. Purchases did not flow into that house as they do into mine. My parents made do with one teapot. I own four of varying sizes. Two of them are gifts. People used not to give casual presents, or send cards, or spend money where there was no necessity. It was not expected. People finished off the tea in the caddy before buying another quarter-pound, and the leaves would be loose in a brown paper bag, not in a packet with a free gift to end up in the bottom drawer. My parents' debris was made up not of broken plastic roses and loose batteries, but of bags of hand-knitted woollen babies' garments, shrunk and yellowed; bent metal from dart boards, incomplete sets of cards, stiffened leather golf bags, stray tent poles and ancient canvas rucksacks, the Bakelite food bowls of long-gone family pets, stored jam jars full of spider webs. And gloves. Odd gloves, kept in case the other one turned up. They had gloves: we have socks. Who wears gloves in these days of central heating? You need your fingers free to slip in the credit card to collect your money from the cashpoint machine: to turn the many keys in the many locks.

My parents' house was only ever locked when they went on holiday. Mostly, as they got older, they went on cruises. My mother met the golfer when the cruise ship docked some-where in Barbados. She fell and twisted her ankle: the handsome golfer picked her up, literally.

In that particular house-clearance I found an envelope stuffed with love letters from my father's secretary. Always something. Once my mother had vanished from the scene the secretary thought my father would marry her. He did not. I found no letters from Tony's one-time girlfriend in the debris of our joint past, but perhaps he valued them, perhaps he took them with him? I wonder who will dispose of them? She never left her husband, when it came to it.

*       *       *

Houses I have left. The mind goes blank, as with childbirth. If you remembered too clearly you'd never do it again. In student days it was fill a car – a friend's, your parents' – and run. That was easy. Later, as material possessions accumulated, and humans too, I ran away from a husband, an earlier one than Tony, tucking my child under my arm. I did not have the courage to tell him I was off: I thought he would hit me. I had no reason to be frightened. It's just that when women wrong men they suddenly remember that men are bigger than they are. That time I smuggled suitcases out of the house before I left. He didn't even notice. I took that as evidence that he didn't much care what happened next. There was no sex between us: I really cannot remember why we were married, or shared a house, other than my desire to give my otherwise unfathered little boy a home. I remember being thankful I could now leave the curtains behind: pale green silk, the first household furnishings I ever bought, a monument to youthful bad taste and impracticality.

Did I once burn a house down, or was that in a book I read? The sense that everything went suddenly one day, that there was nothing left, is overwhelming. It may not relate to actual fire, more to my emotions on coming back from a trip, opening my bedroom door and finding Tony in bed with my best friend. How vulgar, how commonplace: almost too much so to hurt. But hurt it did; friendship is important too. When they'd fled in guilt and disarray – they had that much decency – I found their coffee cups beneath the bed, hers was lipstick smeared, his just ordinarily encrusted with coffee dribble. How horrible everyday things can look. I smashed and threw the mugs away at once, not even waiting to move house to do it. They were the mugs she liked, the ones I'd use when she'd call round. In collusion with Tony she had unstitched my past. They had done it between them, on purpose. How could they?

They would, they could, and so could I. I've done it too, in my time: swept by and savaged the nest, someone else's nest: cracked the feathery, gluey coating of bird droppings and saliva, built up over years; perched to unpick the network of twigs that the wrigglings and writhings of living things had compacted. Then I'd got bored with the task, and just tipped what was left down onto the ground to rot, and flown off. Easy peasy.

I moved into another woman's nest once, still warm from her going: drank coffee and cream from the cute little cups her mother had made as a present for the newlyweds: threw out her hairpins from under the bed and settled into it. Knowingly I plonked my callous rump in her favourite chair. When my new dishwasher came the pottery cups broke and crumbled under the pressure of the first hot wash. Four house-moves on and I find I'm still using their saucers for my pot plants. The saucers must have been fired better than the cups. I honour them, and she who made them. It is all I can do for her. She must have grieved for her daughter.

My new lover waits outside, in his smart car; he is my answer to my mother's golfer. If you do it, so can I. Now I have done the initial sorting, got rid of what's most shameful, I will let the professionals do the rest. Everything will go into some repository somewhere; I have not even enquired as to its location: all I have is the telephone number. I will not exactly be dead, just reborn. My new lover wants me to start again, without a past. I will do my best, but I suspect all I have to offer is leftover life. He will have the scrapings of good meals once eaten.

My father, now living in a home for the elderly, picks at his food: there is always more left behind on the plate than he eats. I watched him the other day. He parted the roast potato with his fork, ate the floury bit inside, but left the crunchy outer coating for the waste disposal. Yet surely that's the most delicious part? Perhaps the very crispness reminds him, as it does me, of the broken bird's nest: anything will do as a focus for guilty remembrance. He must punish himself for ever. What a mess we make of things. And children follow parents, wherever they go.

# NEW YEAR'S DAY

The phone rang and woke Clare. She reached over Alan's sleeping body to take the call.

'Your wake-up call,' said the computer voice. 'The time is zero five hours and six seconds.'

'I didn't ask for a wake-up call,' said Clare, but what use is it to protest to a disembodied voice? She replaced the phone. She did not wake Alan. Why be unkind? She loved him. They had not got to bed until past two, exhausted, the sound of Auld Lang Syne drifting up from the street outside. Three hours sleep. She was headachy, and her skin itched where it touched Alan's. She must have drunk too much bad red wine. Last night they'd been to a party given by Alan's best friend Dave.

'I don't want to go,' she'd said. 'It will be terrible.'

'It's the only one on offer,' he'd said, 'and we can hardly sit at home like your mother to see the New Year in.'

Clare had been right. Dave and Dave's flat were designed for TV viewing and microwave cooking, not parties. All there'd been to do was drink. Too many of the guests were Amy's friends; they'd moved away when Clare approached. Amy had been invited, but had gone home at once when someone told her Clare was there with Alan. People were very strange. Amy was the one to have broken up the relationship: Amy had walked out on Alan, not the other way round. Why should Alan not bring his new partner along? Clare had no objection to Amy; she had nothing against her: she even thought she rather liked Amy's taste in mugs, plates, bed linen, and so on. Why should Amy be upset? This was the end of the twentieth century: people changed partners: it was a fact of life. Love ebbed and flowed; you went with the current.

Amy was pregnant but it was her own doing. Alan had made it clear from the beginning he didn't want to be a father. Amy had lost Alan's love; by trying to make him one. Love abhors a vacuum: Clare had replaced Amy in Alan's affections. It was natural and inevitable. Clare slept.

'Happy New Year!' said Alan. It was ten-fifteen. He'd brought up a breakfast tray. Coffee, milk, toast, butter, jam. She'd have to wean him off butter and on to margarine. Amy, from the photographs Clare had found in the kitchen drawer, had been at least a stone overweight. Beach photographs: Amy in a bikini. You had to be very sure of love in the eye of the beholder if you were to trust yourself, a stone overweight, in a bikini, to a camera. Safer to lose weight.

Clare skimmed butter on to her toast. She put milk in the coffee. Drank. She felt her mouth puckering.

'This milk is sour,' said Clare.

'It can't be,' said Alan. 'I got it from the doorstep only just now.'

'It must have been there since yesterday,' said Clare. 'No one delivers milk on New Year's Day.'

'I'm sure it wasn't there last night. I'd have noticed,' said Alan.

Clare drank her coffee black. She told Alan about the
5 a.m. wake-up call. Alan said that sometimes did happen at
the exchange, though rarely. You could get an impulse
contact from adjacent wires, and receive someone else's
call. Since Alan worked for a telephone company Clare
supposed he knew what he was talking about. She was in
PR herself, an altogether livelier occupation, all speculation,
very little fact.

'An impulse contact,' she said, 'I suppose that's like a
contact high in the drug world.'

Alan laughed, but uneasily. She moved the tray off the bed
and drew him down beside her. She thought he'd lived a
sheltered life. She would re-educate him. He was only thirty.
He'd been with Amy for seven years. His lovemaking was
remarkably enthusiastic and uncorrupt. Amy hadn't taught
him much. In time he would come round to wanting a baby.
Since Clare was thirty-two she hoped it would be soon. Clare
had had lovers but never lived with a man before.

She ought to say to him now, as they told you to in the
magazines, touch me here and touch me there, but somehow
she couldn't bring herself so to do. It was different if you
knew a man was going home after breakfast; then such
instructions didn't hang around the house to embarrass
you. It seemed easier now just to pretend satisfaction.

The front door bell rang. Clare put on a pink silk wrap Amy
had left behind and went down to answer the door. It was the
police. They said they'd had a report of noise and domestic
violence from the house. Alan followed Clare down in his
pyjamas: they made an obviously quiet and peaceable pair.

'But we had two phone calls allegedly from separate
neighbours,' the police said. They made a few notes, a phone

call or so on their mobiles. They had a dog with them, which squatted to make a long soft turd on the path.

'Someone fed her whisky last night,' said the younger policeman. 'This is always the worst weekend for practical jokes.' They left.

'I hope this isn't going to be the pattern of the next year,' said Clare, trying to find the wherewithal to clean up the dog's mess in Amy's cupboards. They weren't Amy's cupboards, technically, but Alan's. Alan and Amy hadn't married: Amy had moved in with Alan seven years back and had since been paying her share in food, petrol for the car, holidays, music, and so forth. Amy worked as a librarian for the local authority. She didn't get paid much. Unless you had a child within a relationship you had no rights as a common-law wife. Alan didn't see why he should pay for a baby he had specifically asked someone he wasn't married to not to have.

Clare found paper, knife, bucket, mop, and so forth, and soon the path was clean again.

'Alan,' said Clare, 'you do seem to take it for granted that I'm the one to clean things up.'

'Darling,' said Alan, 'you're right and I'm wrong. One of my New Year resolutions is to help more about the house.'

They went back to bed. The telephone rang. When Clare picked it up it went dead.

'Impact contact,' said Alan. 'It must be at the exchange.'

'I suppose so,' said Clare. 'But a wake-up call at five in the morning, one sour bottle of milk on the step, two phone calls to the police? Do you think someone doesn't like us?'

'Can't think who,' said Alan. It occurred to Clare that she'd paid for the taxi the night before. They hadn't gone in

Alan's car because he hated the whole idea of designated drivers. Alan had patted his pockets and said 'No change. I hate carrying change.' When she thought about it Alan very seldom carried any change. His suits hung beautifully: they were expensive. The sheets beneath her were real linen: creamy white and a slightly roughish texture. Amy's choice.

'I suppose Amy will be coming back to collect her things,' said Clare. 'I'll be sorry to lose the sheets.'

'Oh no she won't,' said Alan. 'She came with a suitcase and left with a suitcase.'

'Like I will?' Clare asked, sadly.

'You don't understand. I love you,' he said, his long, lean, bare body close against hers. 'I never really loved Amy. I mean to marry you.' Clare felt great joy. She'd put her flat on the market the day he'd asked her to move in with him. The place had sold within the week, to everyone's surprise, for the asking price. No time for second thoughts. Once the mortgage was paid off she'd even pocketed £10,400. Now it sat in her bank. Ten years' worth of hard work, long hours, doing what you didn't really want.

'If I pay off your mortgage,' she said to Alan, 'we could put this place in our joint names.'

'Don't talk about money,' he said. 'Talk about love. Don't think about mortgages, think about going to the Bahamas.' She was ashamed of herself.

The smoke alarm went off. Clare went downstairs. The kitchen was full of smoke. Something was burning in the oven. It was a bread roll she'd forgotten to take out the night before. She'd cooked Alan *coq au vin*. A celebratory dinner. She'd slipped into the shops on the way home from the office, lugged everything back. How much had she spent on food? More than thirty quid. In two weeks ten thousand four hundred was already down to nine thousand and something, one way and another.

The smoke alarm shrieked on. Clare held her nose and fetched out the cindery black oval from the oven, using Amy's kitchen tongs. Stainless steel kitchen tongs! What a luxury. She dunked the crisp black thing under the tap, and it softened and smelled even worse. Alan came down to the kitchen. He stood on a chair and took the battery from the alarm. The quiet was wonderful.

'You can get alarms you shut off from a switch on the wall,' he said.

'Aren't they very expensive?' she asked.

'They're smart and good-looking,' he said. 'Quality's worth paying for. And standing on chairs is dangerous.'

'I'll look out for one,' she said. 'But this is so spooky. I swear I turned the oven off last night.' But when she looked, its little red light still glowed. She turned it off. 'Amy could have got in,' said Clare, 'after she left the party. She could have turned the oven on. I expect she still has a key.'

'I changed the locks,' said Alan. 'My, you are paranoid! You'd better clean the oven out really well, or the smell will linger. Of course, Amy could always get in the loo window, if she forgot her key. But I hate talking about Amy. She's gone, gone, gone. This is your place now.'

'Shall we fix a day for the wedding?' she asked. He said he'd always wanted to get married in the summer. Perhaps when they went to the Bahamas, they could have a beach wedding.

Clare felt fidgety and irritated, short of sleep and hangovery. She ate a lot of toast and jam, she wasn't quite sure why, after she'd opened the front door and the windows and flapped away most of the burnt bread smell with Amy's apron. Alan buttered the toast for her, really thickly. It melted in and tasted delicious.

'Um, um, um,' he said, 'I love to see a woman eating.'

Someone was coming up the stairs; a tall lugubrious man with a cavernous face and a dark suit.

'The front door was open,' he said, 'so I came in. Where's the body?'

'Who are you?' asked Alan.

'I'm the undertaker,' he said. 'I had a call to say someone had died. I came right out. Always open for death, even on New Year's Day, that's me.'

'A male or a female body?' asked Clare.

'That's a funny question,' said Alan.

'Not to me,' said Clare.

'A female,' said the undertaker. 'A young woman dead from strangulation.'

'It's a hoax,' said Clare, feeling her neck. 'You can see I'm alive. I must have an ill wisher.'

'It's New Year's Day, love,' said the undertaker. 'I always expect this sort of thing on public holidays. It's the parties plus the hangovers; it turns people sour.'

As he left the undertaker pointed out that the metal No 6 on the door had fallen, and was hanging from one nail, so it looked like a 9. They watched him go to the house across the road, the real No 9, and knock. The door was opened and he went in. There was a police car and an ambulance outside.

Later Clare and Alan went for a walk in the park, holding hands. It was a beautiful winter's day, crisp and bright. The air was like nectar: Alan said so. Clare wondered what nectar was.

'We're so lucky to have each other,' said Alan. 'I have

never been so happy in all my life. Let's just get to the top of the hill before we turn back.'

But when they got to the top of the hill it was only Alan who stopped: Clare unhooked her hand and found herself just going on walking. She walked and walked till she thought it was safe to look back, and Alan was a small startled figure dwindling against a setting sun. After that she went on walking, knowing what she was doing, all the way to her mother's, and never looked back once.

'My lucky day,' said Clare to her mother, 'New Year's Day. Thank you God and thank you Amy, for sending so much luck.'

# INSPECTOR REMORSE

Sociopaths don't feel remorse. That's how the condition is diagnosed. This does not mean that everyone who fails to feel remorse is a sociopath. In the world of logic that's an error known as the fallacy of the undistributed middle. You could, for example, not feel remorseful not because you were a sociopath but because you had nothing to be remorseful about. You were a saint.

Here I sit, a rather elegant woman of around forty in a neat grey suit in a large empty Victorian church on Easter Friday, between services. I ponder these things, inspecting my soul for remorse, in the hope of finding just a trace of it, but failing. I conclude I am either very good or very bad. One has to be rigorous in this kind of moral inspection, worry away at clues like a detective to make sure one hasn't missed a thing. Saint, sinner or sociopath. Which? A case for Inspector Remorse! Is that a tingling of proper emotion I detect inside? A flicker of anxiety and shame mixed – which I suppose is what remorse is? An internalised wail – 'I shouldn't have done that: oh, I'm sorry, I'm sorry: don't do the same to me. Forgive me, I knew not what I did.' No.

*    *    *

# A HARD TIME TO BE A FATHER

Easter Friday, Yom Kippur, Ramadan – all religions have a time for remorse, a ritual for atonement. One belief structure, they told me at school, was much like any other. So I have ended up with a cosy mish-mash of beliefs, a Munchkin religion; God is Good, Death is Not Final, Reincarnation offers Justice. Take the Ten Commandments minus the one about adultery, mix up with Wheel of Life and Tantric Yoga, the Quest for the Inner Child, the Brilliance of the Ineffable. Don't we all?

Everyone I meet believes they're good, does the best he or she can in the circumstances. But if everyone's good why is the world in such a state? And why should I not suffer from the same common delusion, that of my own goodness?

How this place echoes. Just a footstep is enough to make me jump.

Bleep, bleep, bleep, there goes my mobile phone. In a church of all places. They ought to be banned. 'Hello, hello, oh it's you, Ian. No, I can't speak now. I'm in a church . . . Just sitting, contemplating my navel, considering my sins, if any. It suits me, it suits the day . . . I won't be here long, the cold is getting into my bones. I must go. Goodbye.' Click. Off. Bleep. Beat the breast and smear the ashes.

It would be sensible to leave. I'm not sure why I stay. The cold is easing through the soles of my shoes. Little lace-up pointy boots, built for fashion not for cold stone floors. Is that the sin of vanity? Do I feel remorse for this? No, I have pretty feet, why shouldn't I show them off? Besides, I suffer for it. I pay for my pleasure. Cold feet, fear of being alive.

The cold heart I sometimes show to Ian, who loves me more than I love him, so I have power over him. I abuse it, I make him suffer. He flushes, he creeps, he is eaten up with sexual jealousy. Do I feel remorse for this? No. Ian should know better than to love me: it's his doing, not mine. A wimp, a wimp, Ian is a wimp. He is also a banker, and older than me, and rich.

Prelates flutter by in white gowns; others stride in thick-soled boots. Clump, clump. Easter Friday is a busy day in the Anglican church, just bleak and cold as my heart. An un-flowered place, till Sunday.

Bleep, bleep, Ian again. Something he forgot to say. Switch it off. I want my thoughts, not his. Sociopath or saint. Inspector Remorse, still not a sign of you. Lost in a flurry of priests.

My breath begins to show up as mist. I can't believe this church is so cold. Perhaps the chill comes from me, emanates from me. I am aware of sin.

Lucy Brown died because of me. No, that's absurd. Lucy died because she had cold feet: she was afraid to go on living. If you're afraid of life you deserve to die.

Exmoor is a cold, wild, cruel place; all heather and bog and grass that snaps and crackles beneath the feet in winter. It's always winter. Forget the tourists, forget the sweet Exmoor ponies: the devil rides them bareback on stormy nights: listen hard: that's not the howl of the wind: that's the devil shrieking his delight. I have a sweet face, Ian says, lovely lips. If only my breath didn't fog the air so.

I'd never have chosen to live on the edge of Exmoor. But then I'm an art critic not a creative person: what do I know. Hard weather and stone floors, enough to depress anyone. Lucy

107

Brown was certainly depressed: she was married to Terry Brown. They were artists: he was successful, she was not. Terry won the Rome prize – she won nothing. When I met them I was only twenty-five but already powerful; I had a weekly column in *The Times*, in which I could make or break an up-and-coming painter. I enjoyed the power. I feel no remorse for that. What is power but something to use? If people deserved it I praised them: if they were crap I said so. I still do. And I am right. When and if I turn up at a show the room falls silent. I would rather be feared than loved. It's what I am, how I am.

I have long, long legs, I know how to sit, how to attract, how to repel: I always have. I first met them at Terry's private view. Lucy was a quiet, proud, plain thing: fifteen years older than me, edgy, awkward, hating the publicity, loathing the fuss, wanting to get home to the cottage on Exmoor and the snails which came up the drainpipe into the sink. They had a little daughter, Hilda. Exmoor, Terry, Lucy and Hilda. It sounded so cosy.

'Terry's good enough,' I said to Lucy, 'but I've seen your work too. You're in the first division. He's just top of the second where all the glitter is.' Her eyes lit up. She begged me and Ian to go down and visit. She had paintings to show me: she wanted my advice. That is to say she wanted some recognition and her name in the papers. She was intolerably vain. I asked Ian; he wanted to go; he's a sucker for creative folk. He's like some soft puppy. He likes to please: he's for ever wriggling. I sit still and calm, look beautiful and seldom smile, so people feel the need to placate me. I get the best seat in restaurants, get upgraded at airports; smokers stub out their fags at my approach.

\*　　\*　　\*

Terry and Lucy's cottage was the usual kind of artist's home. Messy, beautiful, unkempt, crowded, nice pieces of furniture in need of polish. It began to snow. We couldn't leave, we had to stay overnight. That pleased them. When the power lines came down there were candles to hand: they built a wood fire in the grate. They were excited by discomfort: I was horrified. I told Lucy I wouldn't look at her paintings this time around. It was too cold to concentrate. I'd come down again in the summer, I said, take pics and do a proper article when the fuss over Terry was over.

Do I feel remorse for this random spite? No. I was annoyed by her sullen patience. How could she possibly merit the love Terry showed her? Terry was charismatic, tall, talented, good-looking, he could have had anyone, even me. But all he seemed to want was Lucy. And all I had was Ian, a dolt. I have to have someone rich: I have a high standard of living. Art critics don't earn much, apart from a lot of abuse. How can I be remorseful for something which is just a fact? That night, I sat on the floor by the fire in a long diaphanous dress, with bare feet, and my hair flowing and played the flute and sang sweet songs. Men are such suckers they usually fall for it. But Terry just left the room in the middle of my song because he said he heard little Hilda crying.

The next day Lucy really annoyed me. She told me to go and fetch wood for the fire. She already had Ian peeling potatoes. I am not a servant to be ordered about. I lost my temper with her and heard the Cockney whine of my beginnings in my voice, and hated to hear it.

'You're just jealous,' she said, and laughed, 'because you're a critic and I'm a painter, and Ian is dull and Terry takes no notice of you. Calm down.'

And I managed to smile at her and apologise, but it was unforgivable that she knew so much about me. And later I went upstairs and found Terry sitting by the sleeping Hilda's bed, and brushed my breast past his cheek, which usually works, and it did. He looked at me thereafter in a different way. I don't think he liked me, but what does that matter? It is interesting to see lust and distaste battle it out in a man's eyes, and watch the wife watching too, to see which one wins. Lust won. It usually does. Ian noticed nothing at all. He is not sensitive to atmosphere.

The snow turned to sleet, sleet turned to rain, the power came back on: Ian and I dug the car out of mud and went home to our apartment, thankfully and carefully minimalist.

A couple of days later Terry called me. I was expecting it. He was coming to town: could he see me. It's not up to me to feel remorse for a thing like that. He called me, I didn't call him. He acted, I responded. Besides, the thing was greater than both of us. I told him so and he believed me. It's easy to relieve a man of his guilt. To me that's doing a kindness, not compounding a sin. Who wants to go to heaven anyway: such a boring place: people behaving properly. How white and thick my breath is upon the air.

Bleep, bleep, bleep. Ian, is that you? Yes, just about stopped communing, I'm coming home in a minute. Pour me a drink; make sure the gin is icy cold. I've inspected my life and find no cause for remorse.

I want to celebrate my sainthood now, not wait till Easter Sunday.

\*       \*       \*

Terry joined me in the minimalist flat. Ian was away in Brussels. Sex has a logic of its own. No sociopath feels remorse, but not all who feel no remorse are sociopaths. That figures. Terry asked when he would see me again and I said never, and hid his watch so he forgot to put it back on, and when he had gone I rang Lucy, and said, Oh, Lucy, Terry was here and left his watch, and there was a silence at the end of the phone, and then she put the receiver down. It annoys me the way men expect you to keep their secrets. Not to tell. Why shouldn't I tell? Serve Ian right for being away, even if he did find out, which he didn't.

Later that night, the phone rang and it was Terry saying bitch, bitch, bitch. I wish I could feel remorse, I really do. Perhaps it's too far in the past: fifteen years ago. By the time Terry got home, I heard later, Lucy was in a coma. Whisky and sleeping pills: a note. Terry got her to hospital and they stomach-pumped her, but it was too late. What she did was unforgivable. She did it to spite Terry, because she was jealous of his success, and to harm Hilda because Terry loved her, and to get back the attention to herself, to get her paintings posthumously recognised, which was what happened, though not through any doing of mine. As for Terry, he never painted anything in particular after that, and he wasn't up to much in the first place. Or that's what I tell myself.

Sergeant Doubt, is that you? Yes. And here comes your friend at last, Inspector Remorse, clump, clump, clumping down the aisle. I see you.

Bleep, bleep. Ian is that you? I have a confession to make. Remember Lucy Brown the one who killed herself? The painter? It was because of me, because of what I did, what I made Terry do. Can you forgive me that, or is it going to be the last straw? What, can't you hear me? Too distorted? The batteries must be going. Forget it, Ian, nothing important. I'm on my way home. People are coming in for the next service. I don't know what I'm doing here anyway. 'Bye.

Gone again, Inspector Remorse, and just as well.

It's warming up in here. I can't see my breath any more. Time to go. Not a saint, not a sinner, just an ordinary sociopath.

No sociopath feels remorse, but not all those who fail to feel remorse are sociopaths. Let us at least get the logic right.

# MOTHERS
# AND SISTERS

MY MOTHER SAID

A LIBATION OF BLOOD

PYROCLASTIC FLOW

# MY MOTHER SAID

The pair of them, Anne and Anthony, started as nothing and turned, for a time, into something. Getting back to being nothing again was painful, for both of them.

Anne's mother Lorna had warned her from the beginning about the pain of existence: the life-caution required to avoid it. Anne did her best to ignore her mother's words, but random bits and pieces must have stuck, for all their in-built contradiction.

'You're nothing as a woman if you don't have a husband,' Lorna would say to little Anne. Five minutes later, her slow mind still mulling over the statement, she'd say something like, 'Mind you, a woman who marries simply throws away her life.' Little Anne would get terrible headaches, though they cleared when she was thirteen and realised her mother was not offering wisdom, but expressing anxiety. Lorna would call as witness the common sense of the world, and no sooner had it in the dock than she'd dismiss it, in the light of her own experience. Understanding this, Anne could at last stop puzzling, abandon the attempt to reconcile the unreconcilable.

'The higher you go, the further you fall: remember that,

Anne,' Lorna would say over the cake-making. And then, 'Nothing ventured, nothing gained. If you don't *do* something, nothing happens.' And she'd put too much baking powder in the mix so the cake rose and rose in the oven and then collapsed as soon as it met the cold air outside. Which proved something, but what?

'Anne proposes to marry Anthony,' Lorna said, 'but he has no real career prospects. Isn't being an interior decorator a risky kind of business?' Then two minutes later, 'But of course love's the only important thing.' And presently, 'Are you sure he's not gay? Most people in that profession are. Not that I have anything against gay people.' And then, 'Isn't homosexuality hereditary? You have to think of that,' and then, 'Of course, if you're too choosy, you can miss your chance,' and later, 'No good just holding your nose and jumping, Anne. This is *life*, not a hockey game.'

Anne had been good at hockey and captain of the school team. This preferment had worried Lorna greatly. Better for Anne just to be one of the team. Perhaps Anne couldn't cope, would end up captaining her side to defeat? If she took games too seriously she'd develop large calves and larger thighs: a girl had to look after her looks – though, five minutes earlier, Lorna had claimed personality counted for more. And might not Anne be raped on the way home from practice? Anne gave up playing hockey, forswore the pleasure of hacking away at enemy ankles, not because she feared the future, but to save her mother anxiety.

'Why did you call me Anne?' she asked Lorna once.

'It's the kind of name which doesn't draw attention,' said her mother. 'A middle kind of name.'

*       *       *

Anne decided early on that she would not live as her parents did, in some small back street with a neat well-weeded back garden where only the most conventional vegetables grew – cabbages, onions, carrots and tomatoes – and never a courgette or even a mangetout in sight.

She went to university. She defied her mother, and stepped into the unknown.

'You'll educate yourself out of your place,' warned Lorna.

'You won't fit in anywhere. Isn't that so, Harry?'

Anne's father Harry had little to say on this or any subject. He was grey and agreeable, and would nod his consent to everything his wife said.

'Your mother's right,' he'd say, and if a teenage Anne retorted, 'But she said the opposite a minute ago and you said that was right too,' he'd add, 'She's a very wise woman.'

Harry worked in the Highways Department of the local Council, and Lorna worked in a solicitor's office. She wore brown tweed skirts, grey blouses and sensible shoes.

Bath water at home trickled mingily from a gas-fired device called a geyser, installed in 1938. It operated by slipping a coin into the slot; a 1937 penny used over and over no matter how the currency changed, kept on a chipped, tiled ledge in the bathroom. Hot water fell into a great high-walled, rough-bottomed bath, cooling as it fell. The bath stood on claw legs. Every now and then the geyser would puff little explosive bursts of accumulated soot over the naked bather. There was no telling when it would happen. The bathroom was un-heated. There was one little slit window. The green lino beneath the bath had rotted and broken away as if a mad dog had been gnawing at it.

'When I grow up,' Anne told her mother, 'the best and brightest room in the house will be the bathroom; unlimited hot water will flow on demand; the towels will always be fluffy and warm, and I'll step out onto carpet.'

'You'll have to marry money then,' said Lorna, and a little later on, 'No sensible man would put up with a carpet in the bathroom. If you want your own way you'd best stay single.'

Anne met Anthony on the second day of her first term at university. He was tall, dark, and had large mild eyes. She was fair and a little dumpy, and her calves were big by nature, forget hockey. They went to bed within an hour of meeting and she forgot at once that he had the edge on her, lookswise. It wasn't looks that counted, or even personality, it was the ability to receive and give pleasure. Nineteen years of virginity gone without reflection – what a waste, Lorna might have said, if she'd been told.

'Where do you come from?' he asked.

'From nowhere,' she said, 'absolutely nowhere you could tell from anywhere else.'

'That's a coincidence,' he said. 'It's the same for me.'

The implication was that together they might go somewhere. And so indeed they did: Anthony and Anne, one of those couples, together from the beginning, grown into each other, even their names as one, tripping off the tongue, 'Anthony-nAnne.' They went hand in hand through the years, as equals. If Anne looked after the house and the children and Anthony earned, it was not because society had decided that these were appropriate roles, but because Anne liked being a housewife and Anthony was good at his job and earning money came easily to him. It was a rational division of labour. He started his own firm and became Designer of Choice at first for the rich and staid; later for minor celebrities with wilder tastes. He was away from home a lot.

'Keep an eye on him,' said her mother, 'you know what men are. You don't want to end up divorced. No one asks divorced women to dinner,' and the next Sunday, apropos of nothing in particular, 'Of course women alone have the best lives, these days.'

Both statements seemed quite irrelevant – Anthony and Anne laughed. They were happy and un-anxious: they would be together forever, everyone knew. Of course there were minor tensions. Anne wasn't tidy: Anthony was. Anne was healthy, Anthony hypochondriacal. Anne wanted to go abroad for holidays, Anthony preferred the Scottish highlands. Anne wanted the children – Alice and Andrew – to go to state schools, Anthony wanted them to go through the private system. He won. He made a lot of money. It was reasonable enough. Alice had a pony. Andrew, who was musical, had a music room full of state-of-the-art recording equipment. They were happy, stable children, mildly difficult teenagers. Whose weren't? Anne's bathroom was spectacular in marble and mahogany. She had warm fluffy towels. She served aubergine in olive oil for starters. Anne felt dull.

Anne found a note in Anthony's pocket. He was having an affair with one of his clients; a tall, skinny woman with a rasping voice and enormous eyes. She was a minimalist: she couldn't bear clutter. This seemed to be the way to Anthony's heart.

'She's just so interesting,' said Anthony. 'She has such a

sense of style. Be reasonable, Anne. We've been married seventeen years. We can't both go through life having only ever had one sexual partner. It's absurd.'

It didn't seem absurd to Anne, though she could see it was unusual. Anthony said the relationship with Big Eyes would stop since it upset Anne, and he gave her leave to have a brief balancing affair if that was what she wanted. OK, but who with? How would she set about it?

When she was sixteen in the sixties and there'd been a sudden, brief fashion for topless dresses, Anne had gone bare-breasted to a party. That is to say the neck of the dress was so low her nipples showed.

'If you've got it, flaunt it,' said her mother, unusually cheerful, as Anne stood at the top of the stairs. But as Anne went out the front door Lorna said 'Don't do it. You'll catch your death of cold.' Anne did it, in defiance, and had to run home away from the groping hands, ashamed, and had indeed caught the most dreadful cold. She had dressed and acted modestly ever since. 'Learned your lesson!' said her mother. Anne had managed to get to bed with Anthony but that was about the limit of it. She had never learned the art of flirtation.

'I'm not interested,' said Anne to Anthony, 'in anyone but you.'

Anne wondered whether infidelity ran in families. Anthony's father kept a mistress. The mistress had come to Anthony and Anne's wedding along with the wife, Anthony's mother. No one had seemed to mind, at least on Anthony's side of the church. Of course, increasingly, weddings were out of fashion. People lived in *à seul, or à deux*, or even *à trois*.

Anthony had another affair with another client; then another, then with a male client. Someone suggested to Anne that this was the way Anthony had reached the top of his profession: he had slept his way there. She could not believe that: people were just envious. Anne suffered from sexual jealousy; it was a torment. She became quite thin.

'Jealousy is a despicable emotion,' said Anthony. 'I love you, you know that: these other people mean nothing.' He suggested she went to see a therapist and she did. The therapist told her much the same thing; jealousy was a negative emotion. Its cause was lack of self-esteem: she must build hers up, and yes, intimate relationships with men other than her husband might be useful. Anne thought perhaps the therapist meant himself, for a start, and stopped going to see him. Later she found it was the same therapist that the skinny minimalist consulted. Perhaps Anthony had got the name from her. Perhaps Big Eyes had been given the same advice.

Anne's childhood had seemed grey: but now the world was a maze of violent colours, slashes of blue and mauve and acid green, splashed by crimson streaks like blood. She longed for grey; everything would return to restful grey if she left Anthony. But it was such a rich life, with him, full of friends, good dinners and cheerful events. She didn't want to lose it. She couldn't upset the children. And perhaps it was, as Anthony said, just a small thing, an unimportant sexual thing; she was unreasonable to let his infidelities upset her. And he always came back to her, Anne; and she'd get his clothes cleaned, and he'd talk to her about work, and sometimes about his lovers.

'You're like myself, Anne,' he said once, 'so close to me we're one and the same person. I'm talking to myself, but I can do it aloud. You don't mind, do you? I won't be able to see her for another month. She's gone to Switzerland. Her waist's so tiny if I stretch my hands I can just about encompass it.'

Anne wept in the greenhouse. Alice, the girl, and Andrew, the boy, found her there.

'What's going on?' they asked.

'Just marriage to a man,' she said. They stared at her, baffled, and drifted off.

One night there was a phone call at half past two in the morning. It was Harry. Lorna had collapsed. It was her heart. He was phoning from the hospital. Anne was alone in the house. Anthony was off somewhere; the children staying with friends. They did that a lot. The swimming pools were larger elsewhere, or the ponies cuter, or the music studios better equipped; whatever. Anne took a taxi to the hospital. Just before she died Lorna sat upright, looked straight at Anne and said, 'Half a woman is better than no woman at all. Do be careful, Anne.'

'I'll be careful, Mum,' said Anne. 'Do stop worrying.'

Lorna lay down, smiled, and died.

In the interval between the death and the funeral Anne had fearsome headaches, which got her through the worst intensities of grief. Alice and Andrew did not come to the funeral: they had other engagements, and besides, as Anthony pointed out, funerals would depress them. He was meant to be coming along but something or someone detained him at the last minute. When Anne had finished with the cups of tea and scones at the wake, and settled her father, she went home, rang a solicitor, and sued Anthony for divorce. The headaches stopped. The courts were good to her. Anne kept the house, an income, and the children. Anthony felt betrayed: laid waste: he couldn't understand it. Why, after so long?

On the first weekend of the first Open University course, Anne met Jack, a cabinet-maker, and Anthony was to feel for the first time what jealousy was, and apologised. It did him no good: within a couple of months, Anne was married to Jack. 'It's not a happy ending,' she explained to friends, 'it's not that without a man I'm nothing and have now become something again. It's just nice to know sometimes you can stick your head above the parapet and not get shot at.'

To Anthony, still looking for an explanation, Anne said, 'Sometimes mothers have to die to set their children free. Lorna died: I became myself. I wonder what I do to Alice and Andrew, and don't notice?'

# A LIBATION OF BLOOD

'Mum,' said Alison, 'give me some advice.' Mum was sixty-five and Alison was thirty-nine. Mum was widowed, which is never a nice thing to be, but what can you expect? Women outlive men.

'You?' asked Mum in some astonishment. '*Me* give *you* advice?' Mum had left school at sixteen and gone into the WRAC and packed parachutes. That was as far as her education and training had gone. Alison had gone to college and taken a degree and then a diploma in the Social Sciences. Mum had one child: Alison had three. 'What can I possibly know that you don't know, Alison?' Alison began to cry. Mum, astonished, made her a cup of tea. Mum had a touch of arthritis in her fingers. She lived, as she had always done, in a bungalow on the outskirts of a quiet cathedral town, where Dad had left Mum well provided for. Dad had run a TV repair business. Alison lived in London, worked and earned well. She was employed by a charity to raise funds for mentally disabled children, and ran a small specialist agency of her own, which provided research material on disablement for other charities. She was tall, energetic, good-looking, usually laughing; and now suddenly here she was, out of town, in Mum's small kitchen, laughing and crying at the same time.

'Tea's no answer,' said Alison.

'Tea never was an answer,' said Mum, 'but it was always something to do with your hands, while you got your act together.'

'Like smoking,' said Alison.

Do not suppose that because Mum was sixty-five and had had little education, and no other lover (or so Alison supposed) than her husband, that Mum was stupid or ill-informed. The television and the library make one knowledgeable nation of us all.

'When I press my breast it hurts,' complained Alison. 'Do you think I've got cancer? And I can't make sense of what's going on in my head.'

'You're probably pregnant,' said Mum, 'forget cancer.'

'I can't possibly be pregnant,' said Alison. 'Bobby and I take precautions.' On the telephone to her mother only a week ago Alison had been all set to move in with Bobby. Bobby was a crusader for the handicapped. He was famous up and down the country for his goodwill and good works. He had money. Marriage was spoken of. What a wonder! True love at last – and for a woman of thirty-nine with three children and two marriages behind her.

'Precautions, schmecautions,' said Mum. 'Condoms, schondoms. When did they ever not break? How do you think you began?'

'You're so frivolous,' complained Alison. Whoever liked to believe they had arrived so accidentally in the world? She asked Mum if she'd come up next week and baby-sit Caroline, aged nine, and Wendy and Wyndham, her five-year-old twins. William, the twins' father, had been taken into hospital for his varicose veins, and William's new wife Annabel had declared she wouldn't take the twins if William wasn't in the house, and Alison had a conference she couldn't miss and what with one thing and another she couldn't cope.

'Just cool it, Alison,' said Mum, 'you'll give yourself a heart attack. OK, OK, I'll come up for the week and child-mind but you didn't come all this way to ask me that. You could have done it on the phone.'

'I wanted some peace on the train,' said Alison. 'I wanted my own space. Just a couple of hours.'

'I suppose you travelled first class, or you wouldn't be talking about space.'

'Why not? I can afford it.'

'And thousands starving in Africa!' said Mum. 'Sometimes I think you earn too much for your own good.'

'You'd never say that to a man,' said Alison, and wept again. It was true. Her head was all to pieces. She'd been all set to move in with Bobby, give up her own house, her independence, everything: all for love. But now she wasn't sure she wanted to: supposing it all went wrong? She couldn't bear it. Better not to try, than try and fail. This way and that, things went in her head. Yet wasn't little Caroline happy with the idea: Bobby for a father! Wasn't that reassuring? Of course William wasn't happy about it one bit but nothing made William happy; not now the self-righteous Annabel was whispering in his ear all the time, setting up Alison as a bad mother. What difference could it make if the twins visited their mother alone every second weekend, or their-mother-with-Bobby: she, Alison, put up with Annabel not to mention Annabel's horde of mimsy little children when she visited the twins; why should William not put up with Bobby? Alison wanted a whiff of home, in fact, where nothing ever happened, except in her mother's head, and all was always the same, even the brand of tea. PG Tips.

'Multiple marriages,' said Mum. 'All change, but all the

same! Why didn't you stay with Andrew?' She'd liked Andrew, in the way mothers do seem to like their daughters' first husbands. Or perhaps it was just the pattern of names from the beginning. Alison and Andrew, Andrew and Alison – they'd got used to it, that was all. 'He was a mass murderer,' said Alison, 'that's why.' Andrew had worked as a designer for a firm which produced, amongst other things, leaflets for a cigarette company.

'Now who's being frivolous?' said Mum. Andrew had pronounced himself bisexual and Alison had left, running shrieking into the night, Caroline under her arm, straight into William's all-but-maternal arms. Had she been right, had she been wrong? Should she have stayed? What is intolerable, what is not? Was a bisexual natural father better for Caroline than a heterosexual stepfather? Andrew hadn't kept in touch with Caroline, or Alison for that matter, though he rang Mum from time to time, feeling the need of a mother. Well, these days, who doesn't?

'How can you even speak to Andrew?' Alison would shriek, in the early days of their parting, when she was still flayed red and raw.

'But you didn't *want* him to keep in touch with Caroline,' Mum would remind her. 'He's only doing what you wanted. And you're right, he is a very sexually confused young man. But I am not going to condemn him for that. Surely you wouldn't want me to? And it's all turning out for the best, now you're married to William. Surely?'

Well, perhaps. Perhaps not. Alison's next baby, by William, was a Down's Syndrome child, and the hospital saved its life, whereupon Alison rejected it. She said since the hospital had saved the baby, the hospital should look after the baby, a reaction which shocked the noble and right thinking very much, and William was nothing if not a noble thinker. But he bit back his thoughts, rather noticeably, for love of Alison, and supported her, and the baby died at three months, anyway, never well enough to come home. After that there was a lot of clinic-visiting, genetic testing and detailing of hereditary factors. The odds of William and Alison's next baby being born similarly affected were declared at one in fifteen. But the couple could take advantage of a newish procedure called amniocentesis by which babies could be tested in the womb at four months and aborted if necessary. So you only had the worry for four months. Then if anything was wrong – terminate! Of course by that time it was like going into proper labour.

'At four months?' Mum had asked, in horror. 'Aborted at four months? Babies are practically smiling by then.'

'Especially if it's Down's Syndrome,' said Alison. 'You know what gutsy little smilers they are!' William raised his eyebrows when Alison said things like this; but no doubt she was still in shock; how patient he was with her, everyone agreed.

Four months was the best the medical profession could do at the time. And not even the pro-lifers made much of a fuss at aborting imperfect babies, though Alison couldn't quite understand their rationale. Life in itself being so important, according to them, not the quality of life. William wished she'd just shut up about it all. And in the midst of the discussions there Alison was, pregnant again, somehow or other, in spite of her Dutch cap (the pill bloated her: the coil made her bleed and hurt) while they were still trying to make up their minds to risk or not to risk. William and Alison rejoiced – well, almost. You know what these things are. They'd rather have trusted their judgement than their luck. Who, well and properly informed, would not?

\*     \*     \*

# A LIBATION OF BLOOD

At seven weeks the doctors diagnosed a twin pregnancy, which meant that the odds of at least one baby being Down's Syndrome went up to one in eight: and if the twins were identical, one in six. And Alison was having morning sickness not just in the mornings but at lunch time, tea time, dinner time and all night too, and Caroline, aged four, was coming out in sympathy and kept banging her mother's tummy with her head and saying she hated the baby and no one had the heart to say 'babies, actually,' and the temptation just to terminate now, and not later – whoosh, the good baby going out with the bad, should such there be – though the likelihood of them both being Down's was now up to one in five, because Mum reminded her of a Down's great-uncle, never before discussed, plus identical twin great-aunts on William's side – good lord, those sessions at genetic counselling, William staring at Alison, Alison at William, each wondering whose the bad seed was, and the whole weight of society (not to mention William) blaming the mother, though it's often enough old fathers, not old mothers, who produce Down's Syndrome babies – as the specialist was at pains to point out. Not that maternal or paternal age affected their particular case. Though Mum wouldn't have that. 'The thing about William,' Mum said later, 'is that he was just plain *born* old' – she'd just plain liked Andrew, sexual ambiguity and all, and that was the fact of it. Andrew had needed a mother and William was all the mother to himself he'd needed – just watch him bandage his own cut finger, cosseting and comforting! Anyway, William and Alison kept their courage going and Alison took time off work – 'Caroline needs you at home,' said William, 'at a time like this' – and got through to the amniocentesis at four months – only Alison had flu and then the clinic had been closed because of some virus – and then the twins had actually got to nineteen weeks before the test, and Alison was pretty much bonded with them in spite of her efforts not to be: and in went the needle once, into the amniotic sac – ping! – one baby done – and in went the needle twice – second baby done.

'I say,' said Alison, 'when you got the first one it moved, you know. Didn't like it one bit. You got the baby as well as the sac. I hope it wasn't an eye!'

'Nonsense!' they said. What a mother! Pity the poor father, with a woman who could joke at such times.

'Joke?' said Alison. 'I wasn't *joking*.' They put her on tranquillisers until the results came through. She was very thin, what with the vomiting and the flu, and Caroline's little arms curling round her legs whenever she tried to leave the room. But the test results came through in three weeks or so – two boys, both OK – no Down's, no spina bifida. ('Any tests for blindness in one eye?' asked Alison.)

'Isn't that wonderful!' said the doctors. 'Aren't you relieved? We certainly are! You were taking quite a chance.' Ah, the wonder of modern science.

'Wonderful,' said Alison, but one or other of the babies was pressing on the sciatic nerve, or they were taking it in turns, those two healthy, crowded boys, and the pain was terrible.

Well, Alison was worrying. That never helps, does it? The trauma of the previous baby's birth was still with her, of course, but more than that: she was troubled by the nature of the universe. In hospitals other than the one she'd attended, she'd been told, efforts to save severely handicapped babies were not nearly so strenuous. Luck of the draw, all luck of the draw. This hospital, that. Her birth, Andrew's dual sexuality (genetically determined, he maintained, no matter how she shrieked, 'You're doing it on purpose!'), Caroline's wilting nature, her imperfect baby's survival, the twin pregnancy, William just being there waiting with reassuring arms: luck, luck! Work wasn't luck. Cause and effect operated in offices. Effort was rewarded by money. She pulled herself together and dragged herself to work every morning.

Her father died. A stroke – luck again. The blood clot was incapacitating or not, fatal or not, depending on where in the brain it happened to stick. It stuck in a bad place. That was that. She watched her mother carefully. Mum wept, mourned, recovered properly. It had been a good marriage. Death was, they said, more easily survived in such circumstances. Consciences were clear. Luck again. When you married, who you married, staying married: luck, all luck. The genetic counselling clinic denied luck and claimed probability, but Alison thought she'd rather just hang a lucky charm around her neck.

Mum came up to be with her before the twins were born. A long and painful affair, but at least relieving the pain in the sciatic nerve. The first twin was a boy, the second a girl.

'Oops!' said the hospital.

'You tested the same baby twice,' said Alison. 'Told you so. See, two puncture marks. One on his chin, one on his ear. Lucky you missed the eye. Just test the girl for Down's, will you.' She went back to sleep. Ungrateful and difficult, they decided. The girl had the right number of chromosomes, so all was well. (Better luck than Alison deserved, one or two muttered.) Of course, amniocentesis was in its infancy. It is more sophisticated today. Don't worry. They can do it earlier, and the risk of its causing a miscarriage is down from one in twenty, to one in a hundred, and the proportion of false-positive decreases. A bit.

Well, twins! Something in Alison's attitude upset William. It wasn't that she hadn't bonded. ('Have you bonded yet, mother?' Sister actually asked Alison. '*Both* twins, you're sure?' 'Quite sure, thank you, Sister,' said Alison, primly.) She longed to be up and active now the sheer physical weight of the pregnancy, not to mention the pain and the anxiety, was gone, and William had his two perfect children, the pigeon pair, and even Caroline seemed to find the reality of the twins quite tolerable, and her little white face had become pink again, and she'd been to stay with Mum down in Exeter for a whole week without howling for home. In fact Alison's spirits had been so high, back in the world of cause and effect, not just luck, that the twins had been three before the marriage broke up. Alison wouldn't stay home, that was the trouble: she would go out to work. William took her absence as an insult. He'd lost his job – he worked as an accountant with a small firm which unexpectedly merged with a large firm.

'Luck!' cried William.

'No,' said Alison, 'cause and effect. You could have seen it coming. If you'd looked. Which you didn't.' And William wouldn't even try to get another, having gone off figures anyway and wanting to be a writer, and Alison argued that someone had to bring the money in, but he'd argued that it was better for them all to live off Social Security, and how could he look after twins *and* write, and so on and so forth, and it had all ended up as musical chairs, with him in one household, sometimes with the twins, sometimes not, and Alison and Caroline and an au pair in another and Alison going out to work – 'Unsatisfactory,' said William, 'but I suppose it's what Alison wants and what Alison wants she gets' (a lot of aggro and acrimony there) and somehow or other within a month or so William was living with this Annabel, about whom Alison had never known – but perhaps she should have seen it coming – who had a little money of her own and could stay home with William so he could find the time to write – and Alison, who was earning good money, found herself legally obliged to support both households (and morally obliged, of course. Hadn't her unreasonable attitude been the cause of the marital break-up?). And what more reasonable than that he should take the twins?

Alison grieved for the twins in their absence, of course she did, but she had her sanity to think about (well, didn't she?) not to mention Caroline, who wasn't even William's child (as he kept saying both in public and private, once the arguments started) and both households to support and fortunately Annabel turned out to be both kind and competent (though financially rather over-careful, by Alison's standards) and the twins liked her and she had the knack of somehow turning William's motherliness into fatherliness, but anyway all that was in the past. Alison had met Bobby, and she was happy, and her future was in her own hands, whatever she did with it, and seeing her mother had cleared her head, and she thought perhaps she'd just move in with Bobby but put off marrying him for a few months until she was absolutely sure it was all going to work – then she would be acting responsibly and not trusting to luck. That decision made, she and her mother travelled back to London first class, so she could get to her conference *and* take the twins while William was in hospital.

'I'm perfectly happy going second,' said Mum. 'Why don't you save your money for more important things?' Well,

Mum was like that. It made Alison feel quite safe and happy. Except on the journey up she was sick, twice.

'Pregnant,' said Mum.

'Travel sick,' said Alison, but she felt her breasts and they were sore. She almost wished it was cancer.

She went to her conference, and it was wonderful coming home to Caroline and the twins and Mum, with Bobby visiting, staying the night. Mum liked Bobby, and he liked her and it all felt like home and Alison wondered why she was still hesitating, and forgot to wonder why she'd suddenly gone right off wine and coffee. And when William came out of hospital – his varicose veins stripped – 'Isn't he rather *young* for varicose veins?' asked Mum. 'But I suppose as he was just born old, it's got to his legs first' – the twins went regretfully but happily enough back to their other home, and Alison felt that even though they liked and appreciated Annabel, who kept their socks so clean and organised, it was she, Alison, their real mother whom they loved, and what's more now they were just a little older, less babies, more people, Alison was beginning to come to terms with them and to forget the trauma and anxiety they had caused, not to mention the months they'd spent leaning on her sciatic nerve. Alison blamed the hospital for making what was blind and instinctive somehow rational and required, so the mind cut in and observed the body, just when it shouldn't. Really, she thought, the way things were going in the gynaecological world, new human beings should just be grown in Petri dishes, sperm joined to egg, forget love between man and woman, let alone parent and child, the once dark, once secret act of procreation now so brilliantly, clinically lit.

'Love you, Mummy,' said first Wendy, then Wyndham, when Alison came home from the conference.

'I love you too,' said Alison.

'So do I,' said Caroline. 'And I love William a little bit, I expect. But I love Bobby more.'

'Isn't that all nice,' said Mum, who had quite come round to the modern habit of expressing love through words. She who had never in her youth or middle age been demonstrative could now see the rewards of being so. Everyone changed.

'Come along little ones,' said Annabel, briskly. 'Daddy's waiting in the car with Saul and Rachel and Dodie. Daddy's got to walk two miles every single day for a whole month. Think of that!' They thought of that.

'Ooh!' they said. And William, pale and brave, framed in the car window, spoke kindly to Caroline, who beamed and blossomed in his regard. He spoke civilly, almost affectionately, to Alison as well. So everything was just fine except there was no denying now that Alison, somehow or other, was pregnant. She did a home test and sat and through a slanting mirror watched the little orange ring forming out of yellow dust and wondered whether the new baby would increase the sum of the world's good, or do the opposite? No twins in Bobby's family, let alone Down's Syndrome (or as far as she knew) which helped: but once you had one set of twins the likelihood of another multiple pregnancy leapt up and with it the dramatic halving of the odds against a perfect baby, and of course every year that passed, even with a single baby, put up the odds of it being Down's, having already had one, and how old was she now – thirty-nine? – there was a kind of compound interest going on here: some exponential cosmic penalty for happiness.

'What shall I do?' she asked her mother.

'Trust to luck,' said Mum. Luck! Good God! What good had luck ever done her?

'You must do what you want,' said Bobby. 'Though, of course I want us to have a baby. Very much.' And of course now the baby could be tested at ten weeks, through the cervix, so that took at least some of the anxiety out of it, not to mention risk to the baby, should the pregnancy proceed and they decide to go ahead. No termination, not yet. They postponed rejoicing until after the test. It could be done. Just. You went on pretending morning sickness was food poisoning and not referring to it. The baby was not a baby, just a growth, until declared a valid human being by medical decree. But it was OK. Bobby and Alison loved each other. That much was now certain. At eight weeks, yes, a scan showed twins. Two sacs.

'What will I do?' pleaded Alison. 'I can't go through all that again! Not twins!'

'I might as well tell you,' said Mum, 'since you're already in such a state, you're one of twin girls. You had a sister. She died at birth. Of course these days they'd have saved her, but goodness knows how I'd have coped. Your father was better with a TV set than with a baby.'

'But why didn't you tell me?' Alison was astounded. 'You knew it would alter the odds. You must have known it would.'

'But knowing the odds made no difference,' observed Mum, 'since you got pregnant by accident, anyway. All knowing ever did was worry you more. Now you know that you're terminating two, if that's what you're going to do, all that's happened is the decision's twice as hard. No one likes doing away with a perfect baby. Better wait till they're born, if you ask me, then do away with the one that isn't right, if it isn't, and keep the one that is. 'You go to prison, and I couldn't possibly do any such thing. Kill a baby, once it's born! Allow it to die – that's different. That's natural.'

'Might as well tell you,' said Mum, 'your twin wasn't right, mongol as we called them then, and the midwife did away with her. That's what midwives were for. That's why we had our babies at home. More danger but less interference.'

'She couldn't have been identical,' said Alison, too obsessed by these genetic matters to worry about Mum's deceit, let alone the real function of midwives, 'or I'd have been Down's too.'

'Would you?' asked Mum. 'Down's schmown's, a baby's a baby.'

'Bet you were glad yours didn't live, all the same.' My sister, she felt. The sister I never had, always thought I ought to have, was killed by my own mother. 'Murderers!'

'I was glad,' said Mum. 'Your father would never have stood for it.'

'You may be right there,' said Alison. Statistics certainly showed babies that weren't right broke up families quicker than anything. The disabled ended up with mothers, seldom fathers, hardly ever both. And she thought sadly of William, whose good opinion she still somehow couldn't quite seem to do without, and grieved for her poor second baby, with his extra chromosome and dicey lungs, who had clung so studiously to life, and for so long – long after others would have given up and allowed themselves to be sluiced away in a flood of pre-natal blood. But the conversation, though it shortened, or was it lengthened, the odds, strengthened her mind. Termination. To go ahead with twins was absurd. She didn't have the physical strength, either before or after the birth. She just didn't.

'Oh!' said the specialist, 'if it's twins that worry you, these days we can terminate one and let the other go to term.'

'Which one?' Alison asked.

'The first one we come to,' said the specialist, a little stiffly.

'You mean you can't test both and remove the one with Down's?'

'Not yet. Though no doubt soon we'll be able to. And of course we must look on the bright side. Neither might be Down's.'

'I don't think that's the bright side,' said Alison. 'I don't think terminating a perfect baby can ever be called the bright side.' Difficult, wasn't she. Well, wouldn't you be?

'We would recommend a selective termination in any case: you might have trouble carrying two babies to term. We do it often, nowadays. The procedure's been developed to cope with the number of multiple pregnancies we get nowadays – the result of fertility drugs.'

'That's different,' said Alison. 'This baby of mine – these babies – were created naturally. Conceived in love and passion, if by accident. How can I possibly terminate one? It might be the wrong one. And if it was OK, how could I tell the one that lived, when it came to their turn for genetic counselling, that I'd got rid of the other? What would it think of me?'

'It would at least be alive to do the thinking. I could terminate one now,' said the specialist kindly, 'and test the other at sixteen weeks, when things have settled down, though there would still be an increased risk of miscarriage, and dispose of it for you if it were Down's.' Sixteen weeks! 'No, no,' said Alison. 'Never. No counselling, no testing, I'll have them both and trust to luck.' She could already feel the pain of the sciatic nerve but she didn't care. She'd never said or felt such a thing before. It quite shocked her to hear herself speaking so loud and clear. And as it happened, the gods of chance must have heard, and looked down on her, or somebody or something; at any rate as she left the clinic she felt the first sticky flow of blood, and presently more and more, so much blood there seemed no end to it, so many regrets, so much relief, and within twenty-four messy painful hours the putative twins were gone, male or female, good or bad, identical or fraternal, no one was ever to know, in such a flow of welter and crimson even the hospital was surprised.

'So much blood!' exclaimed the au pair, in the ambulance.

'Don't look,' cried Alison, 'it might put you off.'

Later on, when she was feeling steadier, she'd try again, and trust to luck it wasn't twins. Caroline, Wendy and Wyndham were all just fine – weren't they?

'Just as well,' said Mum, 'though I don't suppose you want to hear that. You have quite enough to think about as it is. How is the inside of your head?'

'Clearer,' said Alison. 'It's the sudden drop of oestrogen.'

'Reminds me of the time I miscarried the first lot of twins,' said Mum, who was, as ever, full of surprises. 'Just as well I did. They weren't even your father's. Now drink a lot of water, and replace the lost blood, and here's to better luck next time. It'll happen. Blood's the libation the God of Chance requires. Lots and lots of blood. Always has, always will. Afterwards things go better. Didn't I have you? Aren't I pleased I gave birth to you?'

# PYROCLASTIC FLOW

'Pyroclastic flow, Miss Jacobs, is the vulcanologist's term for what we loosely call lava. Pyro from the Greek 'fire'; clastic from the Greek 'klastos', broken; lava from the Latin 'labes', to fall, though that seems one of those rather desperately-arrived-at derivations to me. 'Pyroclastic flow' gets used a lot in Montserrat, these days, or what's left of Montserrat, because of the useful way it rhymes with vol-can-o in the many reggae songs now devoted to the subject. But that's by the by. What I am offering you now, Miss Jacobs, is my own pyroclastic flow, the stream of words issuing from my mouth, in free association. Blow the top, relieve pressure, and the stuff pours out. You told me to free associate: you're the therapist: I suppose you know what you're doing. My doctor thinks you do, trusting as he does that a few sessions with you will relieve me of a pain in the neck with no observable physical cause. Like those who claim lava is derived from labes, he is searching for unavailable answers to unimportant questions.

The pyroclastic flow of Mount Montserrat, or what's left of it, travels at 120 miles an hour, at a temperature of between 600 and 800 degrees Celsius. You'd better watch out, if it's coming your way. Run your hardest, it will still catch you up. Jump over the harbour wall into the blue Caribbean and the lava still comes after you, sizzling and bubbling, hardening like toffee in cold water when you test it, and that's you, boiled to death by bits and pieces of accumulated past.

In the first session I gave you my mother, in the second, my father, and my neck still twinges terribly when I turn suddenly. I can't look over my shoulder when I'm driving. Today I shall give up my sister. Such generosity!

My sister Edy is married to a vulcanologist: this is her life's work. He flew off to Montserrat on Monday, charged by the government to find out if the volcano is going to blow the rest of its top and pyroclastic flow pour down into the 'safe' side of the island, or whether it's worth 'redeveloping' as the remaining inhabitants demand. Once the rich holidayed in Montserrat; now only the poor and the stubborn remain. George Martin's studio, where once the Rolling Stones and The Who recorded, is by all accounts now gaunt, hollow and silent, shrouded in ash.

Edy's husband Rolo says the answer is, 'Don't know.' No one knows what a volcano is going to do next until it does it. The worldwide sample of active volcanoes simply isn't large enough for sensible deductions to be made. Ruapeho did this, St Helena did that, Krakatoa was altogether different: so what. I suggested to Edy that her husband was misappropriating public money in flying out to Montserrat to bring back an answer he knew already. I was half-joking but she put the phone down on me. Edy has no sense of humour, which I believe to be a character trait of elder siblings. She flew with Rolo to Montserrat on Monday morning, though I believe she paid for her own ticket.

Edy is two and a half years older than me, and not yet at any age when this is a disadvantage. I don't think it will ever be, in fact; I can see my time will never come. Perhaps to be thirty-seven and a half when one's sister turns forty might be seen as a good thing; but any number with an 'O' feels like a new beginning, while seven and a half feels like protesting too much. And to be eighty-six when one's sister is eighty-eight is nothing like the advantage eight has over six. I'll never get those years back, ever. I feel she deprived me of them. Edy could walk, talk, learn her tables before me. All I did ahead of her was menstruate, and grow breasts and a bum which were an embarrassment to me. I was 'big for my age': she was small. She was neat and composed and competent while I fumbled and stumbled from lack of years, and too much growth.

Ouch. I moved my head too fast. This is what happens. When I talked to you about my father I could detect no memories of abuse. When I talked about my mother's death I failed to pierce the wall of indifference with which, according to you, I protect myself. When I speak about my sister I get a pain in the neck. Well, there's the answer. She's to blame.

Yes, my sister Edy is a pain in the neck. She is so much better than me. She is brave, noble and sensitive, slender, beautiful; she moves gracefully where I clump-clump. I am younger, plumper, bigger, slipperier than she, and could no more stand at my husband's side at the foot of an active volcano with ash whirling all around, bits of burning forest hurtling through the air, in the possible path of a pyroclastic flow travelling at 100 miles an hour, and helicopters swarming in and out of smoke, than I could fly. What a pain!

Edy phoned me from Montserrat in the middle of last night to ask if I was OK, say they'd arrived safely and to apologise for putting the phone down. Oh yes, we're close: divided only by two and a half years and the fact that since her marriage to Rolo she seems to have no public or personal morality left. I

142

put it to her again on the phone last night that Rolo had no business accepting money from the government to find out an answer he already knew: she said but these days governments had to have the backing of scientists and experts before they did a thing: everything has to be re-found-out, to keep up to date. I said I thought that was a specious argument, the least she could have done was not condone her husband's actions by flying with him, and we lost the connection in a lot of crackle, which I hope was not the terminal pyroclastic flow arriving, accompanied as it is by bursts of gas along the periphery. Edy's way of getting out of an ideological fix.

Edy always maintains I suffer from sibling envy. Personally I think I suffer from rage. Terminal rage. Edy likes to diminish the severity of my condition by applying the jargon of family therapy. It ought to be, she pointed out to me on the day of our great row, the other way round. She is meant to be jealous of me, because I came along and stole my parents' attention. But she's not jealous of me. There is, as she delighted in telling me that day, nothing to be jealous of. Edy is a truth-teller of a wounding kind.

'I only say it because it's true,' she'll say, having pointed out my zits or my too tight skirt, or whatever.

To which I say, 'Telling the truth is just an excuse for hurting people,' and she'll come back, if I'm not careful, with, 'Mum told me on her death bed to tell you a home truth or two, someone had to.'

I don't believe Mum said this, any more than I believe in Diana's last words to Al Fayed. But Edy likes to say them: they hurt. You know how it is; those mysterious words people say to you so you think there's something wrong with what you are, not just what you do, and there's no mending it.

143

What happened was that three years back Mum had a stroke, and Edy and I were meant to be travelling up north together to be at her side, and were to meet on the train, but I waited on the wrong platform, had to get a later train, and by the time I got there Mum had just died, and I was in no position to check out what her last words, if any, actually were. Edy was impatient and called the undertaker because Dad couldn't find his glasses, and in the end ran the whole funeral. No one else had a look-in. I'm Daddy's girl. Edy's Mummy's girl. I haven't cried over her death. The grief counsellors don't know what to do with me.

'Face it, Sally,' said Edy on the day of the great row. 'You didn't love Mother and she didn't love you. How could she? You were unlovable.'

A lot of pyroclastic flow came out of Edy that day. I couldn't dodge. It overwhelmed me.

'You're not even a real artist,' said Edy. 'You've sold out. All you do is dress shop windows for money. A nine-to-five person.'

I have a good job designing display windows for Liberty's. It's one of the most sought-after jobs in London, but what does she care? Edy and I both went to Goldsmiths. She said I was copying her, as usual, but all I was doing was going to the best place around. I got a better degree than her but of course she got hers first. Edy is now a Fine Artist – she does morally superior, semi-figurative pictures which have frames around them, and every now and then sells one. She can afford to be so grand: she has Rolo's salary to live on. I'm on my own: I have to support myself.

My mother was a painter. She died at her easel, staring into a space which wasn't even there any more. She seldom looked at me; though she'd sometimes sketch Edy, who inherited her Pre-Raphaelite hair and looks – quantities of crinkled red hair, a high, pale forehead and hooded eyes. It wasn't that I was ugly; I'm perfectly personable. I just looked too much like my beetle-browed father, whose role in life was to support and admire my mother, to be seen to exist in my own right.

I hope the ground in Montserrat rocks under my sister's feet. How dare she say these things to me! She who accompanies her husband on illicit outings at the taxpayers' expense. I hope she is smothered by ash, and dies terrified. She put a pillow over my face when I was two and tried to suffocate me but I struggled free. She was jealous, in spite of what she claims. On the day of the row she said she wasn't punished for trying to kill me, my mother wanted me dead too, I was such an ugly, whiny, spoil-sport; a party-pooper from the day I was born.

Bits and pieces, bits and pieces; the pyroclastic flow of the past hot off the press.

All I'd done to upset her was try to demonstrate to Edy that Rolo, like so many men, had no moral fibre. That he wasn't worthy of her, that she shouldn't marry him. I did my best to seduce him and almost succeeded – he likes a bit of bosom – and then he went and told her, to salve his own conscience. What an idiot! But I was only doing it for her sake: she had no business losing her temper and saying all those horrible things to me. His accepting the freebie to Montserrat proves I was right to do what I did. I had at least to try. She knows I love her. I pleaded drunkenness, and we're all still friends, but there is a pressure there in her, waiting to blow.

You raise your eyebrows at me, Miss Jacobs. Oh, all right, I know when I'm defeated, when my own words betray me. The pain in my neck is not Edy. I am the pain in her neck. The little sister who hangs around it like an albatross, and won't let go. She puts down the phone: I tell a home truth, she tells a home truth. She's right, I'm in the wrong. I get the pain. It is natural justice. The pyroclastic flow grows cool and slows. I'm lucky Edy phones me at all. The volcano is quiescent. Perhaps.

I can't say the pain in my neck is gone; no such luck. Miracle cures are not so easy. But I suppose understanding what goes on is a step forward. Thank you. I shan't make another appointment now, but there's no knowing what's going to happen next. There she blows! I'll just take a raincheck if that's OK.

# OTHER PLACES, OTHER GENDERS

SPIRITS FLY SOUTH

STASI

A GREAT ANTIPODEAN SCANDAL

# SPIRITS FLY SOUTH

I know about old houses. I know it's them or you. Some years back I held a lighter to the thatch of my cottage in Devon and said if you don't sell yourself within the week I'm going to fire you. I don't have the money to get rid of your dry rot; I don't have the money to renew your thatch; all I can do is raze you to the ground, claim the insurance, and be off. You have driven me to the end of my tether; you are becoming increasingly vicious. See how I am limping and bandaged. Not content, I said, with getting rid of my wife – who, I must agree, was better equipped for living in a Manhattan apartment block than an English country cottage – on the Tuesday you tripped me up over your threshold and sprained my ankle, and on the Wednesday you slammed a latticed window and sent shards of glass flying in my direction. Presently, as I attempt to rewire you myself because I can't afford both alimony and qualified craftsmen – a detail you overlooked, and are as furious as me to discover – you will throw me across the room and break my back, or worse, my neck. And kill me. So here's my ultimatum – sell, or burn.

I meant it. You have to mean it, with houses as with children.

*       *       *

149

# A HARD TIME TO BE A FATHER

Within the week a buyer had flown in from Hong Kong. I suspected he wanted the place as a drug processing plant – it was the seclusion and the size of the barns which seemed to attract him, but what was that to me? The man from Hong Kong left me to stew for a couple of days and then came again, this time with a surveyor and a master builder, so I knew he was serious. He declared loudly that the cost of renovation would end up more than the price of the property. This may well have been said in an attempt to get the price down but it was convincing enough for the house. It sold itself. It made itself look as tempting as it could, brooding peacefully and timelessly in its English garden, edged by hollyhocks, delphiniums and roses; there wasn't even a wasp in sight; aphids flew off and earwigs and woodlice fled. The cottage had even organised for itself the kind of languorous summer evening in which it always looked its best, with the shadows long and deep enough to hide the black spot on the roses and the worm in the front door. Swallows swooped around the barns, so that they, not the rotten beams, caught the eye. Such was the evening – naturally – when I had first seen the place, and bought it, to suffer thereafter. The buyer from Hong Kong paid cash.

One of the removal people tripped on an uneven flagstone as they carried my furniture out, and tried to sue me, and the correspondence went on for years, following me to the antipodes. Otherwise the cottage let me off lightly. I had, honestly, done my best. It just wasn't good enough.

After the cottage sold itself I took up a post as a lecturer in English Literature at the University of Auckland. Auckland is the city at the top of the North Island of New Zealand. In the antipodes read hot for North, and cold for South; Christmas for mid-summer, July for mid-winter and day for night. It takes some time to get used to the reversal, but I liked the country from the beginning. If you feel the need to start a new life, New Zealand is the place to be. You know that while you sleep the woman you once loved, and still obsesses you, is awake, working and walking and not in bed with someone else. Or at least not so likely to be. Mattie was certainly never one for sex in the daytime: it took her too long to adjust her dress and re-coif her hair. The nights of the rejected and abandoned and frankly jealous are best spent in the antipodes, amongst the volcanoes.

Don't all come at once: we don't want too many people here in New Zealand: one of the most agreeable features of the place is the amount of space per person, the sense of non-crush, of time that stretches properly and is not unnaturally compressed, of long white empty beaches along which the temperamental Pacific ripples or crashes at will: of white gannet cliffs red-fringed by the fronds of pohutukawa trees, and inland the total silence of the dense dark green bush, and the brilliance of stars in a high black sky. In Europe the overlapping arcs of city nightlight obscure the heavens: no, we don't want that to happen here. Within six months, you notice, I was part of the 'we'. New Zealanders are a tolerant people, who look for the good in everything and everyone.

They have ghosts, however. I had thought in a new country perhaps they'd have fewer. New Zealand rose out of the sea – a superior atoll – late in the geological history of the world. Inhabited at first (or so some say) by Scandinavian pirates, who arrived in longboats – the Vikings got *everywhere* – and later by sea-going Polynesians who drifted here in error, and only in the first decades of the nineteenth century by Eur-

151

opeans – the place scarcely seemed to have had time to acquire many ghosts. Here in this new Paradise there could be no nameless dreads, no night-time terrors, no poltergeist activity; this would not be hair-turned-white-by-morning land: not here the headless horseman on the country road; the sudden unexplained sensation of cold upon the stair; the person-who-was-not-there turning up on the film you get developed at Boots the Chemist. I was wrong. Kiwi ghosts were everywhere. Perhaps they had been driven South, out of the Northern Hemisphere, by extreme exorcist activity: or intensive psychotherapeutic work on the souls of those sensitive to paranormal phenomena. If you can learn to express your fear and resentment of your parents or your spouse, get rid of the woodworm and the dry rot of your beginnings, why bother to see the ghost? It will simply depart, and end up, I began to think, in New Zealand – so many apparitions were seen, and so casually, by those around me.

Australia is not so plagued. Perhaps the climate's too hot for spectres, or the Aboriginals so thoroughly possess the – what shall we call it? The desert parasphere? – that they feel uncomfortable and depart. But these dear, accommodating, uncynical New Zealanders, perhaps feeling it unkind to disbelieve in the restless spirits of the departed, are prepared to put up with the paucity of their existence, and give them leave to be. And so they come, like me, and stay, like me.

I fell in love with one of my students. Let me put that differently. She fell in love with me, and my state of mind was such, post-Mattie, that I responded. We had one of those intense, nervy, dreamy yet erotic affairs, which obsess one at the time but get forgotten as life moves on and one practicality or another gets in the way of the relationship and forbids it settling down into matrimony, household and children. It was not a forbidden or a hopeless relationship. There was nothing secret about it, or particularly inappropriate. I was young to be a lecturer – thirty-five – and Mila was old to be a student – twenty-eight. Both of us were free. So long as we did not push the affair under the noses of the university authorities, so long as I did not take it into my head to give a clearly B-standard student – she was better at netball than Eng. Lit. – straight A's, it would be OK by them. No scandal, you guys – and be as happy as you like.

I had bought a small house in Rosemary Street, Ponsonby, overlooking St Mary's Bay. Auckland is a harbour city, like Sydney, or Rio, or Vancouver – stunning cities all of them. Why live anywhere else, when such brilliant seascape vistas exist to please the waking eye? It was a new house – only six years old – and in perfect condition. Everything fitted, everything worked: nothing rotted, frayed or disintegrated. Nothing needed painting. Everything was plain and perfect cream and blue: cheerful and bright and, yes, boring; boring to a natural handyman like me, but never mind.

I had learned my lesson. I would never buy an old house again: they are too easily disgruntled. Every penny you spend on yourself is grudged: buy a new pair of shoes and it thinks you should have replaced a bannister instead: you will find yourself snagging your hand horribly on the bannister rail. Give a party, when the money should have gone towards renewing the bedroom sash cords – a wasp will crawl in the gap between frame and sill and get you on the tongue and mean a journey to hospital and anti-histamine injections while they save you. I tell you, you are lucky to live if your old house takes against you. And yet I missed it. I missed my cottage. I missed it as I missed Mattie. The thing you love wants to destroy you – so what? Except you find you do want to live, and take steps to save yourself. Sell, or burn. How cruel I had been, as cruel as I had been to Mattie. 'Live here or lose me,' I had said.

'Number 22's a very sensible buy,' said Mila, annoying me, 'but it's not quite you.'

At twenty-eight, she was moving out of her parents' home – a step I encouraged. She had taken a long time growing up. Sport, she acknowledged, had blunted her early erotic sensibilities. Too much netball can lead to a too hearty approach to sex, at least for a European taste. Mila's initial appreciation of me had been entirely and frankly sexual; that is to say her conviction was that if she had a sexual itch – and she did – I was the one to scratch it. It was only after repeated scratchings that she developed a more sensuous appreciation of me, and indeed I of her. Mila was a stunningly pretty girl in an athletic kind of way, her legs perhaps too muscly for perfection. But she wanted to be perfect for me: that touched me. Nothing would do, in our first few weeks, but she'd leap out of bed immediately after sex, wash (she was very clean) and be across the room to do some limbering and stretching exercises for the sake of her legs. While I, for my part, even mid-sex, would never at first quite be able to forget Mattie, essays to mark, bills to pay and so forth, and would find myself wondering why I had let myself get involved with so exhausting a girl. But we both got better at being in love: soon, sex over, we would lie around in bed together, in a state of bliss, and as the months passed we drifted into the pleasantest hand-in-handedness, loin-to-loinedness imaginable.

\*　　\*　　\*

154

We became the kind of couple who for ever touch each other in public, each enchanted by the other. We tried not to, but that's what we did. Every now and then I would remember the clause in my contract which stipulated that I must not bring the name of my college into disgrace. 'No scandal.' Now what that meant was anyone's guess, as Flora, a rather attractive colleague of mine at the University, was quick to point out. I was in a strange country, for all I now claimed it as my own. What is the expression of love to one, is scandal to another.

One way and another it seemed best that Mila did not move in to live with me when she left her parents' place. We would give people time to get used to the idea of our togetherness. So with her friend, Wendy, Mila rented No. 12 Rosemary Street, five doors down from my own at number 22. The plan was that Mila would spend nights and days with me when appropriate; go to her own home as she saw fit. As an arrangement, we both thought, it should work well. It would be a learning experience. Our temperaments were so very different – we would need time to adapt to one another. My tendency to accumulate irritated Mila – I am reluctant to throw anything away. She loves to clear out and throw out. I like the bathroom warm, soapy and human; Mila likes it cold, clean and smelling of Dettol. And so forth. But we both assumed that with time we would grow closer rather than further apart – that eventually we would live together at No. 22; even marry, should we decide to have children.

One way and another I had learned the folly of impulsiveness. I had met and married Mattie within six weeks. I had seen and bought the cottage in Devon within the same period. Now news came from home that the place had

burned down. Rumour had it that the owner's drug paraphernalia had caught fire in one of the barns; flames had
caught the cottage thatch, and that was the end. I was oddly
sorry: I suppose once you have talked to a house, no matter
how cruelly, it takes on human aspects. I even wept.

No. 12, where Mila lived, was the oldest house in Rosemary
Street. It was charming, quirky and instantly likeable; it had
been built in the last decade of the last century. There was a
tiled roof which someone had patched with corrugated iron;
its floorboards were made of kauri wood – the hardest of
hard timbers. (The giant kauri, now a protected species, there
being so few of them left, takes at least five hundred years to
grow to maturity.) The house was fronted with a charming
but crumbling late Victorian verandah, full of cobwebs,
spiders and a brilliant white clematis which grew in from
outside. Roots pushed up the stone slabs of the front porch;
above that were the elaborate iron railings – original Coal-
brookdale, brought over as ballast for ships which would
return to England full of butter, cheese and wool – which you
see so often in these antipodean cities. The bathroom out-
house, built on to the back of the house sometime in the
twenties, needed rebuilding entirely: the foliage of the cliff
wall behind it now pushed up so closely against the structure
there was no wonder it dripped with damp. I told Mila that I
got a whiff of dry rot from this back bathroom, but she did
not comprehend the deep seriousness of what I was telling
her. What did she know or care about dry rot? She just loved
the house. And after all she and Wendy were only renting the
place – from, as it happened, my friend Flora, who was its
owner and lived next door in No. 10. Mila said she'd shut the
door on the damp back bathroom if that made me happy,
and use the shower room on the landing instead. Showers

were healthier than baths anyway. There was nothing what-
soever wrong with No. 12; it was old and had been empty for
four years and it showed, that was all. I was to stop
whingeing.

'Dry rot flourishes,' I told her, 'in damp places that have been
dried out – you're asking for trouble,' but Mila was off: she
wouldn't stay even until I'd finished talking. Mila never liked
to listen to what she didn't want to hear. She went next door
to No. 10 instead, to watch Christchurch play Wellington at
hockey on TV, and cheer her friends on. Mila knew everyone
who was anybody in the world of sports, as she kept telling
me. Sometimes I felt positively puny.

No. 12's previous owner had lived in the place since the
nineteen thirties. Four years ago, aged eighty-two, she'd
broken a thigh bone when a section of the balcony ironwork
– eaten through with rust – had collapsed beneath her small
weight. She'd died in hospital: the house had stood empty
since then. When the property finally came on the market
Flora had succumbed to impulse and made it her own. Flora
was Professor of Statistics in the Department of Psychology;
she was unmarried, one of those grey-haired but still pretty,
fine-boned, intelligent, choosy women you find in university
departments everywhere. Her pension bonus came through
in four years' time; her plan was to wait till then, renovate
No. 12, sell at a vast profit, and live comfortably ever after.
In the meantime she'd let the place out to students. Mila and
Wendy were to be her first tenants.

'I hope four years isn't too late for the house,' I said, when
Flora first showed me round it.
    'If it all falls down,' replied Flora cheerfully, 'so much the

better. I'll just get planning permission, clear it away and put up something sensible. Old houses can't last for ever.'

'That may be true,' I said, 'but don't say so in their presence. Nice house!' I said, patting it as I would a dog. 'Good house!' And Flora laughed. Mila would have made puking noises. Had Mila not come along I might have drifted Florawards. But she was ten years older than me and senior in status: the university 'no scandal' rule still intimidated me. I had found so much so suddenly I could not bear to lose it, through carelessness, not again.

A weta flew in the open door while I was helping Mila and Wendy move into No. 12. Even I was disconcerted, and Mila and Wendy both screamed so loudly and became so helpless I had to summon Flora to help me catch the creature and remove it. We used the glass and card method while the girls screamed at us to kill it, slaughter it, and we ignored them.

A weta is a kind of ugly flying dragon which tends to drop off trees into the hair of passers-by. Mila and Wendy could bungee-jump, surf tidal waves, outface avalanches and shear sheep but neither could face wetas. They just wanted them to die. Flora observed that wetas put pakehas (NZ for whites) in mind of Maori warriors in full gear, their faces made hideous the better to frighten their enemies. Of course, said Flora, the whites wanted wetas slaughtered. Wetas made pakehas feel guilty.

'What for?' I asked.

'Genocide,' said Flora.

Mila sucked air and snorted. Flora did not seem to like Mila very much, though she was always courteous.

\*　　\*　　\*

Apart from this incident all went well. Flora had given No. 12's interior a brisk coating of white paint, to cheer it up. The rooms were bright, large and elegantly proportioned. A staircase ran up out of the wide central hall and split at the top; two galleries ran along to either side, with the upstairs rooms leading out of them. Wendy was twenty-six and a tenderer-looking girl than Mila: white-skinned and soft-bosomed, with bright blue eyes and a receding chin. As with so many New Zealand girls, her looks belied her temperament. She was training as an air pilot. She was also a New Ager – no coffee, no alcohol, no antibiotics – just crystals, horoscopes, meditation and peace and love to all. This did not seem to conflict with her evident ambition to get on in the world. Mila also leaned gracefully towards the naturalism of the New Age – for fear of heavy-metal poisoning she'd recently had all the old mercury-based fillings lifted out of her teeth. Elaborate precautions had been taken the while to avoid inhaling the gas released when the fillings were drilled – Mila had pronounced the operation worthwhile, albeit expensive. No more fits of lassitude, she claimed – not that I'd ever noticed any. Mila had no ambition, really, other than to feel good, play ball games well and be happy with me. Which was flattering.

Mattie called me once to say she was marrying again – an interior designer working out of Minneapolis – and to wish me well in my new life. I told her about Mila and Mattie said she hoped I wasn't on the rebound, it sounded suspiciously like it, and I said I imagined no more than she, Mattie, was. I hoped Mattie was being sensible – weren't most interior designers gay – and she put down the phone.

Be that as it may, I cheerfully helped Mila and Wendy move in to No. 12, shifted furniture, fitted their hard Japanese style beds back together for them, stocked the kitchen, locked the damp back bathroom – the bolt was old and rusty – and checked that the door to the unsafe balcony was securely wedged shut. Then I helped the girls place their ornaments and comfort-objects here or there – a long and elaborate process. Mila collected soft-toy cats and Wendy china pigs. I Blu-Tacked their posters on the walls and drove in nails for their framed family photographs.

When all was done, Wendy set about preparing a little house-warming ceremony with candles, crystals, borage tea and so on. They had actually asked friends round – they didn't seem in the least tired. I was exhausted. They warned me there would be chanting. I didn't particularly want to stay, in any case. I am too easily embarrassed, and start to laugh, which even I can see spoils the atmosphere they have gone to so much trouble to establish.

I liked to think Mila subscribed to these rituals out of loyalty and affection for Wendy, rather than that she believed such ceremonies could in any way tilt the flow of the universe in her direction. I said as much. Mila said I was being over-intellectual. Then she mentioned that she had arranged to spend the next day out of town at an Ultimate Frisbee Fest; she would need to be fresh in the morning and couldn't spend the night with me after all – a decision I had to respect though I rather wished I had been consulted. Ultimate Frisbee is a team game which was, as Mila reminded me, likely to be on the menu at the next Olympics. Mila certainly widened my horizons. I said as much. She said I was not to act sarcastic, it wasn't attractive in a man. We arranged to meet next evening at the party Flora was giving at No. 10 and I went home, considerably out of humour.

\* \* \*

Later, it seems, Mila and Wendy and their five friends, all female, laid a Tibetan cloth in the centre of the hall – the kind with little mirrors inset between bright embroidery – placed candles on it in the form of a pentagram, within which they sat and chanted, burned incense, transmitted good thoughts from one to the other, exchanged gossip, related their various sexual adventures, sipped their borage tea, ate little almond biscuits white-iced in heart shapes, and in general pulled blessings down on the new home.

When the ceremony was over, and the guests gone, Mila and Wendy realised they didn't own a broom to sweep away the crumbs. They set off for the corner store to buy this useful and essential item, and obtain other cleaning materials as well. What once had been mothers' work, they realised, was now theirs. They made sure they had the key, closed their own new proud front door carefully behind them, and walked down the wormy wooden steps and along the pretty garden path to Rosemary Street. The evening sun shone serenely: a thin new moon could just be seen the other side of the harbour. Both at that moment, as never before, were conscious of the beneficence of a fate that had brought them to this time and place, healthy and happy: Mila in love with me and surely about to win at Hamilton and make the National Ultimate Frisbee team; Wendy at peace with the spirits and with her commercial flying certificate in the post. They had a home of their own, a life of their own making, and nothing to trouble them. They put all those thoughts into a simple exchange of 'wows!' but both knew what the other meant.

Later that evening they were to be seen crouched in the corner of Flora's living room, no better than terrified animals, clutching each other. What had happened was worse than a weta in the hair. They'd returned to No. 12, Wendy had unlocked the door and held it open so Mila could go ahead with her brooms and dustpans. But as Mila crossed the threshold, a blast of something like a surge of electricity (Mila) or a wave of earth energy (Wendy) had flung Mila, brooms and all, halfway to the end of the garden, and sent Wendy staggering off-balance down the wooden steps. Mila sat shocked on the path for at least two minutes, before recovering her wits sufficiently to start searching for cuts and bruises or anything more serious that might stop her playing in tomorrow's match. She supposed there had been some kind of explosion. Wendy ran next door to call the emergency services. The police came and discovered no signs of anything untoward. The firemen checked gas and electricity. Nothing. No leaks, no shorts. The ambulance men found some nasty bruises on Mila's bum but not much else. Everyone went away.

When they felt better the girls went bravely back into No. 12. They found the Tibetan cloth rolled into a ball in a corner at the foot of the stairs, but otherwise everything else as they had left it. Wendy, who was shivering, complained that the atmosphere of the house had changed, but Mila would have none of it.

'All that's happened,' said Mila, 'is that the wind changed, and there was some sort of build-up of static electricity inside the house which was released when we opened the front door. Poor house!' And Mila went round stroking walls and making coo-ing noises at the panelling; it was probably the worst thing she could have done. It isn't wise to imbue non-organic forms with personalities; they get above themselves. I know I do it all the time, but it isn't always safe. You have to know what you're doing. I did. Mila didn't.

I was away in Coromandel for the day, teaching creative writing classes and was to know nothing about these events until later. It seems the evening went placidly by: Mila and Wendy sat on the floor of the living room and watched TV. Wendy wrapped herself in a rug. The curtains started billowing. Mila checked, and found the French windows fitting so badly that now the wind had changed and blew from the Antarctic south, they could hardly do anything else but billow. She believed what she wanted to believe. Who doesn't, unless trained to it?

Wendy wouldn't sleep alone so they pulled and pushed her bed into Mila's room. Mila too found it a relief not to be on her own. She too had gotten jumpy. They would share a room just this one night, they told each other. No. 12 Rosemary Street was a beautiful house with a friendly atmosphere and that was that.

They talked themselves to sleep, overcoming with an effort their natural reluctance to talk about what they called 'spooky things'. Neither really believed in ghosts – but on the other hand supposing the old lady who'd died falling off the balcony hated them? Supposing whoever had built the back extension was angry at the locked door? Supposing there were other occupants, further back, who'd died miserably? Maori souls who couldn't settle?

Both fell asleep at the same time and slept soundly; they woke to a brilliant day and with all fearful night fancies fled away. Just a pity that as Mila came down the stairs looking forward to breakfast she felt what seemed like a lot of little children's

163

hands pushing into the small of her back, so she had to hold on to the bannister to stop herself pitching forward. A pity that two pieces of toast jumped out of the toaster, smoking black and flew right across the room, when Wendy was certain she hadn't even switched the thing on. A pity that when Mila unrolled and smoothed out the Tibetan cloth, all the little mirrors were cracked and dark. Though Wendy said that was just as well: if they still reflected, God knew what they'd show if you stared into them. Still they tried to laugh it off, make light of it.

'Hello, ghost!' called Wendy. 'You be our friend, we'll be yours!'

'Ghosts!' Mila amended, thinking of the myriad little hands in the small of her back. Either way there was no reply. Wendy stayed unduly cold. There was nothing to fear, Mila told her, except fear itself, and possibly damp, which could trigger off arthritis and put paid to sporting activity. Mila declared herself to be perfectly warm. She was due to take the ten o'clock train to Hamilton for Ultimate Frisbee. She felt bad about leaving Wendy on her own. But Wendy said that was OK; if there was any more trouble all she had to do was go next door to Flora.

Mila caught her train, and by eleven Wendy was indeed at Flora's. Shortly after Mila had left, the dustpan and brush, sitting under the sink, had started to vibrate of their own accord, rattling together, and set off such further vibrations that the very structure of the house had begun to shake and rattle. There was a noise like that of a million little falling stones: pigs, cats and ornaments had toppled from shelves; and framed photographs leapt off the walls. Blu-Tack flew about the room. Wendy had run outside, thinking it must be an earthquake. But everything along the street was peaceful and still, calm in the morning sun. If it was an earthquake, it was the house's own. Wendy fled next door.

Flora rang the Catholic priest, Father Ivor, and asked him to come round to perform an exorcism. He said he could come next day if it was urgent, but he was booked up, one exorcism after another, there'd been so much trouble in the neighbourhood lately. Flora asked why he thought that was, and was told it was either an increase in sin, which Father Ivor rather doubted – the volume of sin in the world was a moveable east; like a balloon: squash it there and it came up here – or that the intense drought of the previous summer had led to subsidence, and the disturbance of earth spirits. Father Ivor sounded a jolly person. He was not worried that Flora was a Presbyterian – for all he knew, the unquiet spirit was a Catholic who had failed to receive Last Rites and had heard that Father Ivor was practising in the area. The exorcism would cost $100 NZ. Flora reckoned she could put it against tax, and booked Father Ivor for the following week.

As it happened, Father Ivor had a cancellation that very afternoon – a couple who'd discovered that the psychic disturbances they complained of were knowingly manufactured by a teenage daughter (a cry for attention, said Father Ivor). Flora called me to ask if I'd come along with her to the exorcism. This was the first I'd heard of any need for it. Mila had not wanted me told – I would, she claimed, have only said 'I told you so.' Flora had seen fit, thank God, to overrule the younger woman. And that was how Flora, Wendy and myself came to witness the ritual, Mila having deserted us in the interests of Ultimate Frisbee.

\*     \*     \*

Father Ivor, big-bellied and red-faced, drove up in his little 2CV, parked at the entrance to No. 12's driveway, and took out the customary Bell – the same kind of little bell Catholics tinkle at intervals through the Mass – and the Book – a large old illustrated bible that bore the rings of many coffee mugs on its vellum cover. (New Zealanders are not necessarily careful with old things: they have got into the habit of living in the present and the future, and putting the past firmly behind them. They believe that, in general, things get better, not worse. That standards rise, don't inexorably fall. They have no sense of entropy. It's not a land where antique dealers easily grow rich.) The Candle was tall and white and came with a heavy silver-plated candlestick, with the plate half worn-off.

'I'm not the best man in the world to be doing this,' said Father Ivor, 'I'm easily scared.' He asked me to help him in with his things – a man's job – and this I did. As well as the traditional Bell, Book and Candle Father Ivor had brought with him the paraphernalia required for burning incense. For some reason this put me in mind of the kind of equipment I imagined a drug dealer would use to purify his wares. Flora and Wendy stayed outside the house. Flora was looking particularly well, I thought. She loved an intrigue: she adored sudden event: her cheeks were pink: they had lost their normal slightly papery older-woman pallor.

The inside of No. 12 was in a sorry state – as a house might well be after a severe earthquake. The china pigs we had so hopefully placed the day before had slipped off their shelves and shattered: the fluffy cats lay sprawled face down – one had all but lost its head – heaven knew how that had happened. I retrieved it, the easier to lose it. I did not want

Mila reading into a headless cat more than there was to read. Paintings had fallen. Doors swung open on uneven door frames. Old plaster had flaked and fallen.

'A very private earthquake,' Father Ivor murmured, awed. 'Or else a nasty case of subsidence,' I said. 'It's been a long hot summer.'

But I went through with it. Best to be safe. Father Ivor swung incense into corners; he used the Good Book, not to read from but as a source of power: he intoned from memory in some rough kind of Latin. When he paused for longer than a few seconds, I tinkled the bell as if I were some eccentric form of audible computer screen saver. Father Ivor seemed satisfied, and started off up the stairs – got some three steps up and then stopped, as if faced by a glass wall.

'This is too strong for me!' he complained, and came down again fast. He ran past me through the hall, long black gown flying around his ankles, leaving me to pack everything up and follow him out. I was not conscious of any particularly disagreeable atmosphere. It did seem to me that Flora ought to call in a surveyor as well as an exorcist.

I told her so after Father Ivor had departed, pausing only to collect his cheque. But Flora had begun to worry about the party she was giving that night – she had that agreeable habit I have often noticed in women, of abandoning an ongoing major worry in the face of a minor one that's incoming. There was so much to do, she explained. Tables had to be set up, and glasses found, pavlova cases baked, vol-au-vent pastry rolled and left to stand – at least, as I told her, no one would have to worry about a subject for conversation; the haunting of the house next door would do very well.

Mila came back from Hamilton cheerful – her team had won at Ultimate Frisbee – but with no intention, having taken a quick glimpse at the wreckage inside, of setting foot inside No. 12 until it had been properly exorcised. Wendy concurred. The wrong priest had been summoned. They would call in the Tohunga. I admired them both very much. Frightened they might be, but they would not allow themselves to be defeated. Out of any situation, however unfortunate, a New Zealand girl will use her ingenuity and come up smiling.

The Tohunga, summoned by telephone, was a witch doctor from, I believe, the Polynesian island of Samoa, whence come a large proportion of the NZ labouring force. He was even fatter than Father Ivor; he had a truly enormous belly which seemed to hang on to the rest of him, rippling and swaying, clinging on for dear life, in danger of falling off with every step. The Tohunga had, like Father Ivor, a great red drunkard's nose; he wore a thin X-X-X-L size green and blue tie-dyed T-shirt down to his knees, and rubber sandals. His mouth was vast and almost toothless. His day job, he let us know, was as an electricity pylon repairman: he moonlighted as herbalist, shaman and exorcist. He had been very busy lately. Spirits, he said, fly South.

'I told you so,' said Wendy, 'the unquiet spirits are Polynesian. Of course they wouldn't respond to Father Ivor's superstitious nonsense.'

Flora and myself were the only ones who continued to refer to 'ghosts' – to everyone else the word already seemed

vaguely impolite and discriminatory – to have lifeist implica-
tions, if nothing else. 'Spirits' or 'the departed returned' were
now referred to. Since neither Wendy nor Mila would go into
No. 12 with the Tohunga: I had to do it. Flora was by now
too busy with her pastries and home-made elderberry wine to
be much involved. The girls, I was later told, took time off
from helping her to go to a clinic round the corner, each to
enjoy a quick aromatherapy. No such luck for me.

The ghosts seemed impervious to both our presences. I took
the opportunity of cleaning up a little. Nothing out of place
occurred while I did. The Tohunga first cleansed the ground
floor; he paced the perimeter of the rooms, chanting, pausing
at each corner to take great gulps of air, then standing in the
middle of the room to hyperventilate. He unlocked the door
to the damp bathroom and I could almost touch the musty
dry rot smell once again. I'd got a whiff or so of it at the
cottage, before I sold it on to the drug dealer. The Tohunga
gulped mightily, on the threshold of this jerry-built extension.

'Best leave door open,' said the Tohunga. 'Let forces flow.'
He went through the same rituals upstairs, unlocking the
French windows which led to the rusty balcony before
sucking yet more forces into himself. I could see the balcony
would have to be made safe if Flora meant to continue
letting. It would take more than just locking doors and
hoping to make the place habitable.
    'Got it all,' said the Tohunga. 'Time to go.'

When we got back to No. 10, the party was in full swing.
Most New Zealanders don't mix their drinks as Australians
do, but they are not averse to getting drunk. Some already

were. I tried to stop Mila mixing beer with home-made cider, but to no avail. When she had been drinking there was a rather coarse, crude, slack-jawed look about her: I noticed that her nose had caught the sun, and she spoke too loudly and confidently about the kinds of things she knew nothing about – from sex to hauntings. Her youth seemed more off-putting than charming. For all her stretching exercises her bare brown legs were still knotted with muscle. She wore a T-shirt and jeans: she looked hopelessly healthy without eroticism. I had, in fact, fallen out of love with Mila: or perhaps, more like it, as it now occurred to me, I had never been in it. Or why would I now be so critical all of a sudden? Flora appeared at my elbow. She looked tidy, severe, sober and stylish. She wore a grey high-necked dress with a row of unfashionable buttons running over a neat chest, and she had gone to some trouble to arrange her hair. She seemed infinitely desirable.

'Do you actually believe in ghosts?' she asked.

'No,' I said. 'Just in subsidence, and never owning an old house.'

She laid her hand on my own and smiled. Mila caught the smile, and cornered a rugby player with a neck as thick as his thighs and flirted with him to annoy me. The Tohunga had come in to join the party: he drained glass after glass of red wine, and belched at intervals, great geyser spouts of gas from deep down in his belly into the noisy party air. I kept out of his way. I advised others so to do.

Flora suggested she and I went next door to see if the Tohunga had earned his money – $500 NZ – and we did. We went straight up to Wendy's bed – Mila's would not have been right – and we made love. Flora used the phrase – Mila only ever said 'fucked'. The house did not move on its foundations, but I felt I had come home.

Mila came in and found us together. Still there were no manifestations in the house. Just the crunch of already broken glass underfoot, and an odd flake of plaster falling from the ceiling while Mila screamed and beat Flora and myself about our heads. Her hands were strong and brown from too much Ultimate Frisbee; Flora's were neat, small and fluttery.

Mila went home to her parents' house. In fact she left university altogether, to devote her life to sport. Wendy never spoke to me again. Flora and I married. I sold No. 22 and she sold No. 10 and we used the money to do up No. 12. We put in proper foundations, removed all the rotten beams, rewired and re-plumbed and most importantly rooted out the dry rot. We demolished the bathroom extension and put in a conservatory: we renewed the balcony using iron railings from a conservation store. My own opinion is that No. 12 had just got desperate: two careless girl students were not its idea of suitable occupants: I was the better bet. No. 12 was bad to them but good to me.

Perhaps the spirits of dead houses, not just of people, travel South. Perhaps the ghost of my Devon cottage had followed me, to reproach me. I should have found it a better buyer. Perhaps fewer ghosts are reported in Europe these days because most old houses have been 'done up' – and are in good repair and not desperate for their survival. Their spirits are quiet.

Or perhaps it was nothing to do at all with houses and their repair; for all I knew the Tohunga had indeed swallowed up the circling spirits of some ancient Maori burial ground. The new owners of No. 10 did report the occasional phenomena in the room where the Tohunga had done his belching. They'd find a little piece of grit where no grit should reasonably be: a machine-load of washing which managed to get itself into knots, literally: the odd footstep overhead in the bathroom – but nothing much, and all apparently random. I advised the new owners, who had already begun to trip over rugs and catch their elbows and shins on this or that, to try having the upstairs windowsills replaced before the winter set in. They did, and after that all was quiet and pleasant in No. 10. And Flora and I lived happily ever after in No. 12, tinkering away with our home improvements.

# STASI

## An Interview with a Film Actress

I'd tell you the truth if I could, but I can't. No one can. 'Tell me what it's like,' you say. 'Tell me what it feels like.' But no woman can speak the whole truth. She has her husband, her partner, her children, her parents to think of: there are always others to be protected.

Yesterday I read of a woman who finally met up with her son after fifty years searching. She'd been raped by a German soldier in the second world war. She'd been sixteen at the time. The man had fallen upon her in a cornfield, and left her for dead. But she came back to life and had a child to prove it. Whereupon her family turned her out for the guilt of her misfortune, and the authorities took the baby because she had no means of supporting it. 'You can never see him again,' they said. 'We pay, we own.' Decades passed while the mother searched: the patterns of human cruelty and kindness changed; empires foundered and fell. Once she found someone who claimed to be her son but he turned out to be an imposter: the Stasi, the secret police, had stolen her boy's identity: given his name and his passport to another. She'd wondered why the adult's eyes were brown when the child's eyes had been blue. But all babies' eyes are blue when they are born, are they not? Deep, deep blue. She didn't know even that much about babies. In the end she found her true son; he was running a factory in Prague, in what was once Czecho-slovakia but is now the Czech Homelands.

The fifty year break was probably just as well. 'Mummy, tell me what Daddy was like?'

'He was a fine upstanding man, darling, so strong and impetuous. See, I have the marks of his buttons on my ribcage to this day!' No, better to wait fifty years, for the scars to fade a little. A child must think well of his father, or else he'll grow up with a hanging head, a shuffling gait.

Can I give you some coffee? Yes, set up your tape-recorder on this table here. How nicely your English sun shines through the windows. Yes, it is a pretty house: a little large and empty now for our needs: my mother says I'm throwing money away: is that my plan? – she thinks everyone must have a plan. Yes, I know the world is interested in how I feel. Yes, I owe the truth to my audience; yes, I know yours is a respectable and intelligent newspaper; but I must repeat there are individuals it is my duty as a woman to protect.

It is just as bad for men: I am not claiming special privileges for women. What father hasn't looked at his children and wished that he had chosen a different mother for them? Or wished them altogether out of existence, so he could be free? But he takes the same care the mother does not to let them know it.

Once we loved God, or our nation, or felt we would lay down our lives for this cause or that. But now that we have lost our capacity to love outside ourselves and must make do with the personal, we betray each other since that is all we have left to betray. I was betrayed by my husband, who kept a secret file against me in his head.

The secret police are everywhere; people prefer their rules and penalties to be strict and unreasonable. Recently I was told of the fate of a French farming family under German occupation: their teenage son turned up at Gestapo head-quarters and reported, 'My father has a gun.'

The sergeant, a father himself, said three times, 'Go home, boy. I don't want to hear this.'

The son persisted. 'But I tell you, he has a gun!' Bureaucracy took its course. The authorities turned up, took the father away and shot him. So perish the disobedient, betrayed by the obedient: it's the asp in the bosom, not in the grass, which gets you. The boy had his heart's desire, at least until he grew out of it. His heart's desire? Why his mother's undivided attention and no more disturbing noises in the night.

Cruel and oppressive regimes have always benefited from the flow of children all too ready to tell tales against their parents. The informers are always with us: the neighbour who tells the tax-man everything: the wife who shops the maid to immigra-tion; the child who says his uncle fondled him. What ever changes? 'This person is really a Jew.' 'That person speaks against Stalin.' 'My nanny has Hutu blood.' 'My neighbour claims benefit but goes to work.' There's always something. The interrogators get you, squeeze the truth out of you while you scream, inwardly or outwardly, be they the Inquisition with thumbscrews, the KGB with their truth-drug, or the hospital saying, 'And how did your child get that bruise?'

*    *    *

And then there's black-out! Always black-out. 'I'm sorry, our records are private, our deliberations are secret. This is for your own good.' Security, you understand. Personal letters are censored in war, newspapers in peace: censors are always freely available: watchers are everywhere. Watch, watch, Neighbourhood Watch! Scratch away the apparatus of state, of tyrannical political systems, and we're left with our own natures. We cannot endure freedom. I read yesterday in the English newspapers of a two-year-old, still groping for words, who was expelled from his nursery school; he was accused of racism. I tell you the Stasi is now in our own minds, no longer in the body politic; and the more frightening for that. After the fall of the wall, freedom fled West, repression fled East.

Do you take sugar? Milk? I talk a lot; yes, you're right – that way I need say very little. How astute you are. How old are you? Twenty-five, twenty-six? I love your wide belt; your thick, flowing, confident hair. Yes, I've seen your by-line. You are doing very well in the journalistic world. Married, I hear, and a baby, and a career? If you could choose any two, which two would it be? It might come to that. Quite often the choice narrows to one. But you don't want to know that: you believe that in this country you're safe. Well, here's hoping.

Yes, let's get down to business. You're becoming impatient. You have to get back to give the baby its bottle. You have to keep the child-carer happy so she allows the baby to grow up to love you: or to be like you, or better and happier than you, or whatever it is you want for your child. And you'll be going out to dinner tonight, and you can tell them you interviewed me, and what I was like. Keeping up a good front, I hope you will say. My hair is combed; I have my lipstick on.

My husband and I reckoned ourselves more fortunate than most. No, I don't think we were exactly complacent. Certainly, we were regularly presented as the world's most famous happily married couple. My husband wrote the films, I acted in them. No, I don't think there was a real conflict of interest there: I made more money than him but he had more status. I thought we balanced. Yes, I was wrong, as it turned out. Yes, our children follow in our footsteps: the boys acting, the girls writing. Yes, that reversal is strange. Yes, I like to say 'our'. That word is all I have left of my husband. But I'm probably a bit of a downer; not a bundle of laughs, any more, he told me as much: a woman much sobered by the world. Yes, I can see that after twenty-five years, so creative a man might want a change, some new source of inspiration. A touch of spirituality in his life. Yes, long-lasting marriages are unusual these days.

As you know, he had a threatened heart attack. As you may not know, being young as you are, the doctors and nurses gave him the new ritual advice, the viper-whisper they love to utter, the taking-aside, the word of permitting authority in the vulnerable ear, the Stasi sing-song which brings about the second, fatal heart attack sooner than anything. 'You must think about yourself now. Forget the others.'

That is to say, safer now to go it alone, since the source of the stress-related illness, the focus of all blame, lies in others, not in the self. But how does a man of integrity, a family man, a man who loves wife and children, if only by custom and practice, achieve such wickedness? To abandon all others and put himself first? The effort kills him.

People are moral creatures, not just survivors. More than you think would be prepared to die rather than say that black is white, that two and two make five. Dissenters have principle; torturers lack doubt. The Stasi everywhere say that for the sake of others the disobedient must be tamed, must be brought into line, must abandon their random and dangerous fancies, whether they're to do with an anarchist cell, freedom of speech, or simply loving a family. The twist to the torture is the same in oligarchy or democracy: tell us what you know, admit that it was you, or we'll subject your children to this agony too. We know where you live. Do what we say, believe what we believe, or die. But in the doing, in the believing, in the saying, after the heart attack, lies the dying. They don't tell you that.

Yes, that's how it went. The story was in all the newspapers of the world, following where our films had gone. Why am I talking to you at all? I so seldom give interviews these days. I can't imagine how you got beneath my guard. Yes, the hospital sent my husband to a psychotherapist the better to be trained in the art of not loving me, the better to stay alive, the better to think only about himself. And yes, he made her pregnant, as everyone knows. Sex was part of the freeing process, as it now so often is. The cutting of the ties that bind. Yes, I can accept now that the pregnancy was accidental; neither one of them is alive to deny it or confirm it. What difference can it make? The fire that devoured the loins is quenched, if you don't object to a fancy turn of phrase. How long or importantly it burned for either of them is neither here nor there, though it seemed to matter at the time.

\*        \*        \*

And yes, why do you ask, do you think I am foolish enough to reveal some little extra, some tiny scoop? Joanne Dee was found asphyxiated one morning, stifled in bed with the pillow which had propped her patients' heads, she and her unborn baby dead. The big window which opened on to her garden was open. There had been a full moon that night. It must have been so beautiful, so bright, as Joanne sat and gazed out at trees and contemplated her achievements. What do I mean by her achievements? Why the bringing to aloneness of so many. 'A clean break!' she persuaded my husband. 'Make it a clean break.' It will be easier for her like that. The grass was damp with dew, but not enough to take the imprint of the killer's foot. And yes, I was arrested and charged with murder, and brought to court and acquitted, because where was the evidence? It could have been me, need not have been me. Anyone amongst us could have done it; any of us who'd lost our family to her placid scheming, her smiling stupidity. Men from the Stasi would be found mysteriously dead, from time to time.

I sound as if I hated her? I do. I have a right to hate her. She rendered me powerless, my anxiety and love for my husband made me helpless as she plunged around in our lives, laying waste everything delicate and significant. Hate sustains me. Certainly, I hated her enough to kill her, of course I didn't tell the Court that. Would you inform them of such a thing? Hardly! But I didn't kill her. I assured the Court of that. Who wouldn't? If they believed me, why shouldn't you? Yes, I am glad she is dead, and that she took her baby with her into the afterlife. My husband listened to her, not to me. Why should I wish her to continue in this world?

She was the State, I the dissenter. She was Stasi: she removed my husband for interrogation. She went too far with her tortures, and killed him. Well, it happens. His second heart attack was fatal. Of course it was. The waxing moon saw his death; the next full moon hers. It was just. My husband turned up at headquarters to inform against me, talk about me to a hostile stranger, as if I were not flesh of his flesh, bone of his bone, and he also went too far. That is to say, he told her about our sex life, in detail, and so made nothing of it, before they'd even physically touched – though I daresay she anticipated that from the beginning – and so the warmth of our sex and love wasn't there to sustain him when he needed it. Bad-hearted, he fell, icy-cold, and he stayed cold.

You ask me how I feel? I tell you only a little portion of the truth; as much as I can, I assure you, without upsetting new loves and existing children. I watched a group of former East German dissidents speaking on TV the other night. They spoke of the stirring days before liberty was achieved, when free speech and free thought seemed more important than daily bread. One of their own, friend and comrade, confidante and love, now mysteriously dead, had revealed himself after the fall of the wall to be a Stasi informer. These innocents on TV, still stunned, shocked! 'How could he have done such a thing? Why? Why?'

'He believed in the proper authority,' said the man from the Stasi, calmly, by way of explanation, 'and besides, we paid him well.' The woman the traitor had lived with went down to Stasi Headquarters, when that authority finally opened its files, to see what her lover had said about her. She read a list of her failings, as reported by this man who had so enjoyed her bed.

'What did you feel like,' asked the TV interviewer, 'when you read this account of yourself?'

'I felt as if my brain had been transplanted,' she said.

\*      \*      \*

And that's what I feel like too. I feel as if my brain has been transplanted. Put that in your paper and print it. I am not the person I thought I was. All the years of my past are an irrelevance, nothing to do with me: there is no truth in them. I am negated. It can't upset the children too much, can it, to say that? I don't want them to start losing their jobs, their marriages, to hang their heads and start stumbling, like the political prisoners of long ago, lining up, walking the prison yard.

# A GREAT
# ANTIPODEAN SCANDAL
## A Bedtime Story

Let me tell you about your great-grandparents, Cordelia,
while we wait for baby Helen to go to sleep. You need to
know more about them, in case Helen inherits the Stanway
temperament. How they quarrelled, Cordelia, Lord, how
they rowed and raved! By night, the sound of their sobs
and shrieks, slaps and counter-slaps, would rise through the
clear Antipodean skies and make the Southern Cross trem-
ble. That was back in the thirties, when the heavens were
pollution-free, and the constellations seemed further away
and more clear cut. Nowadays the stars are nearer and
muzzier. Those were the days when the Pacific broke its
furious rollers against empty beaches, and you could gallop a
horse along the sands and not have to deflect its stride to
avoid picnickers, or hippies, or a single jogger in a black
tracksuit with a white stripe up the side of the leg; and there
wasn't a café or a cream tea in sight, or a 'This way to the
bungee-jump' or an old beer can either.

*  *  *

How wild the seas seemed to be, in the first half of the century. New Zealand rose from the seas long after the rest of the world was formed: only in the last fifty years the tides have become reconciled to the fact of New Zealand's existence; now they break upon its shores more languidly.

Yes, nature these days has lost quite a lot of its oomph: the spirit has gone out of it. It may be no more than the way a shiny haze of oil now coats the sea, the land, the sky, and dampens everything down. All that stuff that swilled about beneath the surface of the earth, unnaturally brought to the surface, like the damp of exhalation inside a balloon which is suddenly turned inside out.

But that's just a fancy, isn't it, Cordelia? Whatever happens to nature, the babies still get born lively enough, burst into the world shrieking and furious. It's all you can do to get today's babies to sleep. I don't think the murmur of my voice will excite baby Helen more than she is excited already. We could just go away and leave her to cry. No? You are storing up trouble for yourself later on, but never mind, that's only my opinion. I never had children myself. What do I know?

What was I saying? Yes, how Reg and Harriette rowed! Your great-grandfather and great-grandmother. They were famous for it, and forgiven, which was strange enough when you think of the community they lived in: in the little town of Christchurch, on the edge of the Canterbury plain; back in the thirties; the squarest place you can imagine, its very streets squared off as those of planned new cities are, fanning out from a town square with a Victorian church and a copper steeple turned green with age. Not very much age, in those days. Fifty years at most, but still the oldest building in the town, indeed in the whole country, except the Quaker Meeting House, which dated from 1840. Parties of school children would be taken to marvel at the antiquity of the Meeting House.

The story goes that your great-grandmother Harriette said to her daughter Pippy, your grandmother, back in 1932, 'Antiquity means the Greeks or Romans: it does not relate to some Victorian chapel in a dull colonial town at the ends of the earth, that is to say, here.' And so saying she showed Pippy a Wedgwood vase on which white naked male Greeks cavorted. She'd brought the vase with her from 'home' which was how England was referred to, in those days. Pippy managed to break the vase. She liked New Zealand, though her mother did not.

Harriette's not liking New Zealand was mostly what she quarrelled with Reg about. Though I suspect anything would have done. Reg loved the place. Harriette didn't. Pippy did. But then Pippy knew nothing better, as Harriette remarked: how can you miss what you don't know? Little Pippy, Harriette would complain bitterly to Reg, had even begun to speak through her nose, like any ordinary New Zealand child, afraid no doubt of opening her mouth properly in case a tuft of wool blew into it. Canterbury lamb was the nation's export. First they were sheared, the poor pitiful plentiful things, and the wool sold off; then they were eaten. One sheep per bleak acre of tough tussocky grass. At shearing time, or so Harriette swore, wool blew with the hot South-Western wind and blurred the eyesight and stuffed the mouth. Open your lips, and bleats came out.

By day, Reg and Harriette were as peaceable with one another as lambs: loving as doves – a species unknown in

New Zealand, so the comparison was not often made. Only by night did they row, did they rant and rave, so that the sound of their quarrels rose to the Southern Cross.

'Noise never stops,' Reg famously once told Pippy. Pippy would lie in her bed on the verandah, listening to parental shrieks, shouts and sobs. 'Noise just leaves you and travels out to space; it goes on forever into infinity. Where there are ears to hear, it will be heard.'

A child can ask and ask, but if the question is simple it will never get a proper answer. In the end the child stops asking, feeling foolish, but the truth is that nobody knows. Does sound fade? Where does space end? Why are we here? Where was I before I was born? Such a complexity of civilisation is built upon our ignorance.

Reg edited the *Christchurch Evening Star*. Harriette and Reg Stanway were a popular couple in Christchurch society. They were artistic, albeit English, and were excused their noisy altercations on this account. Moreover, Harriette was an inspired, if part-time, doctor: she could excise a tick and detect a louse better than anyone, and treat scabies and ringworm with something other than gentian violet, thus saving the children from much humiliation. She approached such problems with a horror and distaste equal to the children's own. She was rich, elegant and beautiful as well; fine-boned, clear-skinned and wide-eyed; unlike any doctor the New Zealanders – only later did they come to call themselves, self-dismissively, Kiwis – had met before, male or female, and she and Reg presented masques and gala operettas on the smooth banks of the river Avon, in the grounds of Bishop's House, which they rented from the Presbyterian Assembly. Reg, an altogether livelier and fleshier type than his wife, had sympathies with the unemployed and the underdog: he was known to have socialist tendencies. There was a rumour that he was Jewish and the name was originally Steinway, but no one had the heart to pursue it, to add this complication to those already in existence. By and large the couple presented so erratic a spectrum of attitude and behaviour, combined with so high a profile, the town just gave up bitching and forgave them their faults. Harriette's money and instinct for entertaining no doubt helped. The Stanways held parties in the grounds of Bishop's House; they employed domestic staff to keep the supply of vol-au-vents, eclairs and cheese straws flowing. Wine was all but unknown to the nation, not yet a hundred years old, but there was always beer, gin and whisky on offer and, what is more, and after the bars had closed, as well. Closing time in those days was half past five in the afternoon, and a source of misery for everybody.

You might well ask why, Cordelia, if Harriette hated the place and only Reg loved it, and Harriette had the money, did they stay in New Zealand? Why did Harriette not make a run for civilisation, get back to her academic and arty friends, her well-born, highly cultured family? Because in those days, Cordelia, women did not leave husbands; a divorce was a thing apart and a divorcée was a scarlet woman, and even Harriette was afraid. Besides, she loved him. And in those days men and women would fight and spat and there was no one to explain to them that such behaviour was unhealthy, or likely to upset the children.

Was little Pippy much upset? Of course she was: children like to grow up into a happy world, and seldom do, though I can see you are doing your best for little Helen here. I think she's giving up: I think her eyes are closing. Today's children are reluctant to sleep, in case the world is different when they wake. Everything moves so fast. Then it sauntered along.

In the morning, over a serene breakfast table, Pippy would watch her remorseful parents, Harriette's perfect face blotchily sullen, Reg's fleshy face so pale and stunned that the black hairs which sprouted round chin and jowls seemed more pronounced than ever. She'd watch them embrace, press into one another as if hoping to be the other, to get inside the other's skin, and it may have been that this upset her even more – both the inconsistency of their behaviour and the thought that love and hate are so closely linked. Pippy, like all children, longed for consistency, longed for justice, hoped to see virtue rewarded and wrong punished, and noted that only in story books was it ever so.

By day, Harriette claimed it was love for Reg which kept her in New Zealand; by night she denied the love and gave as her reason that war in Europe was clearly on its way. The Germans would soon be at it again. How could she take Pippy into such a situation, and where Harriette went Pippy went, no matter what Reg or the law had to say about the matter.

By the time Pippy had got to be seventeen, the European war had indeed started, and there was then no way Harriette could get home even if she'd wanted to: ships no longer carried civilians, only troops from one war theatre to another. You could get by a flying boat from Auckland to Sydney, but any further North than that and you would be mixed up in jungle warfare. The world was a much more real place in those days, Cordelia, and more dangerous, let me tell you. Distances meant something.

*    *    *

How did your grandmother Pippy get her name? She was called after the little shellfish which live on those Antipodean beaches, burying themselves in the fine dark damp sand just below the tide line – when the sea recedes you can tell their presence because they blow bubbles to the surface. Pipi hunters watch and wait, and dig quickly where the tiny bubbles appear, and there they find them, solitary creatures, two little fine white fluted shells clamped together, and a delicate living morsel inside. Surely nothing dangerous can happen to it now it's safely closed? But it can, it can; it does. The pipi has betrayed itself, by breathing out.

Pippy nearly got caught, couldn't help herself; betrayed herself by a breath of dangerous emotion. She was saved in the nick of time, oddly enough, by the most tremendous of Reg and Harriette's rows. Pippy, who later came to England and changed her name to Hypatia, and became a Greek scholar and married a clergyman, your grandfather, very nearly ruined her life. In those days it was easy for a girl to ruin her life. Now if a girl gets pregnant she can get unpregnant: if she gets married she can get unmarried. Money can save her from most disasters. But it was different then. Fall in love with the wrong man, and you'd had it for life.

Pippy died before your mother Trixie gave birth to you, Cordelia. Do you have this family history straight? This child in its cradle, who in the modern fashion just won't go to sleep, is Pippy's great-grandchild. Harriette's great-great-grandchild. I'm no relative: I'm just a friend of the family. I carry its history in my head. Why are you confused? Didn't you know about the great Antipodean scandal? So great that poor Harriette and Reg were driven out of Bishop's House?

On the positive side, it served to stop Pippy ruining her life. What opposed her, also saved her.

I would have thought the present would relish this tale of the past: but on second thoughts no – the present relies on the past to exist as some boring and respectable country – a kind of New Zealand amongst other nations – by comparison to which they can see themselves as brave, daring and unconventional. Let me remind you, Cordelia, that the blood of Virginia Woolf runs in your veins, of cross-gendered folk with artistic abilities and infinite cultural grandeur, at least in their own eyes. Don't ever think you have your life in order: you won't have: there is too much trauma in your past, too much trouble in your genes for you to live the quiet life you occasionally think you want.

When Pippy got to seventeen, she was in her last year at Christchurch Girls' High School, where scholastic standards were high. If Harriette had had her way, her daughter would have gone to St Margaret's, the town's fee-paying school, and worn a green uniform, or even Rangi-Ruru, up-country, and worn orange, but Reg insisted that the state grammar school and its navy blue was more ideologically sound. Not that the phrase was current then. 'More appropriate to socialist principles' was how it was put.

'Hypocrite!' Harriette would charge.

'Snob,' he'd respond.

'You don't mind living off my private income –' though that would be hours into the quarrel '– you just don't want Pippy to benefit from it! Pimp, gigolo!'

'Bitch.'

And so on. Reg won, and it ended up with Pippy at the Girls High, wearing a navy blue gym tunic and a white shirt, chanting:

'Rangi-Ruri rotten rats
Go to school in Panama hats,
Do they stink? Yes, they do.
Like the monkeys in the zoo!'

and falling hopelessly and unhealthily in love with a prefect, and writing her love letters which Harriette discovered, rifling through her drawers, as mothers did in those days without compunction.

'She's turning into a lesbian, Reg, but what did you expect? That school is a hellhole of perversity!'

'Your side of the family, Harriette, not mine – a long line of lesbians –'

'Bastard! You'd rather score a point off me than look after your own child.'

'Harriette, can we calm down? She doesn't even know what men and women do together, let alone women and women.'

Which was true enough.

It may have been Pippy's desire to prove to her mother that she was not a lesbian – in those days a source of shame, not pride – which led her to fall in love with Malcolm Mackay, a twenty-three-year-old farmer's son from Southland. His homestead was a hundred thousand acres of the plains south of Canterbury, a desolate land indeed: next stop Antarctica and the South Pole! Malcolm's father had died when his horse had stumbled and thrown him, its foot in a pot-hole, his head on a yellow-lichened stone. Now Malcolm helped his mother run the ranch, with its hundred thousand sheep. One per acre. He had come by boat up the coast to Christchurch, quite openly looking for a wife to help his mother out, and his eye had, perversely enough, fallen upon Pippy.

Perversely, I say, since in his head he wanted a good stolid, no-nonsense, hard-working girl who could bake a dinner for a dozen sheep-shearers with one hand while making clothes for her kids with the other. But no, Cordelia, his eyes must fall upon your great-grandmother Pippy, who was petite, pretty, immensely clever, highly academic and carried an erotic charge she would not lose to the end of her days, and all sense deserted him. Her eye, alas, also fell upon Malcolm. He was well set up, and with a good mouth and chin, which many New Zealanders do not have. His teeth were firm, white and strong and all there – there is apparently a lack of iodine in that soil which makes good teeth a rarity. Many of Pippy's friends were given sets of false teeth by their fathers for their seventeenth birthday, and were overjoyed; the trouble and pain of a lifetime's dentistry spared them. Pippy and Malcolm clasped one another: his horny but young hands held her fine ones and – he in stumbling tones and she in poetic ones – they swore eternal love.

'If you don't let me marry him,' said Pippy to Harriette, 'I'll get pregnant by him. Then we'll all be up shit-creek without a paddle!'

She'd talk like this to annoy Harriette and make Reg laugh. Getting pregnant was the threat girls held over their parents heads' in the days of respectability before contraception; when virginity was the good girl's path to future happiness.

'It's obviously true love,' said Reg to Harriette bitterly, 'and there's no escape from it. Bet you're sorry now your daughter doesn't take more after her great-aunt Virginia. Girls should marry young or they get ideas in their heads. But he's a nice steady young man and it will do Pippy good to learn what real life is like.'

Though, actually, Reg too was appalled. But he didn't

want Harriette to know. Or she'd have said (she did): 'This is what comes of sending her to a State school.'

The date of the wedding was fixed. It was to be a big do. The Southland relatives were to come up the coast, by the dozen; the cream of Christchurch society was to attend. The bride was to wear white as befitted her virginal state: for the women, formal dress; for the men, white tie. Presents to Bishop's House, flowers by courtesy of the Christchurch Botanical Gardens: excitement was general, as Reg and Harriette, everyone agreed, were to be assimilated properly and finally into the community by way of Pippy.

Pippy stoutly maintained her love for Malcolm over the six months of the engagement, and he for her, though his mother, Mrs Matilda Mackay – her grandmother had come over from Scotland in one of the early waves of immigration – was shaken by her son's choice of bride. She doubted Pippy could bake a decent sponge, let alone rear a lamb, or mend a tractor, or milk a cow, or any of the things Mrs Mackay did as of rote in her daily life. But perhaps the girl would learn. She'd have to. She'd be eighty miles from the nearest neighbour and there'd be no one to help, and no one to put on airs for, let alone Malcolm, who'd get tired of her nonsense after a week; that is, if he took after his father.

'You're so fragile, so perfect,' muttered Malcolm in Pippy's ear, and if he had a doubt or so, he subdued them.

'You're so strong and peaceful,' murmured Pippy in Malcolm's ear. 'I know we'll never quarrel. I'm sorry about my family. I know they're peculiar.'

'I can put up with them,' said Malcolm. 'They're pommies,

and can't help it. But you're a regular bloke; you were born here, after all.'

The day of the wedding dawned, as it should, bright and fair, and even the Southern-West Arch had left the sky, which meant even the wind was on the young couple's side: zephyr-fresh, not at all hot and dusty. On days like this nature seemed to have forgiven the two islands (three if you include Stewart Island, that afterthought of an afterthought) for existing out of turn: indeed, even to want to make it up to the inhabitants. Up in the North Island, Mount Cook – in those days still perfectly formed; its main peak properly balanced by two smaller peaks: one was to blow itself up in the eighties, in the same way a foolish and careless terrorist can maim himself with his own explosives – Mount Cook, as I say, Cordelia, let off the merest wispy cloud of smoke to show it wasn't angry, merely alive – and the Kiwis snuffled and grunted and came out from under cover, and one was captured by the Wellington Zoo, and the Taniwha – the Maoris' mythical monster – refrained from shaking the ground with his foot. That is to say there wasn't even an earthquake anywhere that day. Puff pastry rose properly in ovens, cream did not turn sour for no reason, sheep refrained from spraining their ankles in rabbit holes.

But Harriette and Reg rowed on. Their anger with one another had not for once got appeased by sex, so great was their pre-nuptial anxiety. Wedding nerves! Forget Pippy, what about the parents?

On the morning of the wedding, their clothes were laid out by the maid on the double bed in the spare room. (The maid, Ellie, was later to become an Olympic swimmer: she regularly kept wanting days off for practice, which Harriette would regularly refuse her: she did not follow the Stanways into exile, as they had expected her to do.) Reg's dress-shirt was clean and starched: his tuxedo, with its purple cummerbund, all present and correct. Reg had had no occasion to wear it for some three years. The war had, to his relief, led to less formality in Canterbury society: it had taken a big wedding to restore it. A long time since an invitation had asked for formal attire.

Harriette was to wear a little pale green silk suit, with gold-buttoned jacket and swinging skirt, and a dark green cloche hat with a veil. She had put on some weight lately; she had in fact to have the suit let out for the occasion. You don't understand 'letting out', Cordelia? In those days clothes had hems and the seams were generous: they could be made bigger and smaller at will. You could get as much as four inches more round hips and waistband. Women *sewed*, Cordelia.

The night had led to actual fisticuffs between the Stanway parents. Reg suddenly changed his position regarding the wedding and said he disapproved of the match; it made him sick to his heart. Pippy was ruining her life. He blamed Harriette; she had impetuously and unkindly accused Pippy of being a covert lesbian: now of course the girl was determined to leave home.

'You said she didn't know what I was referring to,' pointed out Harriette acidly, 'so how can I have upset her? If it's anyone's fault it's yours. You are much too possessive of her – it's unhealthy. Of course she has to leave home!'

And so it had begun. Harriette had become hysterical. She had slapped Reg: Reg had slapped her back. There had been much running around Bishop's House and slamming of doors all night while Pippy and the servants lay awake and listened, and longed for their beauty sleep.

Pippy herself had almost decided to call the marriage off; perhaps she need simply not show up at the ceremony? She was worried about her dress. Mrs Mackay had produced her grandmother's white – well, yellowy – wedding dress, circa 1860 – and insisted that she wear it. It would save unnecessary expense, as well as being in the family tradition, though it turned out that Pippy was in fact the first Mackay bride small enough to get into the dress, for all its seams, since the original, wraith-thin, New Zealand Mackay had managed it. The dress seemed to Pippy to be ill-omened, since the poor girl had died of TB within three years of her wedding: Malcolm and his mother both poo-poohed her sensibilities. Pippy could see that her sensibilities would always be much poo-poohed down on the farm. Perhaps her mother was right: perhaps she should not give up her education, her place at University? At Canterbury College, where the great Karl Popper lectured? Malcolm at least loved her; he did not see through her. If Pippy lost him, who would ever take her seriously again? The sound of the shrieks and the slamming doors on her pre-nuptial night made Pippy put away doubt. She would marry Malcolm Mackay first, worry second.

Eight o'clock in the morning came. The wedding was at eleven. The maids were up and about: the marquee was going up on the lawn: flower arrangements were in hand: caterers' vans delivered tables, chairs, even food; the Post Office delivered telegrams and presents. The hairdresser – only one in all the town, so sensible and practical were its inhabitants – had arrived to do the bride's and the bride's mother's hair. And still Reg and Harriette had not turned up to make their apologies and perform what Malcolm called their lovey-dovey act.

Pippy began to be worried. She felt tearful. Her hair was done: her mother's wasn't. She was in her dress. She even liked it. The vicar, Mr Hollycroft, turned up for a few last-minute instructions. He assured Pippy that the ceremony could take place without her parents if it came to it, since they had already signed the necessary consent forms. Nevertheless, he looked troubled. Were the Stanway parents ill? What was the matter? Shrieks and shouts could be heard from upstairs.

Mr Hollycroft and Pippy waited until the last moment, and then went upstairs to stand outside the spare-room door. Pippy knocked but was not heard. They listened.
    'Bastard! You said I was fat!'
    'I did not say you were fat. I said you were always too thin for my taste. That is wholly different.'
    'I wish I'd never married you!'
    'I assure you it is mutual.'
    'You've ruined my life. You look ridiculous in a purple cummerbund. Dressed up like a monkey for these provincials.'
    'At least I'm not bursting out of my clothes, as you are, Harriette. Look at you! It's absurd. The buttons will hardly meet. Put on something else decent, for God's sake.'
    'I have nothing else decent. I suppose you want me to go naked.'
    'I certainly don't want you to go naked. You don't have the figure for it.'

'You didn't care about my figure the night before last.'

'I kept my eyes shut. But then I always do these days. In bed with you, who would want to open them?'

And so on, and so on. And then, from Reg: 'Very well, I shan't wear a purple cummerbund. You are quite right, it makes me look ridiculous. I'm the one who's going naked to the wedding. Put that in your pipe and smoke it.'

And then, from Harriette: 'Then I'm not going at all. I am not going to stand and watch my daughter ruin her life at your behest.'

'At your behest, my dear, neither am I!'

The Reverend Hollycroft and Pippy crept away. Pippy struck away a tear or two, and Mr Hollycroft got hold of his brother to give the bride away.

'We'll say they've got food poisoning,' he said. 'People will understand. The important thing, my dear, is that for you this is a day to remember.'

Word was got to Malcolm, staying in the Cathedral Square Hostelry – Christchurch's one hotel – that the bride's parents had food-poisoning and were not going to the wedding.

'It's bad blood,' wept Mrs Mackay. 'You're marrying into bad blood. This wedding will be a disaster. You'll have peculiar children.'

'Peculiar', then as now, was about the worst thing you could say about anyone in New Zealand society. Malcolm was shaken but determined to go ahead.

'Look, Mum,' he said, 'it's her I'm marrying, not her parents.'

Malcolm was standing at the altar with his best man when Pippy walked up the aisle. He thought she looked perfectly lovely: his great-grandmother's wedding dress was just fine. Even he had had his doubts. Pippy glanced over her shoulder and dimpled at her husband-to-be. It was going to be all right. The church was packed with a congregation who also all surely knew, or they wouldn't have been there in their best bib-and-tucker, that it was going to be all right.

The groom stood by the bride's side. The Reverend Hollycroft began to speak. Then his voice faltered and stopped. The congregation rustled and murmured. Malcolm and Pippy turned.

Harriette and Reg stood in the entrance of the church: the door was open and bright antipodean light shone upon them, dispelling all sepulchral gloom. The light in New Zealand is always bright: there's so much ocean all around for it to glance off. Reg slapped Harriette with his silver handbag. Harriette beat Reg about the head. Harriette was wearing Reg's tuxedo, cummerbund, white dress shirt, bow tie and all. She looked terrific. She had rolled up sleeves and trousers. She wore Reg's black polished shoes. And Reg, Reg was wearing Harriette's pale green suit: the gold-buttoned jacket was strained across his hairy chest; the pleated skirt came to just above the knee. His bare legs were sturdy and hairy. He wore her high-heeled pumps in apple-green satin. He wore her little cloche and veil, or had, except that now Harriette's blows had knocked it off. He held her hand aloft to stop her.

'Bastard!' said he to her.

'Bitch!' said she to him.

They realised where they were: a kind of sanity returned. They looked at one another, at the congregation, and decided they must go through with what they had begun. The quarrel was over: now they would have to act together. They walked up the aisle towards the altar. Mrs Mackay, in the front row, screamed her son's name aloud.

Pippy looked at Malcolm, Malcolm looked at Pippy. Malcolm dashed the ring he held in his hand to the ground, and turned and ran. Mrs Mackay ran after him: waddle, waddle, big strong hip this way, big strong hip that way, on unaccustomed high heels. Malcolm thrust Harriette and Reg apart as he ran: Mrs Mackay did the same. Reg and Harriette joined up again and went on walking altarward. The congregation's paralysis held until Reg and Harriette stood either side of Pippy. Then there was an unpleasant laughter, a tittering; cries of 'perverts', hisses, boos. The Reverend Hollycroft leaned back against his frugal altar, too appalled to quieten or calm his flock. His congregation departed, standing not upon the order of their going.

'Well,' said Harriette. 'That settled that.'

'It certainly did,' said Reg.

Both seemed rather amused. Pippy did what she should have done a long time back: she slapped them both, hard. First mother's cheek, then father's.

There now, Cordelia, I think that child has gone to sleep at last. Why does my mind turn so resolutely to slapping? What happened next? The Reverend Hollycroft organised the distribution of the wedding bakemeats to the poor, the Mackays and their party retreated back to Southland, congratulating themselves on their lucky escape, and the Presbyterian Assembly did not renew its lease of Bishop's House. Harriette's patients no longer came for treatment; Reg was obliged to resign from his newspaper. The Stanways went to live in Wellington, that hilly, windy, rocking city, in modest retirement. The Taniwha seems to have a special down on Wellington.

Yes, there was a great scandal. Pippy went on with her studies in Christchurch – the young are always more forgiving than the old: they have not yet discovered the necessity of condemnation – and took the first boat to England after the war, in 1946, to do her classical studies there. She became one of the first – and last – woman professors of Greek Literature in the world: the species was endangered, shortly to be extinct, but no one had told her that. All things change.

Today Harriette and Reg could dress up in one another's clothes with impunity, and would not have to quarrel so much or so long to achieve their ambition. Pippy was later to say that that day of her almost-wedding, that parental quarrel which endured out of the night into the morning, that apotheosis of all previous rows – was what they had been moving towards all their married lives and had finally achieved. They were cross-dressers in a world in which the concept had not yet been verbalised.

And, what is more, by facing their own natures, they saved Pippy from ruining her life. They changed the course of it. And just think, Cordelia, by so doing they allowed Trixie to come into existence, and after that you, and now this sweet little baby too. Though I always think a baby who cries and won't sleep when there is absolutely nothing wrong with it is simply ego-centric.

# HOSPITAL

NEW ADVANCES

NOISY INTO THE NIGHT

A HARD TIME TO BE A FATHER

# NEW ADVANCES
## A Short Story in Fifty Words

'I don't want a fashion house, I want a baby,' moaned famous, beautiful, busy designer Annie, fifty-three.

'Too late now,' whimpered Belinda. 'You can't have your cake and eat it too.'

'Can so,' said Annie, and went to Rome where, thanks to advances in gynaecological technology, she had a baby.

# NOISY INTO THE NIGHT

More women seem to die than men, though of course that can only be illusion. We peg out in equal number. But when men do die, what an uproar! Women are dying all the time, clogging up the cancer wards, no one taking much notice, the family saying what a blessed relief it's finally over; a small private funeral, a rummage through the old hat box, a flick through the family photographs: 'Remember when! Remember when!' A trip to Oxfam with the better things, a quarrel over meagre possessions and past promises, a minor upsurge of sibling rivalry and everything's over; the corpse, the female corpse, has settled down into soil or drifted as ashes over the waters of some familiar river or in the park where she walked her little dog.

But the men don't lie down so quiet and silent, oh no! For them the heart ward and the hi-tech rescue, the drama of alarm bells, the shouts of resuscitation teams, obituaries; they died intestate like as not, unwilling to believe the world can go on without them. Rows of tearful women line up at the grave: ex-wives, mistresses. 'Who's she? Who's she?'

\*　　\*　　\*

Don't think you count as the one and only wife, till you see who turns up at the Crematorium, tearful over your old man.

Unusual to find a weeping cluster of ex-husbands, and ex-lovers at a female funeral – not unless you're Marilyn Monroe or Jackie Kennedy and the media requires it and has old pics it wants an opportunity to pull out. Female Monarchs make it to a State Funeral, of course; Queen Elizabeth, Queen Victoria; solemn music, specially composed, threnodies, goose-stepping by ranked males, guns pointed earthward, but it's scarcely personal. Woman as symbol of nation looks good on a coin; see it like that; see it as necessity – there hasn't been a decent male profile since Caesar. All men may be equal in death, but in this case man doesn't include women, and there's the truth of it.

'Nothing like the thought of your own funeral for reviving the feminist spirit,' observed Trixie. The old 'Not fair, not fair!' Did she argue too hard: should she make out a case for the opposite? Probably, but Trixie didn't want to; she hardly had the energy. She wouldn't even, at Imp's urgent request – 'Think about it, Trixie, think about it!' – consider the fact that women outlive men, notice the way men tend to die suddenly, stricken in the full flood of sex and anger; she just wouldn't see the unfairness in that. All Trixie could think about was the way women tended to die alone, yanked out of bedsitting rooms, thrown into hospitals, as she had been, 'defeated by surplus', as she told Imp.

'What do you mean, defeated by surplus?' asked Imp. Imp and Trixie had ended up in adjacent beds. They preferred to call it by its proper name – Terminal Mixed. Whatever fault you could find with Imp and Trixie, and many did, they were seldom afraid. 'Oh, she's in Uppingham Mixed, I'm afraid,' tactless girls at the Customer Information Desk would say to enquiring relatives. The 'I'm afraid' gave the game away, spoiling the myth. The game? That none of us die. The myth? That hospitals cure, don't just add decency and non-disclosure to the end of our lives. All men die, as Trixie said, and women too, but you'd never know it, and this ward, like this life, is Terminal.

'A surplus of undirected growth,' said Trixie, 'that's all cancer is; an overflow of body energy, a surplus of cells made so dizzy over time they can no longer distinguish between good and bad, what's appropriate and what isn't, rendered punch drunk by the requirements of female life. Daughter, wife, mother: hear the death-words toll! No wonder so many women these days simply refuse to participate.'

'Give your life for a family and that's exactly what you do,' said Trixie. 'There's no stopping the process once it's underway, nor is there a reward for sacrifice. That's it. The family woman fades away: there is nothing left to mourn, so well the family she created incorporates her. The better you do it, the less they notice your existence. Give a child what it wants and it's gone for ever. Grudge it, and it's yours for life. Herein lies the bitterness: that in the very invisibility the woman sets out to achieve, in the forswearing of her human rights, in the gritting of her teeth, the shovelling of the shit, lies the non-reverence that is her lot.'

'I can't even remember my grandmother's Christian name,' complained Trixie. 'And why not? Because in the end there was nothing left of her to remember. The family had gobbled it up.'

\*      \*      \*

Trixie sat at the end of Imp's bed, thereby settling the bedclothes too heavily on the electrodes attached to his ankles. If his ex-wife were not careful, Imp realised, the leads to the monitor would disconnect and its bleeper start pealing false alarms and nurses come running – if he was lucky. Imp remembered now why he had divorced Trixie: she had argued too much, been far too noisy; all over the place, like a heart faultily connected to its leads, messy, setting off too many alarms. He had fallen in love with Rosemary in simple self-defence.

Chance and adjacency by alphabet had brought Imp and Trixie, after many medical adventures, to lie side by side in Uppingham Mixed, Terminal. Trixie was post-operative after the removal of her womb, but there were secondaries everywhere; Imp was recovering from his second heart attack, waiting for a quadruple bypass. There wasn't much hope for either of them.

'Errata,' said Trixie, condescendingly. 'All women die and you'd never know it. All men die and you certainly do.'

Earlier, realising his first wife's proximity, Imp had asked to be moved to another ward. He had explained the circumstances: stress was not good for him: his third wife, Isobel, would be visiting; so would his child by his second wife Rosemary – more dramas – it was an intolerable situation. He had done his best, if only for Isobel's sake, but when Authority had declared nothing could be done, he had accepted its verdict without argument. The fact was that Imp found himself oddly comforted by their side-by-sideness, in this their joint extremis. Imp-and-Trixie had always sounded right, had fitted, as if Trixie, for all her dreadfulness, her noisy feminism, had been the true and proper wife. Imp-and-Isobel, third time round, sounded fit for a dinner party; it betokened a calmness and a dull orthodoxy in bed, and would do; Imp-and-Rosemary had never worked. The strung-together words did not suit, had no staying power. Imp-and-Trixie sounded like a good dying partnership in a mixed ward. Not that gender, so important in life, weighed much with anyone in Uppingham. A withered breast exposed, or a shrunken penis suddenly visible – who cared any more? Yet, oddly, people did. Modesty, Imp decided, was inborn, or so habitual it might as well be inborn. Seeing is seizing, seeing is knowledge, knowledge is control: so cover up! The new world taught you some new things.

Imp and Trixie. Imperator and Imperatrix. Emperor and Empress. Master and Mistress. Father and Mother, in charge of all they surveyed, by virtue of the grace invested in them by God above. Paul and Helena Race. Helena's father the Rev. Gibbs, newly a widower, renamed them Imp and Trixie at their wedding, back in 1957, wishing on the couple the central role they did indeed come to hold in the lives of others. The mantle of the parents' household fell, and the names stuck, surviving Imps' free-loving Sixties, Trixie's feminist Seventies, till skinny-hipped Rosemary had come along and wooed and won Imp, and Trixie had gone into bitter and angry exile. But Imp in his turn had been exiled by Rosemary, thrown out; thoroughly King Lear'd. The second wife took game, match and empire – that is to say the Rev. Gibbs' well-sited and by now valuable vicarage. That's when Imp had his first heart attack, in 1980, in the act of moving out what a Court referred to as his 'personal possessions', denied all pomp and circumstance by his Her Majesty's usurper. 'Trust you!' was all Rosemary said, calling an ambulance and going out to dine with her new lover.

'Serve you right,' said Trixie to Imp at the hospital then, charitably visiting her ex, 'for breeding a child by a woman other than me, then divorcing me and marrying her; what was she but a self-interested yuppie bitch who let the black spot get the better of my grandmother's climbing roses? I can never remember her name but at least I cherished her climbers. Of course Rosemary shafted you, as you shafted me. Biters get bitten.'

'Get out of here, you feminist bitch,' was Imp's response. One callousness deserves another: once they begin, how can you stop?

'No one asked you to visit. Your time is well and truly over.'

Then as now the monitor trace had bounced about all over the place, though not for any technological reason, not because leads were being mispositioned by Trixie's hollowed-out weight, but because in those days passions of hate and rage still had the power to overwhelm him, alter the patterns his heart made. Those were the days when Trixie was still powerful, still the Queen in Exile, robust and healthy enough. Took seven years for her to wear out her objections, to roam the edges of a different land. How she'd suffered in the meantime, she told everyone; the proud bitch! Imp had seen to it that she suffered, Trixie claimed: none so finished or worthless in a man's eyes as a dismissed wife. Oh, the pain, the pain! Twenty-two years of royal marriage swept away by a greedy kitchenmaid, a brisk, skinny girl with a Filofax, long, shaved legs and a designer suede skirt pushed out of place by a pregnancy. An early scan showed the brat to be a boy, a prince. Twenty-two years of marriage to Imp and all Trixie had produced was a couple of girls, pretty enough but lacking the gravitas of the male. Or so Trixie would have it. While Imp claimed feminism was the mother's way of unconsciously diminishing her daughters: so emphasising their female disadvantage as to bring that disadvantage about.

'The nuclear family is hell,' Trixie's self-appointed advisors whispered in her ear. She could hardly tell, in retrospect, whether they'd been real or not, these advisors, vague, lumpy shapes looming through a fog full of disembodied voices. 'Let the house go: what do possessions matter? Walk away from the past; save yourself.' Sheer surplus of astonishment, Trixie sometimes thought, at discovering the world to be so dire a place, had triggered off the cancer that now pushed her innards this way and that. By the time she felt better about the world again, had put the marriage to Imp into the past, had actually stopped hovering and walked away, it was too late. No going back, once the processes of despair had gotten underway: the destruction of family.

'She moved out of her own free will,' Imp assured everyone who asked. 'She left me defenceless: walked out on me and the girls. Treason! What kind of wife abandons her husband to the wiles of another woman?'

'The kind whose husband asks his pregnant mistress to tea and says why can't we three get along? He tried to move a concubine into my home,' said Trixie to everyone. 'I couldn't put up with that. There was too much loss of dignity involved. I would have lost my allies: even the girls would have gone over to the usurper. Better to save my face and lose my home.'

\*    \*    \*

210

'Good God,' said Imp to Trixie back then in 1980, 'I am not Henry VIII, you are not Anne Boleyn: you are a contemporary feminist. You are giving me a pain. Do you want to kill me? Is that why you've come? Go back to your coven and your man-hating; leave me to suffer in peace.'

'You have a bad heart,' said Trixie, 'in every sense of the word. One heart attack foretells another. Excuse me while I go back to my coven and stick a few pins in a few more wax images.'

And Trixie left, furious, brushing past the nurse, who, as it happened, presently became Imp's next wife. Breast lightly touched breast. Trixie's leather jacket: Isobel's stiff white uniform. Such a sweet, caring girl, Isobel. Her heart bled for Imp: she took him into her own home when they unhooked him from life-support; she nursed him back to health, both emotional and financial. Imp had lost not just his kingdom and his fortune to Rosemary, but his clients too. Five full years before he was back on his feet.

'Do you hate me as I hate Rosemary?' Trixie received a letter, out of the blue, Imp to Imperatrix, five years on. 'I hope not.' Trixie wrote back with the one word: 'Yes'. One bad act deserves another.

But now once again Trixie sat on Imp's bed, and this time he did not drive her away. The heart monitor bleeped its warning as she wriggled – she could never sit still – and Imp groaned aloud in embarrassment, not pain. The nurse brought him paracetamol at once.

'Men get given painkillers more speedily than do women,' Trixie observed to her first and last husband.

'You just say that,' he complained. 'Where is your statistical evidence? You and your sample of one! Same old problem.'

'First and last! First and last!' Trixie had had liaisons with both men and women since she left Imp to become Empress in Exile, but would not, by remarrying, let him off the hook of his guilt. She'd roamed the boundaries of the kingdom, making Imp and Rosemary uneasy in their first, good days, attributing her presence in the locality to chance. Revenge? You must be joking! No, a talk at the local school on equal opportunities, a visit to an old friend's cat on its deathbed, a local wedding, a former neighbour's child's christening to attend. What could be more civilised? If Trixie's social activities had contributed to the Palace Coup, to Rosemary throwing Imp out, and his consequent Learing, why then Trixie announced herself glad. If they had led to the second major, massive heart attack which had left Imp feeble and finished in Uppingham Mixed without even the strength to move his leg out from under his first wife's haunch, so much the better.

'All your fault,' Imp murmured with some truth, swallowing his paracetamol, though in no observable pain. 'All your fault. Feminist bitch!'

Trixie failed in resolution, momentarily. She wept at her ex-husband, first and last, a little; she snivelled, for both of them.

'Try to be nice to me, just a little,' she implored, 'now we're both so near the end –'

'Damn queen! Intolerable! Speak for yourself!' but Imp's voice caught in his throat: he spluttered. He longed to be 'nice' to her, but was too much out of the habit.

\*　　\*　　\*

212

When they both felt better, that is to say when the companionable habits of twenty-two shared and responsible years upon the throne had managed to cut in, like some sulky motor starting up, Imp repeated the observation that for Trixie to say 'All men died but you'd never know it, it so seldom seemed to happen, what an uproar when it did' was grossly unreasonable and unfair. He could not let the matter lie. Obviously women died as often as men, only later. Women, everyone knew, had the advantage of a couple more years of life expectancy, much good might it do them in their shrivelled-up state. They could hardly enjoy it.

Could not Trixie try to reform now if, as she claimed, her end was nigh; could she not see reason, exonerate men from at least this particular blame? He, Imp, was well aware that, Dworkin-like, Trixie saw all male sex as an attack. Was not this bad enough – and the very attitude that had driven him into Rosemary's arms in the first place – without Trixie now saying that all female deaths were men's fault?

'Look around,' said Trixie, 'use your eyes. Twelve beds in Uppingham Mixed,' she told him, 'seven of them occupied with female cancer patients, sorry, "customers", one female terminal multiple sclerosis, only one male cancer, two male heart patients, and one bed screened, its occupant now thoroughly genderless inasmuch as it was dead and awaiting transport to the morgue' – there was a shortage of porters. 'You could tell this particular customer had been female,' Trixie told Imp, 'because of the absence of fuss at the end; just a little flurry the night before; a stifled sob from a family member, and this morning a scuffed, emptied woman's handbag in the bin in the sluice room, the leather denatured, as flat, throw-away, collapsed and pointless as a cat's body once the spirit has left it.'

'If that person had been male,' Trixie observed, 'no one would have whispered. The whole ward would have been woken, resuscitation equipment brought, priests and lawyers been called, alarm bells and bleepers rung, and medical staff come running – with any luck. Women were encouraged just to slip away out of this life, annoying no one: men were meant to go noisily. As for cancer,' said Trixie, 'why, cancer, that disease of surplus run riot, was what a woman got when she tried to behave.'

Trixie offered Imp both diagnosis and cause, waving her skinny finger in this direction and that around the ward. 'Look there, look there!' She'd spoken to all of them, and these were her conclusions:

Sally Dixon, fifty-six, from throat cancer, from biting back too many words, failing to make too many sharp ripostes, swallowing too many insults, from being too good. Her husband's fault, for being horrid to her.

Miriam Patch, twenty-three, from cancer of the breast run riot, from the death of love and a broken heart and being sad. Her lover's fault, for leaving her. ('Women have died and worms have eaten them, and the worm's name is love,' said Trixie.)

Marlene Briggs, sixty-two, from cancer of the liver, from boredom, too many regrets, too little stress, having played safe all her life. Her son's fault, for not having her to live with him.

Susan Serocynski, forty, from a malignant melanoma, from

too much uprooting and being too sensitive to insult. Her father's fault, for emigrating, for bringing her young into a hostile, sneering land.

Mary Panikar, fifty-one, from cancer of the womb, undiagnosed too long, from childlessness, refusing a smear, believing she was exempted from her female fate. Her own fault, for being too proud: Trixie would acknowledge that. But the finger of blame might well point at the father, or an uncle, but Mary wasn't telling.

Teresa Gallichan, thirty-three, from too much trust in the medical profession, from shock, a fibroid misdiagnosed, an unnecessary hysterectomy. Her surgeon's fault, for taking away bits she wanted without asking.

'Don't go on,' said Imp. 'You're absurd. For every male death you could equally blame a woman. Cancer of the prostate: cause, associating with frigid women. You should know all about that.'

'I was never frigid,' said Trixie. 'You were inept.'

She would never, ever give up, thought Imp. Though even 'never' must have an end. How much did she weigh now? Eighty, ninety pounds? Still enough to discommode his leads by wriggling.

'Why do you waste your last breath in this way?' asked Imp sadly.

'Because you said your illness was my fault,' said Trixie. 'And I want to persuade you to take it back.'

'I take it back,' he said, adding cunningly, 'That is to say, I blame Rosemary for my condition more than I blame you. She was even worse than you.'

'Blame Isobel, too, then,' said Trixie, 'since nothing can be your fault. Isobel failed to save you. Not that I mind Isobel so much. There were only pieces to pick up by the time Rosemary had finished with you, nothing worth having. And now I suppose we're expected, all three wives, to line up at your funeral? Together in your death?'

'Of course,' said Imp blithely. 'In a row, throwing flowers. Isobel can have first go because she's current. You can have last because you were so long ago.'

'Oh thanks,' said Trixie. 'You always did know how to hurt. And if I die first? Will you come to my funeral?'

'How can I possibly?' asked Imp. 'All wired and tubed up as I am? I'm far too ill. It would kill me.'

'You wouldn't come anyway,' said Trixie. 'What, stand in a row with the other lovers? Men don't do that kind of thing. Only the last man in there is required to attend a woman's funeral.'

'But women,' said Imp, 'were meant to act as if life were a game of tennis: go up to the net when it was over and shake hands.'

'But it's not a game, Imp,' said Trixie. 'It's real and it's a fight to the death. I'm not coming to your funeral, don't think I am.'

Having made her point, and because Isobel, red-eyed, face swollen with grief, was now coming down the ward in the company of Rosemary, who looked ruthless, beautiful and short-skirted as ever, Trixie quickly got off Imp's bed and back into her own. She turned her face to the wall and pretended not to be there, not to exist at all, as had always been Imp's ambition for her: and indeed her thinness suggested collusion on her part. Nor did Imp let on, as he received the concubines, that the Queen was present. Trixie took this as some kind of acknowledgement and felt, on the whole, comforted.

'Why did people call them Imp and Trixie,' asked Isobel of Rosemary at Imp's funeral, 'when their names were Paul and Helena?'

'No idea,' said Rosemary. 'There was so much falsehood and lying. All I know is that it was going to Trixie's funeral which killed Imp. First the heart attack, wholly because of her, then this perfectly pointless exertion. It wasn't as if he'd thought about Trixie for years, let alone seen her. Everyone warned him, including myself, but he insisted on going: sheer stubbornness. I blame Trixie for everything that went wrong.'

'Me too,' said Isobel, weeping into the grave, held up on either side by the princesses, Imp and Trixie's daughters; nice girls, Cordelia and Stephanie, but they wouldn't inherit a thing.

# A HARD TIME
# TO BE A FATHER

Once upon a time, DEAR READER, but not so far away or long ago, practically round the corner, in fact, and *fin-de-millénaire*, a young man took his PAIN to a hospital, for the sake of his young wife DELIA.

See the HOSPITAL as a castle, see the CASTLE as a place which immures THE HEALER MAGICIAN; see it in the sense of FAIRY TALE or KAFKA, see it how you will. We are all within SPITTING DISTANCE of castles; spit away, if that's where your experience of institutions leads you, if it makes you feel better.

THE YOUNG MAN had been to art school and now worked as a store-window designer, where being HETEROSEXUAL he stuck out like a sore thumb, but never mind all that. He came to the castle by night: AFTER work but BEFORE the pubs close being the most propitious time to attend CASUALTY, or so Delia told him.

Delia knew better than he how the world worked, or seemed to.

CASUALTY was written in letters of fire which passed across a frosted green panel above the hospital doors, and seemed to offer a welcome, albeit a dangerous one, for the dog CERBERUS roamed the castle gates keeping off all comers. Cerberus had THREE HEADS and all of them were ugly.

'You obviously can't park there, sir,' said the first head. It wore a collar, a tie and spectacles, waved human arms and used CONTEMPT as a weapon. 'These spaces are reserved for DOCTORS. You are attempting to commit an anti-social act. Kindly move on.'

'I'm so sorry,' said the YOUNG MAN, being apologetic by nature – and he drove on round the corner hoping for better LUCK.

'Don't even think of parking there,' said a SECOND HEAD, appearing out of nowhere. Its scalp was shaved, its tongue and lips were ringed: its mien was terrible. 'That's reserved for fucking ambulances. Are you blind?'

'It's true that pain does somewhat blur my vision,' the YOUNG MAN said with heavy irony, but only once the window was UP and his door lock was DOWN. He drove around another corner where amazingly he found an EMPTY SPACE. As he backed into it a THIRD HEAD came along, wearing a hat of the kind a Ruritanian general might wear, all heavy gold and red embroidery. 'Double lines, sir, you can't park there, on penalty of clamping.'

'Then where am I meant to park?' asked the young man.

'Nothing to do with me, sir. I just do my job.'

CERBERUS'S NECK is very long: HEADS spring up all over the place; latterly he has been cloned, they say. He is everywhere: the faces may waver and change, often taking female form, but rest assured he is the same beast. He guards the gates of castles everywhere; even though the castles may be

PHANTASMAGORIC, Cerberus is real enough. Only in parts of London can you cheat him; by parking with your back wheels in WESTMINSTER and your front wheels in CAMDEN; then confused, Cerberus sometimes finds it easier to leave you alone. But such spaces are in hot demand.

PAIN made the young man unusually brave. He just left the car where it was and walked away, the CREATURE FROM RURITANIA taking notes behind him.

Now the young man's name, dear reader, as it happens is CANDIDE, not because your writer is trying to make a point, but merely the better to report a story as told to her in real life by a young couple whose names were in fact Candide and Delia. Blame Candide's parents, not me, should blame be called for: let's get on, now that's out of the way.

The bullet-proof glass doors that admitted walk-ins to casualty were bolted shut against VIOLENT MARAUDERS. Two SECURITY GUARDS flanked the entrance. Candide was checked over visually for suitability for treatment out of PUBLIC FUNDS. The security guards took their TIME.
    'Please! I need help,' mouthed our hero through the glass.
    A nod from ONE to the OTHER: at least the person had the password right. Their eyes were grim and their mouths tight, but they let him through.

CANDIDE saw a SWEET-FACED GIRL behind a counter marked *RECEPTION*; she wore a badge which named her as MIRANDA – *VOLUNTEER. FRIENDS OF MERCY*. In streaks of pinkish fire which travelled ceaselessly above her head, moved the slogan *PLEASE WAIT PATIENTLY. OTHERS MAY BE IN NEED OF MORE URGENT AT-*

*TENTION THAN YOU. THANK YOU FOR CHOOS-*
*ING THE HOSPITAL OF MERCY.*

'What's your problem, sir?' MIRANDA enquired, kindly
enough. She had some small training in dealing with difficult,
even violent, patients. Hospital casualty these days is full of
violent people, but no one knows why.

'Appendix, peritonitis, death, who's to say,' said Candide.

'I appreciate your sense of humour, sir,' said MIRANDA.
'Just wait on one of those chairs over there until a member of
staff is free to attend to you. We are very busy today.'

Candide sat and clutched his BELLY until the pain eased.
Fifty GREEN PLASTIC CHAIRS were ranged in five rows of
ten. Forty were unoccupied, ten occupied. Candide spent his
time counting them. Other SUPPLICANTS slept, breathing
and snorting gently, DINGY GARMENTS trailing and root-
ing on the grey floor. From the far end of the great hall, by the
coffee machine, came a burst of colour, chatter and laughter.
FOUR GIRLS OF EASY VIRTUE – or so Candide supposed
them to be, for their skirts were up to their crotches, their
jewelled handbags swung low, their heels were high, and
their faces heroin white – had worked out a way of extracting
coffee from the machine without paying; one would thump,
the other would kick; another try and catch the coffee as it
spurted. The YOUNGEST GIRL, who was about twelve,
was smoking and not interested in coffee.

'No smoking over there,' cried MIRANDA. 'In the interests of public safety. Don't you understand this is a hospital?'

'Fuck off,' shrieked the SMOKER, in harsh though
Sloaney tones, 'or I'll spit and spread Aids.'

Candide resolved to keep his distance, and even Miranda
paid THE BAD GIRLS no more attention. It takes GIRLS

FROM ALL CLASSES, dear reader, to keep the SEX IN-
DUSTRY going; the trade is BUYER DRIVEN, and VOR-
ACIOUS.

Ten minutes passed: fifteen, twenty, sixty. There was coffee
all over the floor.

A RUGBY PLAYER slept in the last chair of the first row. He
seemed to have been there some time. A red and white striped
scarf was wound round his head: his shirt was striped black
and white, vertically. He murmured in his sleep: he drowsed.
He wore muddy shorts striped horizontally in purple and
yellow. His thighs were vast and muscle-knotted; his socks
could barely stretch around his powerful calves. Beneath his
right knee Candide now noticed a SLIVER of broken shin
bone piercing the flesh. Candide peered and peered again. He
could not be mistaken.

'Nurse, nurse,' called Candide, spying one who passed. She
was a dark-eyed girl with the face of a GRECIAN GOD-
DESS, calm and strong.

'Well? I'm busy. What?' asked NURSE GALINA, for so
her badge named her.

'That rugby player asleep over there –'

'Yeah, we get lots of rugby nuts on Sundays. They bring it
on themselves, like smokers.'

'But his leg is broken. I can see a bone sticking out.'

'Bones often do that when they're broken,' said NURSE
GALINA.

'Shouldn't he see a doctor?' asked Candide. His OWN
PAIN had eased. In fact he was beginning to wonder if he
needed to stay at all, and worrying about the fate of his car
outside, left in the space reserved, he now remembered, for
PATIENT PARTICIPATION OFFICER, GRADE ONE

ONLY. He thought the traffic warden had probably been bluffing, but supposing the PPO was on night shift and turned up to claim his space?

'It's asleep,' said NURSE GALINA. 'A rugby player's like a baby: if it's asleep, don't wake it. It's just asking for trouble.'

'A BABY,' repeated Candide, and all but fainted. NURSE GALINA had to thrust his head between his knees till his head stopped swimming. Candide explained to her that this was part of his TROUBLE. His wife was pregnant. He suffered from recurring STOMACH PAINS which their friends assumed mimicked LABOUR PAINS and were SYM-PATHETIC: well, he could IGNORE these; they were one thing: but the fact that whenever he heard the word 'BABY' he felt DIZZY and PASSED OUT was another. It had become something of a JOKE with his friends, but it was a serious matter. The word was used increasingly all around him; no one could avoid it, as his wife's labour became imminent; he needed to be in TIP-TOP FORM to help her when the time came. This was why he had come to casualty.

His OWN DOCTOR would not take his complaint seriously.

'But there's no one complaining of this kind of thing on my list,' said NURSE GALINA. 'Have you checked in?'

'I don't think so,' said Candide. 'I was told to sit down.'

'That new girl on the desk,' complained NURSE GALI-NA. 'She knows nothing about anything except sex. She's sleeping with the Senior Registrar, they say. You should have checked in with Triage Nurse ages ago. How can she call your name if you're not on her list, let alone pass it to me? Didn't you think about that?'

'I trusted the system,' he said. 'I assumed you knew your business. And who and what is Triage Nurse? I thought Triage was a system used to sort those lying on the battlefield at the end of the day. The dead who need to be buried; those who can be cured to fight again, and those who are better just left as they are.'

'My, how knowledgeable we are,' said Nurse Galina, but she said it kindly and explained that Triage Nurse divided patients into three CATEGORIES: those who were seriously ill and a DOCTOR needed to see QUITE SOON: those who were making a FUSS ABOUT NOTHING and would have to WAIT: and those who were only fit for PSYCHIATRIC anyway. At least that is what he thought she said.

'From the sound of it,' said NURSE GALINA, 'you're ripe for psychiatric.'

'I don't see why,' said Candide, 'Delia and I both look forward to the BIRTH. The pregnancy is PLANNED, we're both halfway up our CAREER LADDERS and on FLEX-ITIME and so forth; we're doing everything RIGHT, I can hardly be MAD. Whatever my problem turns out to be I am sure it's PHYSIOLOGICAL in origin, or I wouldn't be here.'

'My, my, my,' said Nurse Galina, 'in denial, are we, and what big words we use!' – but she took him back to RECEPTION to register.

APPOINTMENTS NURSE was small, skinny and dark. Her name-badge read ISHTAR PATEL. She asked Candide for his NAME, ADDRESS, AGE, RELIGION, PARTNER STA-TUS, SEXUAL ORIENTATION and how he had TRA-VELLED TO THE HOSPITAL.

'I don't see how that latter is relevant,' said Candide.

'You are not expected to see anything,' said ISHTAR. 'This information is needed for our statistics.'

'But I could be DYING,' said the YOUNG MAN. 'I might not have the time to help you with your statistics.'

'Perhaps English isn't your first language,' observed ISH-TAR coolly. 'I may have to wait for our ETHNICITY expert to come back from lunch so she can help me fill in the form. She takes a long lunch.'

'I came by car,' said the YOUNG MAN, sighing, 'and parked it, for all that Cerberus snapped.'

'Definitely psychiatric,' murmured ISHTAR to GALINA, 'as are so many of these fair-haired square-jawed types; off to Triage with him!' And Candide was sent to sit in a different part of the great hall.

Here light was scarce, and the WRETCHED OF THE EARTH, who had somehow sidled around SECURITY and gained an entrance to the WARMTH and SHELTER of the Castle Mercy, huddled in some number in corners. They seemed to murmur and whisper in chorus. Candide tried to make sense of the muted, drifting sound, and thought the words ran thus:

'We are the flotsam, the jetsam of this city,
The drifters, the hopeless, the object of your pity.
You need us to be sorry for;
In triumph we sing our ditty.'

At least that's what Candide thought they murmured and whispered, but who was to say? The faint SMELL of antiseptic dulled his senses to more acrid human scents, and the low HUM of central heating, and the distant clank of trolleys, and CARING FEMALE VOICES, lulled him as he waited, and waited. Thus the castle works its enchantment. The stomach pains had abated. He drowsed. But the plight of the rugby player, whom he could see quite clearly from across the hall, now troubled him more than his own:

he could not rest. A shaft of light glittered on the white sliver of projecting bone.

Nurse Galina passed by again. Once more Candide drew her attention to the rugby player. Apparently the man slept; but supposing he had lapsed into a COMA? Were they keeping an eye on him?

'Why do you care about that great ox?' asked Nurse Galina. 'More like an animal than a human being. He'll be seen in due course. We know well enough what we're doing. Those who inflict damage on themselves, smokers, over-eaters, drinkers, sportsmen, and so forth must take responsibility for their own actions: we've had a memo round. If a male giant throws himself into a scrum and invites a lot of other male giants to stamp on him, he needn't think he can come in here and ask for special privileges from hard-working women.'

Her voice rose in pitch as she spoke. She let it be known she was at the end of her TETHER.

'Hasn't Triage Nurse even seen you yet?' she asked, as if Candide's negligence were responsible; and when Candide shook his head, she sighed heavily.

TRIAGE NURSE, who was little and fair and PRETTY, now emerged from her cubicle, calling for a BABY Longman. Nobody responded to her cry, not Longman mother, not Longman father, so she huffed and puffed her way back into her cubicle as if she were a DRAGON thwarted by the non-appearance of St George. Next time she came out she called for one CANDIDE NEWMAN. Yes indeed, dear reader, NEWMAN is in truth my hero's surname. I promise you I'm not doing it on purpose. His parents just liked the sound of it. Like Fifi or Peaches, or Pixie. Why not?

\*       \*       \*

'Yes, this is me,' Candide replied, coming forward as quickly as he could, so as not to irritate Triage Nurse further. Progress was not as quick as he hoped; he was still recovering from the effect of a new barrage of the word BABY. He staggered and groped through DARKENING VISION.

'You took your time,' snapped Triage Nurse and sat him down facing her. She took Candide's temperature, his pulse, and MARVELLED at the lowness of his blood pressure before she let him describe his SYMPTOMS. He told her much what he had told Nurse Galina.

'Feeling faint when the word BABY is mentioned is not exactly an urgent matter,' she REPROACHED him. 'What do you think your local surgery is for? This is casualty department of a large inner-city hospital: we exist to deal with emergencies. And the most common cause of fleeting stomach pain is WIND.'

Candide found, as sound SWAM and SANG in them, that he had ears to hear her thoughts. Sometimes the UNSPOKEN words of others ring through another's head. It has happened once or twice to me, reader, and I HOPE it never happens to you, as it happened that night to Candide, as TIRED, EXHAUSTED, DEAFENED, and BLINDED by the problems of others as he was, he persisted in his attempts to breach the defences of the Castle.

'Good God, what a wimp, what a poor pathetic wimp,' Triage Nurse thought: and it became very clear to Candide that substantive thought must indeed be preceded by language. 'Pity his poor partner, who'll be left on her own in due course coping with the broken nights and the crashy nappies and the rashy crap. No. The crappy nappies and the nappy rash. Thank God my own baby doesn't have to put up with a father. No, it's the crechey child and the crappy care for my little girl, and trime pine for me when I get home from this the Castle Malaprop. In the meantime this wimp is wasting my time. There's nothing wrong with him; my BP machine's on the blink, that's all. No one can have blood pressure as low as that and stand up.'

'If, as you say, there is nothing wrong with me,' Candide began, but Triage Nurse stopped him short, very short. 'I must ask you to withdraw that allegation. Anything said to that effect might have legal consequences,' she SNAPPED, her pretty little mouth TIGHT and FIRM. 'I did not claim there was nothing wrong with you, I inferred it as a possibility.'

'There is definitely something wrong with that man over there,' said Candide, 'I don't care what you say. I can see a sliver of bone sticking out of his leg and that is that. He must be in agony.'

Triage Nurse seemed to SOFTEN.

'Try and realise that men of that kind don't feel PAIN like we do,' she replied. 'I suspect it's your blood pressure. It's so low you are suffering from optical illusions. I can see no BONE from here. It is true waiting times are a little longer than usual due to the recent DOWNSIZING of our medical team and the fact that our new computer has CRASHED again, but if there was a problem, we'd have seen to it. Let me tell you a JOKE to cheer you up. It comes from a book called MORE FROM RUGBY, which was on my father's shelves when I was a CHILD. My father was a keen rugby player: never at home when he was wanted. This is the joke. TWO MEN are sitting peacefully by the river fishing. They say nothing for the first two hours.

'Then the first angler says, "Weren't here YESTERDAY, then," and the other replies "No."

' "What stopped you?" PERSISTS the first angler.

' "Got MARRIED," says the other. There is a long, long silence. Bees BUZZ, stream RIPPLES, fishes DART. A beautiful day.

' "GOOD LOOKER, is she?" asks the first angler, puzzled.

' "Nope," says the other.

' "Got MONEY then, or what?"

' "Nope."

' "Is she SEXY, is that it?" demands the first.

' "You must be JOKING," says the second angler.

' "Then why on earth?" asks the first angler.

' "She got worms," says the other.'

Triage Nurse asked Candide if he thought the JOKE was FUNNY. Candide said if he had laughed it had been INADVERTENTLY. He assured her he himself was neither an angler nor a rugby player, had never seen the book in question, let alone read it. He was innocent. He was a new man like his name. Ha ha. The nearest he got to any kind of sport was that he and his wife Delia were in the habit of JOGGING round the PARK on a Sunday morning. But Triage Nurse wouldn't have it, she said she was talking GUILT BY ASSOCIATION. A man was a man for all that.

The CASTLE MALAPROP, the one that Triage Nurse inhabited in her head, is full of little DEMONS from the past: they scuttle out and nip the unwary on the ankles. Or nipple out and scut the anwary on the UNCLES. Speech and thought disturbance occurs.

'All you men go about,' said Triage Nurse, or so he thought she said, 'with an albatross around your neck. "Instead of a cross, an albatross around my neck was hung." Samuel

Taylor Coleridge. Aim of the Make-shift Rhymer. I go to crompulsory dug awareness classes every Wednesday evening. My little girl has to go to greighbours who make me eel the fobligation. Life is not easy for the working, unpartnered mother, no matter how noble the calling. Samuel Taylor Coleridge ook topium, you know, an early morph of forfine, a doppy perivative. It shatters the brain. Whoever heard of anyone going round with an albatross around their neck, but there it is, pain as a plikestaff on the page, certainly taken seriously by those who ought to know better. Awareness is balf the hattle. Most preative creople are on drugs. Are you creative? I see that your occupation is written here as "designer". It sounds creative to me.'

'I assure you it isn't,' said Candide.

'My little girl's in cray dare,' said Triage Nurse. 'I don't get much sleep. Their remit is to stimulate her creativity, but when you see what preativity does to creople I wonder why they bother.

> 'Alone, alone, all all alone,
> Alone on a shiny sea!
> And never a soul took pity on
> My soul in agony.

'Was it slimy or shiny? I quite like the poem, for all it was dug cased.'

'Drug crazed?' he asked. 'Do you mean drug crazed?'

'Are you trying to tell me something here?' asked Triage Nurse. 'Research shows that people on drugs refer to them 27 per cent more frequently than those who are not. I should be careful if I were you. Well, I am glad we had our little chat. I did enjoy it. If you go and sit over there by the green swing doors, doctor will see you presently about the stomach pains.

Afterwards I'd recommend you to go through to psychiatric, but doctor will decide.'

From his seat by the green swing doors, so near and yet so far from TREATMENT, Candide heard a chant SWELLING from some point near the coffee machine. It rose from the painted lips of the whores, who had SETTLED in to play cards.

> 'We are the whores, the bad girls of the city,
> And thank you very much, we do not need your pity.
> We save marriages by millions, and in triumph
>     sing this ditty.'

And Candide, quite cheered up, was thinking, well, perhaps this world of ours isn't so bad a place to bring a child into when Triage Nurse came out again and called – 'Baby Longman, Baby Longman, come in Baby Longman' – and again Candide's head swam, his eyes misted and whether he SAW things that were not his to see, and HEARD things he should not hear, and everything was TRUE and REAL or NOT who was to say?

– but there was a sense of movement everywhere and he SAW that the whores were now moving up and down the rows offering their services, falling into CHEERFUL conversation even when rejected. The ragged SHUFFLED along on their haunches, unseen by Reception, BEGGING and BLESSING even when refused alms.

This time it was his own dear wife who pressed his head between his knees as he swayed. She BURGEONED in PREGNANCY like a SMALL ship with a FULL sail: she had a sweet, anxious expression, a high complexion and nut

BROWN hair so CURLY that all you could do was DUNK it under the tap to WASH it and then allow to DRY naturally.

'Poor thing, poor thing,' cried Delia. 'Haven't they even seen you yet? It's beyond belief!'

'I've been triaged,' said Candide. It was his instinct to make the best of things, if he could. He and Delia fought a battle, if that was not too strong a word for it, dear reader, between TRUST and MISTRUST. If he was Pollyanna, she was Cassandra. Between them they managed very well. 'They can't think it's very serious,' he said, 'or they'd have seen me by now.'

'I don't think that's NECESSARILY the case,' said Delia.

'That rugby player over there actually has a bone sticking out of his leg. It's a DISGRACE!'

'Don't make a FUSS, Delia,' begged Candide. 'You will only make things WORSE.'

But Delia MARCHED over to Nurse Galina.

'I work in TV,' she said (a lie), 'and unless SOMETHING IS DONE for the man with the broken leg I will BRING THE CAMERAS IN. I and my unborn child will be in a position to SUE THIS HOSPITAL for post traumatic stress disorder. Surely I have a RIGHT to come in here and not be TRAU-MATISED by what I see?'

'We can't be pleasing everyone all the time or we'd never get through,' said Nurse Galina, but she HURRIED away, as if PERHAPS she meant to do something. Then she was lost in an ANGRY CROWD now clustering around Reception, prevented from getting even so far as Triage, in as much as the SOFTWARE relating to their means of transportation to the hospital had developed a VIRUS, or so Miranda claimed.

'The new computer's crashed,' explained Candide to Delia. The castle had worked its SPELL on him and he felt the need to DEFEND its ways. 'But when it's working it will CUT DOWN waiting times no end.'

'It's still too bad,' said Delia, rather FEEBLY. She was near the end of her TIME, and beginning to have stomach pains at REGULAR INTERVALS. Like so many of us, she could FIGHT for the rights of OTHERS, but did not like to draw attention to herself.

'It's NOT as if I were an URGENT case,' he said. 'You're the one who needs the care.'

'Me? I'm as strong as a horse,' protested Delia.

At which point Triage Nurse came out calling, 'Mr Holifog, Mr Holifog! Anyone here by the name of Holifog?'

'Bet that's the rugby player,' said Delia, and went up to the BULKY, RECUMBENT, much MULTI-STRIPED vaguely human shape and SHOOK him vigorously.

'Nurse did say not to wake him!' said Candide, tentatively, but Delia took no notice, and SHOOK on. Another half inch of BONE slipped through the hairy skin below the knee so she stopped, aghast. Candide did not say 'I TOLD YOU SO' – it was not in his nature – and besides, he had become conscious of the thoughts DRIFTING through the rugby player's HEAD.

'Don't wake me, Mummy, because I'm in heaven! Run for it! Run for the touchdown! Oh the grass is so slippery, oh the green wet shine of it, the slippage: the silage: the sweat, the ache in the calf, the knotting of muscle, the thwack and collision of flesh. Oh, the earth-shaking joy of it. Sling 'em off, fling 'em off, into the scrum and here's mud in your eye! Wash my clothes, mother, wash them real good' – and so on, and on, ponderous as a rhinoceros, and then suddenly Triage Nurse was calling, 'Mr Huggifuss, Mr Huggifuss, anyone there called Mr Huggifuss?' at which the rugby player STIRRED and said, 'Name's Oliphant. Hugo, Oliphant, actually –'

– and Triage Nurse said, 'No one here of the name Huggifuss. I told you he was a WASTE of time, HYPO-CHONDRIACS all these sportsmen. If they knew what women had to put up with during LABOUR, they wouldn't have the NERVE to complain –'

– and Hugo Oliphant called ALOUD for his father, 'Daddy, Daddy, watch me, one day you'll be proud of me –'

– and such a CHURNING of the poor and disaffected rose around Candide's feet, their hands outstretched for alms, that he SHUDDERED but DELIA said, 'Give them what you can, my dear, who knows when a beggar is a prince in disguise!' so he did.

– and Delia persuaded Hugo Oliphant to whisper his TELEPHONE NUMBER in her ear, and then rang his MOTHER collect. Mothers can often NEGOTIATE the CASTLE when passers-by cannot. Whole FORTRESSES will FALL when motherlove is on the WARPATH.

Now outside one of Cerberus's heads was barking loudly at an intruder: a guard dog of a different tune, a PISSER and a RUNNER: vast and clanking, the TOW-AWAY TRUCK.

'You can't park there!' cried the HEAD, 'Hey you!'

'I park where I fucking well please,' said the other DOG.

'That's our ambulance ZONE,' snarled the HEAD.

'Don't swear at us,' yapped the NEW DOG, and at the very notion of US split in two; into driver and mate.

'They PARK, we CLAMP, we LIFT, we take our time, but when we've taken it we MOVE, right, Fred?' said DOG.

'Right,' said Fred, 'let's do the world a FUCKING favour' – by this time Candide and Delia's Fiat Uno was swinging in the air – 'and drop this pile of CRAP. Look at the rust on that UNDERBELLY!'

– But at that moment an AMBULANCE screeched up, backed up and parked ARSE to REAR of the tow-away truck –

– and a tripartite ROW ensued, between ambulance DRIVER and the TWO forms of dog. The ambulance was bringing in a HEART attack victim – a middle-aged man – and had fetched him all the way in, siren SCREAMING, red lights IGNORING, but now declined to fetch him out until the tow-truck MOVED –

Let's leave them there, dear reader, you know how it goes, so what else is new, and return to the castle anterooms where Candide and Delia hold hands and wait.

'I'm afraid our car's been towed, darling,' said Delia, 'I looked out the window just now and saw it swinging in the air. Perhaps you didn't leave her in quite the most sensible place' – and before he could say 'PLEASE DON'T MAKE A FUSS, DARLING' she was out of casualty and into the ambulance bay GESTICULATING, and within minutes was sitting back next to him, the LITTLE CAR had been LOWERED, the clamps REMOVED, the tow-away vehicle GONE and the heart attack VICTIM was being STRETCHERED into the castle.

'But what did you say, darling?' Candide MARVELLED and Delia just said, 'I told them I'd have my BABY then and there: that always works,' and CANDIDE did his best not to faint right away; he was utterly exhausted. During the minutes of Delia's absence he had been KIDNAPPED, ASSAULTED, RESCUED, and RETURNED to his chair. He was OK, just about, but had few psychic or physical RESOURCES left.

\*     \*     \*

# A HARD TIME TO BE A FATHER

This is what happened.

Two soft-voiced, mousey-haired, maternal COSMIC HEA-LERS had set about him, and DRAGGED him into a linen cupboard. Their names were Donna and Jan. Donna had been a TEACHER and Jan a NURSE in what they saw as a previous life, but now, if you asked them, they'd say their original bodies were inhabited by walk-ins from the Dog Star Sirius. It was their mission to heal the sick by ALTERNA-TIVE MEDICINE and they hung around the castle, posing as patients or friends of patients, chasing the UNWARY, anointing them with UNGUENTS, passing CRYSTALS over the CHAKRAS – the points of energy – of the FEEBLE and ANXIOUS, the better to restore them to HEALTH. They fell upon Candide for no better reason than that he was NEAR-EST to the linen cupboard and ALONE. The ENCHAN-TRESS Donna simply crept up behind him and removed the chair from beneath him: her PARAMOUR Jan dragged him off, her strong hands under his shocked armpits.

'Quickly, Jan love, quickly, before he struggles! Juniper oil beneath his nose. And patchouli too!' The door slammed. He was alone with them, and where was Delia?

Strong odours assailed his nostrils: his head SWUM. He felt his garments removed as he lay upon the FLOOR. A cold, sharp surface scratched gently across his chest and other MORE INTIMATE parts.

'Don't be afraid. Relax. Thank God we got to you in time, before the doctors and nurses, the MESSENGERS OF DARK-NESS, invaded the HOLINESS of your body with their needles and POISONS. Do you feel your strength reviving? We have you framed by four crystals, which TRANSFORM and TRANSMUTE all negative energies. How tense you are; MY HANDS can feel how tense you are –'

236

The long soft hair of Donna the ENCHANTRESS brushed his body as she WORKED upon him.

'Don't, don't,' he CRIED. 'I am a married man –'

'Rose quartz upon the heart,' cried Jan, not to be UN-DONE. 'To promote LOVE and EXCITEMENT at the deepest levels; an emerald here at the base of the SACRAL CHAKRA to refine the SEXUAL energies –'

'This is beyond BELIEF,' Candide cried.

'See,' murmured Donna, 'as your MEMBER rises it creates that perfect form which lies at the root of the UNIVERSE – every cell in your body is diffused with a red light: your whole auric field is SCARLET, the petals of a flower UNFOLDING –'

Mercifully the Guardian of the Green Swing Doors happened to be passing, and was alerted by the SCENT of patchouli, which as every ex or indeed current hippie can tell you, gets everywhere. He was male and powerful and hauled the two women off Candide's dazed but EVER-LIVELY MEMBER, crying –

'Not you two witches again! Is nowhere safe?' and the women SCUTTLED SHRIEKING, WITHERING UP, becoming LITTLE and OLD and CARAPACED, like black beetles making for safe CRACKS and CRANNIES between the skirting and the floor: while the Male Nurse, for it was he, SCRUNCHED and STAMPED them beneath his feet: CRACKY on the outside, SOFT in the inside.

'There's always more roaches where they came from,' Male Nurse lamented. 'A regular plague of them!' And Male Nurse helped Candide back into his CLOTHES, keeping his HANDS more or less to himself, and Candide felt quite AT HOME and as if it was all FAMILIAR: it was like being back at work again.

\*       \*       \*

Reader, you must understand that if you were in a position to click your mouse in every uppercase word in this text, whole worlds of fictional delight would allegedly open up to you (and I bet you EVER-LIVELY MEMBER would, if a count were made, get the most clicks of all, or possibly INTIMATE PARTS). But, think of it, you could have a novel based on the doings of the enchantresses' goings-on – if that is what they were, and not just mere projections of Candide's Id – and their connection with the Ultra Natural Healing Front, and the Alternative Medicinites: or a GAY novel based on POWERFUL MALES, or you could call up on your screen a textbook on SACRED CHAKRAS OF THE HEART – or a combination of all three; really there is no end to the permutations. As with evolution itself, fiction ever seeks to diversify, and with the invention of CD Roms and multiple choice novels now has the opportunity. All it lacks is willing reader-clickers: it is, it turns out, rather in the nature of reader-clickers to prefer non-fiction to fiction, with the possible exception of sci-fi, always the FAVOURITE of the NERDS. Are you not reading this fairy-tale, God help you, upon the page, not on your screens? So words in UPPERCASE can merely indicate your author's pattern of interest, and thus, perhaps, enrich the tale. Even as you take issue with authorial decision, you will, by the very act of indignant opposition, find yourself PARTICIPATING. This has been the object of the exercise. Reading, of course, is almost as complex a matter as writing; all CUSTOM and PRACTICE and RESONANCE within the individual's head. But from now on your author will desist from the PRAC-TICE OF UPPER-CASING. Feel free to place such emphasis as best suits your mind-set: for vigour I recommend the verbs, for diversion, adjectives. Be sparing with adverbs.

*     *     *

But let us return to a shocked and exhausted Candide, recovering as best he could, and sitting once again where he was safest, next to his animated, belly-flaunting wife Delia, flushed from her triumph over split and snarling tow-away dog.

Between the rows of chairs now approached none other than Mrs Oliphant, Hugo's mother: her bosom proud as Delia's belly, swathed in the green peacock plumes of a traditional Liberty's fabric, her face as noble, as pained and strong as that of a prize-winning cart-horse.

'What does he ever want to play soccer for anyway?' she asked the assembled halt and sick. 'You have these babies, you devote your life to them; you take them to the doctor at the first sign of a cough; to the clinic for an X-ray every time they fall on their heads; you squeeze them whole oranges and sieve the juice for pips in case one lodges in the appendix; you clear out their toy-boxes; try not to tread on their Lego; you walk them to the school they hate; you save them from strangers; you look out for signs of drug abuse; you get them to twenty-one without a police-record, and what do they do? They self-destruct. They break their teeth in the swimming pool after years of orthodontics, rip their cartilages on the playing field, break every bone in their body and expect mummy to come along and pick up the pieces. Well I will, but he'll get no sympathy from me. Such a hypochondriac,' she said, her strong voice faltering as she spied her slumped son. 'I expect he's making a fuss about nothing. I had to get my sister-in-law to wait in for the delivery man. A new washing machine. It was pay for a new tub or replace the whole machine; they get worn out, don't they, going all the time. All that mud: it gets into the works. A mother's love is a terrible burden –'

She took one look at her son's leg and yelped. She spied a wheelchair. Fetched it, and with Delia's help, heaved her massive son into it, and started running with it towards the green glass doors, all but slipping on a watery surface as she went.

'Oh my God,' cried Delia to her husband, 'my waters have broken! I am going into labour.'

It is sometimes easier to do for others what it seems all but impossible to do for the self. Candide was finally galvanised into action. He too seized a wheelchair, shoved his wife into it, and fell in behind Mrs Oliphant in their mutual race to the inner sanctum, where healing occurred or was alleged to occur. Here surely would be people trained to hazard a guess as to why a man fainted, or had pains in his belly, who could click a bone or two under anaesthetic, or help nature expel a baby from the womb.

Triage Nurse did her best to bar their way: her arms seemed to stretch a hundred miles in every direction. Her white sleeves reached only to her elbows; she wore shorts in the manner of nurses in the summer, and sandals without socks; acres of firm, healthy flesh rippled and dissolved before them: the king's sorcerers were up to their tricks again.

'You haven't been called, you haven't been called!' The voice of Triage Nurse echoed round the vast chamber: it was the Day of Judgement and see, the dead were forbidden to arise. A murmur of anger rose from the patients on the chairs, and the cluster round reception, and the dim dispossessed in the corner, and the four whores rose up magnificent in all their blonde glory, tarty satin and silver chains – and as Mrs Oliphant broke the glass door with her elbow, put her hand in to loose the catch from the other side, and sailed through in blue peacock feathers, followed by Candide pushing the already groaning Delia, so did all the others; a stream of the dead on their way to paradise –

– Triage Nurse stood aside, she was obliged to; she sank to her true size again: much and permanently diminished, she spoke.

– 'I give up this job,' said Triage Nurse. 'Anyone wants it, they can have it. I'm going back to my little girl, who is the only one who has ever truly appreciated me.'

– and she walked right out of the castle, and everyone agreed it was a better place for her going, while appreciating that she was sorely tried and did a good job to the best of her ability.

– 'A baby!' cried Candide, 'my wife's having a baby,' and his head felt clear and his voice was strong, and the dreaded word no longer afflicted him.

Doctors appeared, and nurses too and on the other side of the green swing doors it was indeed like heaven: no wonder it was so difficult to get into, as many said then to each other. Angels of Mercy whisked Hugo Oliphant off to the operating theatre – and you will be glad to know he was back on the playing fields within two months and his mother's washing-machine was delivered, plumbed in and up and running by the time she got home from the hospital. Oh, what a day of Miracles! – Nurses ran to take Delia to the delivery room: it was going to be what they called a lightning birth.

– Male Nurse sidelined Candide, and stood him under a shower to remove the last traces of patchouli, for the health and safety of the coming baby, he said, and admired his body and was content with that.

– and by the time Candide came out of the shower the baby

was born, perfect, healthy and cheerful, washed and wrapped, and frankly Candide was much relieved by the pattern events had taken and Delia didn't seem to mind too much. Some men are just plain happier for not being there at the birth.

– the man who thought he had a heart attack turned out to be having indigestion pains, and was sent home.

– waiting staff cut away the callouses of the homeless, listened to their sad stories, gave them free cups of tea and put them on yet more waiting lists.

– the four whores found willing punters in a quartet of visiting Japanese politicians, here to investigate the workings of a national health service, and all in all it was the happiest fairy tale ending anyone could imagine.

– and the little Uno started first go when Candide started back for home – he'd collect Delia and the baby the next day – and Cerberus didn't even growl.

Cerberus is always happy to see people going, it's when they approach he gets so restless and multi-headed.